SLATE CREEK: JOURNEY TO THE WHITE CLOUDS

This Large Print Book carries the
Seal of Approval of N.A.V.H.

SLATE CREEK: JOURNEY TO THE WHITE CLOUDS

WALLACE J. SWENSON

THORNDIKE PRESS

A part of Gale, a Cengage Company

GALE
A Cengage Company

Farmington Hills, Mich • San Francisco • New York • Waterville, Maine
Meriden, Conn • Mason, Ohio • Chicago

Thorndike Press® Large Print Western.
The text of this Large Print edition is unabridged.
Other aspects of the book may vary from the original edition.
Set in 16 pt. Plantin.

LIBRARY OF CONGRESS CIP DATA ON FILE.
CATALOGUING IN PUBLICATION FOR THIS BOOK
IS AVAILABLE FROM THE LIBRARY OF CONGRESS

ISBN-13: 978-1-4328-5303-7 (hardcover)

Published in 2018 by arrangement with Wallace J. Swenson

Printed in Mexico
1 2 3 4 5 6 7 22 21 20 19 18

SLATE CREEK: JOURNEY TO THE WHITE CLOUDS

CHAPTER 1

The long ride from Fort Laramie to intersect with the Chugwater offered a taxing fusion of purgatory and pleasure for Simon Steele. The drinking, gambling, cheating, and deceit that had defined his life at Fort Laramie for five years played over and over in his mind as he rode. Countering his dark thoughts, the freshness of the air, the clarity of the July sky, and the cacophony of nature's presence eased him along. His dog, Spud, bounded ahead, out of sight for long periods. He'd return with a greeting, only to run off again in search of something new.

As the day wore on, Simon tried to convince himself he'd left behind forever the dim and seamy nights in the saloon, with the soul-rotting knowledge that, for profit, he'd served the base needs of men. No longer did he need to rationalize his collusion; abrasive grit that had ground his integrity down to his bones. He was, at last, free to find his way again, free to cleanse his soul and to make himself feel whole. But could he?

His friends and mentors, Tay Prescott and Walks Fast, the first an older frontiersman and prospector, the second a Shoshoni dreamwalker, had both encouraged and foretold his journey and helped plan the way. With Walks Fast's map in his saddlebag and both men's words of wisdom ingrained in his head, safe for later reflection, he looked forward to his journey. Pushing through the heat of the high plains in summer, Simon at last spotted the thin blue-gray wisps of smoke that suggested the campground at the Chugwater might be near.

Three men sat on the ground, well away from the fire. A covered wagon with the tailgate down stood off to the left. Simon studied the camp for a minute, cautious, then nudged his horse forward. Spud arrived well ahead of him, his exuberance and wagging tail making his acquaintance. A dozen or so horses stood on a rope line well back from the camp. Simon's horse hailed them with a whinny.

"Climb off and shake the kinks out." The voice came from the other side of the wagon, and immediately a man in a dirty apron stepped around the end.

"Thanks." Simon swung down from the saddle and winced at the tingle in his feet.

One of the cowboys stood. "Howdy. You're named Steele." It was not a question. "You run Amos's place over at Laramie."

"That's right. First name's Simon."

"I'm Wayne Goodman. I run a few hundred head of cattle here on the Chug." He stuck out his hand. "This is Vance Hartman and Vernal Carlson." The two men stood. "That there's our cook, Prod Boothe."

The cowboys' wide-brimmed floppy hats shaded faces that hadn't seen a razor in at least a month. The buttoned collars of plain cotton shirts lay hidden behind sweat-stained scarves, dust masks for the drag riders. Vance and Vernal wore wide leather leggings; chaps, big as storm shutters. All three smiled, and Simon shook the offered hands.

"Nice dog," Prod said. "Dern near big as a wolf."

Spud's tail wagged when he heard "dog."

"Yeah, he likes people. Spent a lot of time at the saloon." Simon ruffled Spud's ears.

"So what brings you down here? Going to Cheyenne?" Wayne nodded toward where they had been sitting, the universal and silent invitation to join them.

9

"There and on west." Simon followed Wayne. "Got an itch to see some new country."

"You know, I've wanted to do that myself." The rancher hunkered down on his heels. "I came here in fifty-five from Missouri. Meant to spend the winter, and then carry on to Oregon." He shrugged. "Never got around to it."

"Gonna join us for supper?" Prod asked. "You're more'n welcome."

"That'd be good. I've got some canned peaches."

"Naw, we got plenty," Wayne replied. "Pull the saddle off your horse and tie her up with the rest. Always good to have someone new to talk to."

The five men perched around the fire on makeshift seats, four old friends and a stranger. As darkness pulled its covers over the face of the prairie, a single coyote expressed his loneliness with a plaintive cry. Soon, several others voiced their sympathies, and the night came alive with the mournful music. The men sat silent, mesmerized by the dance of the flickering fire and the eerie call of the coyotes. Spud grumbled at the noise.

Wayne cocked his head to the prairie sound. "Things like that are what draws a man out here," he said. "Evening like this makes the heat of the day tolerable."

Simon looked up at the blaze of stars. "It is beautiful. Did this as a kid back home in Nebraska. Herded cows a couple of summers with some Texans."

"How in hell did you wind up at Amos's place?" Prod asked.

"My best friend and I decided we wanted a change. Just turning eighteen, what did we know? We headed west and found a home there for five years. Amos hired me, hoping I could make him some money, and he hired Buell to make sure he could keep it."

"Buell?" Wayne said. "He that tall feller that always sat on the high chair by the stairs?"

"Yep, that's Buell."

"Now that's one scary character. I was there the night he near beat that German fella to death. Mind you, he had it coming but, damn, he looked like a herd of cows had walked over him . . . in single file." He flashed a grin at his partners.

"Buell's different. I grew up with him . . . same school, same friends, same everything, almost. Strange how a man learns different lessons from the same teachers."

"I've seen that, too. Whatever happened

11

to him? He still there?"

"Nope. I was told he was up in the Black Hills."

"You said you was going on west. Got a spot picked?" Vernal asked.

"Ever heard of the White Cloud Mountains in Idaho Territory?"

"Can't say I have."

"There's an old Indian at Fort Laramie whose people live there. He said it's north and west of Fort Hall. He drew me a map."

"Been to Fort Hall," Vance said. "Dirty place. Real sorry bunch of Indians camp out there. Steal your fork halfway to your mouth."

"How is the trip from Salt Lake?" Simon asked Vance.

"No problem really. Lots of folks headed that way, mostly into Montana Territory for the gold. I wound up in a place called Hungry Hollow. They named that one right. Never did anything but wear myself out digging. Come back here."

"I was told there was a gold find near where I'm going."

"That could be Leesburg. That's north of Fort Hall. I heard about it after I got back. You don't go to Salt Lake, you know, 'less you want to. You head north out of Ogden. The Corinne Road runs from Bear River to

Alder Gulch. That's near Virginia City, and close to where I was. Must be a cutoff to Leesburg there somewhere."

"The map doesn't show roads, just rivers, streams, and some prominent mountains."

"If the old Indian drew it from memory, probably weren't no roads. I'd ask as I went along," Wayne said.

"Suppose that's what I'll do."

Silence settled over the group again, as the conversations became private in each man's head. Lost in thought, they all stared at the fire, content to just sit; now five friends, perched around a campfire.

The crash of a wooden spoon banging the bottom of a wash pan jolted Simon out of a sound sleep. He sat straight up in bed.

"Git up, you lazy bunch o' varmints. I ain't gonna be the only one earning his keep 'round here." Prod banged on the pan again. "Git up!"

"You whack that pan one more time, old man, and you'll wear it around your neck today," Vernal said, rolling over on his back.

"Sure, you kin make threats laying flat on the ground like that. You don't scare me."

Like three half-crippled jacks-in-the-box, the sleepy men sat up in their bedrolls. Using both hands, they all partly untangled their rumpled hair with a quick pass-

13

through, then stuffed wayward tufts past the sweatbands of the hats they jammed on for the day.

"Mornin', Simon," Wayne said. He threw back his cover and stood. "Coffee ready, Prod?"

"What a stupid question. What in hell you think I do for a livin'?" The cook shook his head and spit in the fire.

"Now you know why we call him Prod."

Simon tugged his second boot on. "I was wondering about that."

"I heard that. Well, you don't have to wonder no more. I don't like gettin' up, and I don't care who knows it."

Ten minutes later the four stood at the tailgate of the chuck wagon, silent, one behind the other in line. Prod, very solemn, picked up one plate at a time, loaded it to capacity with bacon and biscuits and gravy, and handed it to a hungry man. Soon they were all busy clearing the plates and emptying coffee cups. The closer they were to done, the wider the grin spread on Prod's face.

"That's about as long as he's on the prod," Wayne said, tapping his plate with a fork. "This is what he lives for."

"Sure tastes good," Simon said. "Appreciate this, Mr. Boothe. First-rate breakfast."

"Jist get it ate up so's I can wash the damn dishes. And the name's Prod." He wrinkled his forehead in a scowl, but somehow the gruffness didn't quite carry through.

Thirty minutes later Simon shook hands all around and swung into the saddle. "Been a real pleasure. You've helped me get this trip off to a good start."

"Take care of yourself, son," Prod said.

"C'mon Spud, let's get going."

Simon touched the brim of his hat, the time-honored salute of friendship, and turned his horse upstream.

Cheyenne lay an easy two days to the south. A trip to the bank there, and he'd be on his way west to put death and betrayal behind him forever.

CHAPTER 2

Simon's visit two years previous did not prepare him for the sight as he approached Cheyenne from the rolling hills north of town. Many times the size of Fort Laramie, it sprawled over the prairie for almost a mile. Leaving his horse at a nearby stable, he made straight for the huge hotel by the train depot. A hot bath and a clean bed sounded wonderful, but first he had business to transact.

The familiar hum of a dozen simultaneous conversations and the smell of tobacco, whiskey, and oiled wood stopped Simon at the door. The bar to his left beckoned, and a whore caught his eye to pitch her sale without saying a word. He considered her for a few seconds. More grit, he thought, then turned away to march across the carpeted lobby to the front desk.

"Could you direct me to the Mercantile Bank?" he asked the clerk. Simon recognized him from the last time he had been there. The imperious attitude was still there.

"I can," the man replied. He paused as though waiting for more specific instructions. Then, "Go two streets west and one and a half north. It's on the right side."

"Thank you." Simon turned and had taken a couple of steps when the clerk spoke again.

"It'll be closed now, though." The man glanced at the clock on the lobby wall, then gave Simon a patently fake smile. "Open at nine."

"Right. Thank you." Simon mentally counted to five.

The clerk continued to stare through him, and then Simon realized how bad he must look, obviously the most poorly dressed man in the lobby. With five days' growth of whisker stubble, hands that looked like he'd been playing in a campfire, and dusty clothes he hadn't taken off in four days, he'd seen cleaner trail bums at Amos's saloon. He stepped back to the counter. "I'd like a room then."

"I think not." The clerk peered at him over his spectacles.

Simon forgot to count to five. "And why the hell not? I've been on the road for three days, need a bath and a shave and a place to sleep. That's what a hotel's for. And you are a hotel, right?" Simon felt thirty pairs of eyes boring into his back, and he could sense the heat rising up his face.

"We are indeed, sir, but we do not allow animals."

Simon resisted the urge to reach across the desk and throttle the obnoxious character. Then he followed the clerk's eyes to his left. Spud, about four steps away, sat in a small dust storm furiously scratching his neck with a hind foot.

"I ... surely you have ... he wouldn't ..."

With every sputtered utterance, the clerk slowly shook his head. "No exceptions." He raised triumphant eyebrows.

Simon gathered up his saddlebags and rifle, and headed across the lobby; muted laughter pushed him out the door. A two-hundred-fifty-pound saloon bouncer could not have been more effective.

"Snotty sonuvabitch," he mumbled as he stepped back into the street. He turned toward the stables.

"Back already?" The liveryman's genuine smile took the sting out of the hotel encounter.

"Yeah. Where can I stay and have a place for my dog?"

"Right here. Got a copper tub, water in the cistern is always warm this time of year. The bunks ain't got no satin sheets but they're clean. If you got a razor, I got a mug and soap. Cost you six bits." The man looked at Spud. "Dog stays for free," he added, and winked.

Simon chuckled. "If it wasn't so outrageous I'd get madder'n hell."

"Hotel didn't like the dog, did they?"

"Not a bit."

"Mostly that's Gibson's fault."

"Gibson?"

"That snooty clerk. Got here about five years ago. Slept right here as a matter of fact. Hobnobbing with the bluenoses has plumb gone to his head."

"You mean I coulda stayed there?"

"Sure. Ladies with them perfumery lapmutts stay there all the time. It's up to Gibson."

"I never give it a thought about my dog. At Fort Laramie he stayed in the saloon a lot."

"I expect if you pushed the matter with the proprietor, you could still stay there. You're welcome here."

"And here I'll stay. Mostly, I was looking for a bath and you got that. Show me where to put my rifle and bags if you would."

19

"Sure. Last name's Jaspar, and that's what folks call me."

"I'm Simon Steele. Pleased to meet you." He shook hands with the man before they entered the dim interior of the barn and walked to the rear.

"Come on in here." Jaspar opened a door to a long hallway with four doors in the right wall. He pointed to the first one. "Put your stuff in there. The bath is the last door. Help yourself."

Simon went in, dropped his bags on the floor, and sat on the bed. "Not bad, Spud. At least we're welcome, and that's worth a lot. You lie down and I'll go get a bath."

The next morning Simon found the Mercantile Bank. A teller directed him to a man sitting at a desk and Simon approached. "Good morning. My name is Simon Steele, and I have a letter of credit I'd like to present."

"Mr. Steele. I'm James Pettingill. Please take a seat." He nodded at a chair in front of the desk. "Let me see the letter."

Simon handed it to him.

"No problem here." He let a gold chain catch his spectacles when he dropped them. "I know Amos. How would you like me to handle this?"

"I'm going west, and I want to take cash

20

with me. I'd like three thousand of that in gold and the rest in notes."

"If you know where you're going Mr. Steele, I can certainly write another letter of credit good in any major city west of here. Four thousand is a lot of cash to carry around."

"I'm not going any further west than Salt Lake, and I'm taking the train there. I think I'll be all right with it."

"Very well, but I feel I'm doing Amos a disservice. We can put the coins in three belts of fifty coins each. If you can come back in an hour or so, I'll have it all ready for you."

"That'd be good. I'm going to the railroad ticket office and see about the schedule."

Two hours later Simon was back at the stable. Spud lay on his belly outside the doors, staring directly at him when Simon rounded the corner.

"Hey," Simon said as he walked up. "Ready for a ride?" The dog wagged its tail and followed Simon into the stable.

"Mr. Steele," Jaspar greeted him. "Some kinda dog you got there. He didn't move the entire time you were gone."

"I've often wondered how long he'd stay after I've told him to."

"Figger out when you're leaving?"

21

"Yeah. Got the same treatment about my dog that I got from the hotel. They don't allow them with the passengers. Best they could do was the baggage car, and then he'd have to be tied up. I'm not gonna to do that to him."

"So?"

"I'm going to ride a freight car." Simon watched for a reaction, but Jaspar appeared noncommittal. Simon continued: "Seems the farther west you go, the more a horse costs."

Jaspar's eyebrows rose. "Whoever told you that is telling you the truth. I can sell you a good horse and saddle for less than a hundred dollars. Cost you nearer two in Salt Lake City."

"So I've arranged for all three of us to ride in a cattle car. The freight master said there's space on one with twenty-five goats going to Nevada Territory. I can put my horse in there and sleep in the fodder box."

"You ever been around goats?"

"Never. I don't think I've seen more than one or two in my life."

Jaspar shook his head and grinned. "I think you're making a mistake. They got to be the most cantankerous animal God ever created."

"Freight man said they're in pens."

"That's what he thinks. Damn things can climb trees. I've seen it. So expect to have visitors, cuz they're curious creatures."

"If that's all, I can put up with it for a day."

"And a night. Besides that, they stink, especially a billy. I mean they really stink."

"Well, it's either that or schedule for another trip, and he said partially loaded cars are hard to come by. I'll just have to put up with it."

"You're a real soldier. When you leavin'?"

"The train's scheduled to arrive at six-thirty tomorrow morning. They have to switch a few cars that're going to Denver, and then we're off."

"Do you have something to eat?" Jaspar asked. "I know for a fact, unless they have a reason to stop, that train will go right on through."

"Hadn't thought about that. I'm about out of canned stuff. And water. Suggestions?"

"Canvas bag. There'll be water for the stock in the car, but you ain't gonna wanna be sharing that with a herd of goats." He wrinkled his nose and grimaced. "Mercantile two streets over."

"Watch my dog again?"

"Sure, nothin' to that. Leave 'em here for

23

good if you've a mind to."

"Nope. He's the only friend I have left. Reckon I'll keep him." Simon stroked the dog's head. "Stay here, Spud. I'll be back soon."

The next morning Simon stood on the loading dock as the car door slid open. His horse stepped back as far as the halter rope would allow. Jaspar had been right about the smell. The assault on his nose was almost physical.

The freight master chuckled. "Looks like your horse don't like 'em much."

"Good grief, can you blame him?" Simon put his hand to his mouth. "I don't think I've smelled anything quite like that. Sorta rotten sweet."

"You kin call it sweet if you like, I guess. Not the word that comes to my mind." Another chuckle.

The man stepped onto the car and checked the water trough. "Kelly, wheel three or four cans of water in here."

A young man pulled back on the handles of a two-wheeled contraption carrying two ten-gallon cans hooked to the front. He maneuvered the device across the loading dock and into the car. Simon heard the water splash as the cans were dumped.

"I'd put your horse on now and let him

get as settled as possible. Tie his head real good. When the train starts to move, some animals don't like it at all, so stay out of his way."

Simon tugged on the lead, and the animal followed him into the car. With nostrils flared, the horse snorted and rolled his eyes at the herd of goats. Twenty-odd pairs of glassy orbs followed their every move without blinking. Board rails stacked on edge halfway to the ceiling partitioned the back half of the car. Simon led the horse into the shadowed interior.

"Tie him head on. And like I said, don't give him any slack."

Simon did as he was told, and then stepped back into the fresh air. He hadn't realized it, but he'd been half-holding his breath, which he expelled with a huff.

"Reckon you can hold it all the way to Ogden?" the freight agent chided.

Simon was beginning to have serious doubts.

"It'll be a lot better once you get going. You're lucky you're in the front."

The second load of water cans came up the ramp, and the boy soon had them emptied inside the car. "That about fills them up," the youngster said to the agent. He turned to Simon. "How 'bout your

25

horse, mister?"

"I hadn't thought about that." Simon shrugged and gave the boy a wan smile.

"Got an old canvas bucket by the pump," the young man offered. "It leaks, but it'll hold water long enough to give him a drink. Want me to get it?"

"That'd be a big help. Thanks."

Simon put his saddlebags, bridle, and horse blanket on the floor, and draped his saddle over the fodder-box rail. The tote sack of food went onto the pile. "C'mon, Spud," he called toward the door. No dog appeared. "Spud! Come here." Simon went to the door.

The dog lay on the dock with a paw over his muzzle, his mournful eyes looking up.

"Oh, for crying out loud. Get in here."

Spud got up and with short, hesitant steps, entered the car. The look in his eyes begged Simon to change his mind, and he stopped just inside the door. Simon pointed to the front of the car. The dog, with an audible sigh, walked the gauntlet of goats, pausing every three or four steps to look back with pleading eye.

"Bleeeaaat!" Several passengers teased him as he made his way to the head of the car.

When the dog got there, he paused for

one more hopeful look. Then, ears down in defeat, he flopped onto the floor beside the pile of baggage.

"Good dog." Simon chuckled and turned back to the door.

"That should do it," the agent said. "You only have five short stops between here and Ogden." The door rumbled sideways to slam shut with a rattling crash, and the railroad man dropped the hasp into place.

Creeping tentacles of apprehension and excitement rippled under Simon's scalp.

CHAPTER 3

Simon couldn't remember spending a longer twenty-three hours. The incessant wind created by the slow-moving train carried the nauseating, sweet stink of the goats out of the car, only to be replaced by frequent blasts of acrid coal-smoke. The constant shifting of the floor as the train made its way over the uneven railbed kept his stomach on the verge of coming up and made sound sleep impossible. After banging his head twice while trying to peer through the sides at the passing countryside, he'd given it up to sit on the floor. There he'd wait out the journey, dejected and stoic.

A few hours after leaving Cheyenne, the train stopped to unhook the extra locomotive that had helped them up the steep grade to Laramie. He managed to doze off once, only to be jerked back by a rumbling growl from Spud. Two billy-goats, feet propped on the fodder-box rail, sniffed him with

28

interest, their eerie, pale eyes unblinking. He snatched off his hat and swatted the closest one in the face. They both jumped back into their pen and glared at him. The train stopped briefly several more times as a car or two were uncoupled and left behind, or water was taken on.

There was no doubt they'd arrived in Ogden. The railway yard they'd stopped in contained more cars than he thought existed. It was about twenty minutes before the door opened and he looked down at four men. One wore an official looking Union Pacific cap.

The agent ran a stubby pencil down a log-sheet, and then looked up. "Says here you have a horse."

"That's right. Do we get off here?" Simon rolled his shoulders to relieve the kinks.

"Soon's I arrange a ramp," the man replied. "Shouldn't be more than ten minutes." He nodded at three strange-looking men. "These fellas want to take a look at the goats. They're the owners. Greeks." The last in response to Simon's quizzical look at the other men.

The three men dressed alike in soft-looking shoes that reminded Simon of house slippers, and voluminous trousers,

29

tight at the ankles and held at the waist by a wide sash. White shirts with bloused sleeves were buttoned to the neck and each man wore a bright multicolored waistcoat. Raven-black hair gleamed in the sun, and six piercing eyes returned Simon's curiosity with friendly but reserved attention.

Two moved to the railcar, and facing one another, stooped and clasped each other's hands. The third stepped into the improvised cradle, and before Simon could figure out what they were doing, was standing upright in the car. The man said something Simon couldn't understand, then climbed over the rail to join the goats on the other side. The three carried on a rapid conversation as the man moved among the animals. He had touched every one of them by the time four men arrived carrying a slatted ramp, which they leaned against the railcar's door sill.

"Head your mount toward the door and get out of the way," the agent said.

Simon untied his horse and turned it around. When she saw the opening, Simon understood the why of the agent's instructions. The horse charged for the exit and was headed out the door when she realized the ground was five feet below. Momentum carried her one step down the ramp before she gathered her hind legs under her haunches and jumped. Simon thought for sure she was going to fall, but after three- or four belly-scraping steps, she recovered to stand upright, snorting indignantly. The agent caught her halter rope and tied it to the railcar. Simon soon had the horse saddled and his bags strapped on.

Half an hour later Simon found the livery stable recommended by a teamster at the rail yard. Three blacksmiths created a horrific din as their work rang the anvils, each with a distinct note. A fine, almost imperceptible veil of dust hung in the air. Behind the barn, an oval corral about a hundred feet long and sixty feet wide held several mules and about a dozen horses. He swung his leg over his saddle and got down.

A squat man stood just inside the stable doors. He wore a collarless blue shirt with rolled-up sleeves, and a round-crowned felt hat, gray with sweat-grime. The bowler sat slightly cocked on his head, giving him a mischievous air. He was talking to a tall man, apparently a teamster judging by the whip he had slung across his chest. When the teamster nodded and stepped into the street, Simon approached the short man.

"Good afternoon, are you the owner?"

"The bank might argue the point. What

kin I do for you?"

"My name is Simon Steele. A driver at the railroad station said you might sell me a mule."

"I got a few." The man shook Simon's extended hand. "Ferguson." He openly scanned Simon and Simon's horse.

Simon had been sized up before. "I need an animal for packing."

"Let's go take a look." The stableman turned, grabbed a short length of rope, and headed out the doors and around to the back of the barn.

Simon looked down at Spud. "You stay here." The dog sat down by the horse and Simon followed Ferguson around the corner.

"What do you think about that one over there?" He pointed at an animal standing away from the rest. The mule's eyelids drooped and its front feet were planted well apart.

Simon wrinkled his nose as he looked at the mule, and then, shaking his head, turned a grin on the stable owner.

"Can't blame a man for trying, now can you?" Ferguson's eyes twinkled.

"No, I guess not." Simon looked at the other mules. They stood clustered together by a water trough to his left, and they all studied him. He walked a dozen paces to the right, put his hat on the corner post, and then walked back to Ferguson. "Get that one with the star on his chest."

Ferguson stepped through the rail fence and into the corral. As he headed toward the mule, the animal stood its ground, one ear on Ferguson, the other turned toward Simon. Catching hold of the side of the halter, he led the mule to the gate. "Who taught you mules?" he asked as he pushed through.

"Good friend of mine in Wyoming."

"Well, you picked a good one. Smart and strong. See the way he followed you with his ears? He's still got an eye on your hat."

Simon ran his hand down the mule's front leg. "How new are his shoes?"

"About a week. New enough?"

"How much? And I'll need a packsaddle."

"Hundred and seventy-five, with the saddle."

Simon stepped back and looked at the mule. "Well, Sonuvabitch, you got new ownership."

"Huh?" Ferguson's eyebrows shot up.

"No, no." Simon put up his hands. "Him." Simon pointed at the mule. "Sonuvabitch. The man who taught me about them called his that. I thought I'd carry on the tradition."

Ferguson laughed and slapped his leg. "Well, if repeating a name is what it takes, he'll soon learn that." He attached the halter rope to the mule.

"I need to know where I can buy some supplies."

"What kind? Farming, hunting . . . what?"

"I'm going to poke around in the mountains north of here, in Idaho Territory."

"Know exactly where?"

"Got a map in my saddlebags. Would you take a look at it?"

"Sure. Let's git this mule round front, and I'll find a packsaddle for you. Mule?" Ferguson said, almost a question, as he gently tugged on the halter rope. The animal followed them around to the front.

Simon retrieved the map from his saddlebag and spread it.

"That's some remote country you got there." Ferguson drew his stubby finger across the map. "I'd head north out of Corinne on the Montana Road. There's lots of freight wagons headed up that way to Virginia City and Helena. And a feller named Fairchild found some gold east of Fort Hall, place they call Cariboo. They're also prospecting some around the Salmon

River country, and that's where you're headed. See if you can join one of those outfits, at least to Taylor's Bridge." Ferguson peered closely at the map again. "I reckon if you was to cross the river there, you'd be able to see those big buttes your friend has marked here. Gotta tell you though, it's gettin' late for heading into the mountains. Late May or June would've been better."

"Too late, you think?"

"You can't know that till it is."

Simon realized he hadn't given the time of year much thought, but the sudden scalp tingle lasted only a moment. "Is this Corinne a fair-sized place?"

"Oh, yeah. Bunch of Gentiles got together to see if they could get the railroad to make it a main stopping place. Ol' Brigham fixed that and made sure the terminal wound up here. Corinne ain't a railhead, but it's where a lot of freight gets loaded for the trip north to Montana. You won't have any trouble findin' what you need up there. And bein' a Gentile myself, I don't mind if the Mormons don't see none of your money. You ain't a Mormon, are you?"

"No. I've heard of 'em, though."

"Good folks but they're a clannish lot. Don't cotton much to outsiders."

"How far to Corinne?"

"Make it in a day if you start early, only 'bout twenty-five miles."

"Well, I appreciate all your help, Mr. Ferguson. Could you direct me to a place where me and the dog might spend a night?"

"Sure. Three cross streets thataway and take a left. Woman named Kearsley runs a bed-n-breakfast place. Know for a fact she has no problem with dogs; hell, she'll even put up with Chinamen."

"That's what I need. Put my horse up, and I'll be back in the morning for her and the mule. I'm much obliged."

"No problem. I'll see to your horse."

Simon untied his saddlebags and pulled his rifle from the scabbard.

"C'mon Spud, let's go find that lady."

The ride to Corinne the next day was a pleasant change from the noisy, rough experience of the cattle car. Wagons, twelve- to twenty-foot-long lumbering affairs drawn by as many as ten horses, took the right-of-way. Small carriages, spindly looking in comparison, moved smartly behind matched pairs of high-stepping prancers. Men on horseback filled the spaces in between. Dust hung over the road, carrying the smell of horse sweat and fresh droppings. Simon found all the commotion exhilarating.

The farms, models of neatness and order, stretched away from the road on either side. More than a few of the houses, some clustered in small communities, stood two stories tall. The fields, now mostly harvested, lay flat and squared off, with irrigation ditches crisscrossing the whole area. Seven hours passed quickly and on July 9th, 1873, he rode into Corinne, Utah Territory.

CHAPTER 4

"Shit!" Simon looked at the pile of goods still lying on the ground beside the heavily packed mule. A sixteen-foot square of folded canvas, the three-gallon can of coal oil, a water bucket, two twenty-five-pound sacks of cornmeal, a ten pound bag of sugar, a . . . he shut his eyes in frustration.

"Ain't gonna fit. Thought as much when you showed me the list."

Simon looked up just in time to see the storekeeper try to cover a loose grin that said *tenderfoot.* "So . . . any suggestions?"

"Reckon you could find some room on one o' these wagons goin' north. Sometimes the drivers take a little extra on the side . . . kind of a bonus, you might say."

"And how do I find one of those co-operative drivers?"

"Reckon I could find one . . . for a price." The loose grin grew tighter.

"Do you think I can find another mule here?"

"Sure, but it'll cost you a lot more than what you'll pay to squeeze a dab like that onto a tailgate. 'Sides that, you hook up with a wagon, and you can travel well into the night. You got a full moon for the next five or six days. You travel by yourself . . . well, that can get unhealthy."

"Meaning what?"

"There's some that'd sooner take what you got than work for it." The man looked directly at the new Model 1873 Winchester and the ten green boxes of ammunition Simon had just paid for in new gold coins.

"Okay, find me a ride. What's the chance of finding one this morning?"

The trader sucked something from between his front teeth, then spit. "Somewheres 'tween none and that bit of bacon."

Simon led the mule into the stable and started to unload it. Another day wasted.

Eight horses stood in the forecourt next morning, hipshot and heads down. The lead horse craned his neck and looked back as Simon walked out of the stable and up to the rear of the wagon. The sun would not rise for another hour or so.

"Like to use that canvas to bundle it all together." The teamster looked as capable and tough as the fourteen-foot wagon he drove.

"Sure. I'm afraid I haven't thought this out very well."

"Ever'body's a beginner in the beginnin', Mr. Steele. Just throw it up here, and we'll start stacking it on." He nimbly levered himself onto the tailgate.

Simon threw the canvas up, and together they arranged the stiff cloth.

"Now, heaviest stuff first. Like that folding stove there."

Thirty minutes later Simon's goods were safely packed and well-secured to the back of the wagon.

"You can ride up there or on your horse." The driver pointed to the high seat. "Ever rode a freight wagon?"

"I have," Simon said. "I'll ride my horse."

"Then tie your mule on, and let's get this rig rollin'."

The teamster clambered up the five-foot-high wheel and into the driver's seat. He waited until Simon tied the mule, then he kicked the brake loose and hollered, "Git up!" The horses leaned easily into their collars, and the wagon rolled out of the stable yard. "Now Haw! Haw!" The team turned left onto the road.

Sunrise threatened the steep mountains to

the east.

They weren't alone on the road. Three or four outfits about a half mile in front of them raised a dust pall that hung in the still morning air. Simon urged his horse ahead of the wagon and set his pace to keep him there, Spud padding alongside. For the first time in nearly a week, he was able to take in some of the sights around him. The slopes to the east climbed quickly to form an impressive line of bare-rock mountains that formed a barrier running north and south. The land to the west lay as flat as anything he'd seen in Nebraska. A haze-obscured line of mountains appeared in the distance. To the southwest there was the lake. People had told him it was so salty in places fish couldn't live in it. And ahead, the land rose gently toward the hills that formed the north end of the valley.

The air warmed as a sultry heat seemed to rise from the ground. Willow and cottonwood trees disclosed the waterways that meandered into the valley from the north and east, and sheep and cattle grazed in abundance. Simon settled into the semiconscious state of a long-distance rider, mind empty of anything important, his body relaxed and in rhythm with the cadence of the horse. Uninterrupted, two hours had slipped by before he knew it. Straightening in his saddle, he stretched, and then reined his horse to the side of the road.

"Wonderin' when you was gonna wanna stop. 'Nuther mile up there's a nice stream to water the horses. Meet ya there." The teamster hollered the last over his shoulder.

A few minutes later Simon tied his horse to the wagon. The driver strode up a well-defined trail, two full canvas buckets sloshing water on his legs. " 'Preciate it if you'd help me water the horses."

"Of course." Simon took one of the buckets.

"You get the offside wheel. They git all the dust so they git first."

"Never did get your name," Simon said.

"Bill Malm."

Simon watched the level in the bucket drop with amazing speed as the horse silently sucked in the water. The five gallons were gone in about two minutes. He went to the creek and soaked his feet getting the bucket full again. Twenty minutes later the lead pair sucked up the last of their water.

"Why not let 'em stand in the water and drink?" Simon asked.

"And spend the afternoon gettin' the wagon out of the mud?" Malm gave him a knowing smile. " 'Sides that, they'd drink

42

too much."

"How much do they need?" Simon looked at his horse.

"Let him drink till he . . . er . . . she, pauses, then git her head up. Now, the mule's a different story. They seem to know."

"How often do you water them?"

"Often as I want water myself. When they's plenty of water, let 'em drink, but they kin go all day if need be, jist like us. Mule longer." Malm climbed up the wheel and caught hold of the jerk line again. "Take your time. We got nice easy goin' for the rest o' the day, and I'll stop ever' once in a while and let 'em stand." He lifted the lines and sent a ripple along them. "Git up now! Lazy galoots, git!"

The rest of the day was a succession of stops, sometimes by a stream, sometimes just by the road for what Malm called "a blow." The land rose up to meet them as they left the Salt Lake valley behind, still relatively level most of the time, but an occasional rise made the horses lean a little heavier into their collars. The sun had been down for two hours when Malm pulled the team to a halt beside another wagon, parked well off the road.

"Hey, Buck, need some company?" Malm

shouted at the wagon.

"Not really, but don't reckon that'll change your mind," someone hollered back.

"You're right, you ornery ol' scut."

"I gather he's not serious," Simon said.

"Naw, we've been friends for years." Malm climbed down from the high seat and arched his back. "By gum, it's a royal pleasure to git off that thing sometimes."

"Can I help you unharness?"

"That'd be real good of you, Mr. Steele."

"Simon . . . please."

"Okay, Simon. Git the feeling you ain't a complete pilgrim."

"I've worked all my life, and I've helped my father do this a lot. Just not eight at a time."

"Take 'em off just like I put 'em on, two at a time."

"Need some help, you old cripple?" A man stepped around the parked wagon and hobbled toward them, clearly visible in the bright moonlight. He listed heavily to one side, his left leg bent out at the knee.

"Who's callin' who what? Levi, meet Mr. Simon Steele. Simon, this here's Levi Buck, best teamster on the road."

"Pleasure." Levi stuck out his hand.

The strength Simon felt in the grip was frightening. He knew without a doubt that

44

bones would break if the stocky man decided they should.

"Mr. Buck. You been the one just ahead of us all day?"

"Nope, I pulled over about an hour ago. Two rigs passed me since. I went to work this mornin' when an honest man should. Can't abide a feller that lays 'round half the mornin'." Levi shot Malm a grin.

"Had to load Simon's gear on the tailgate, else you'd be eatin' my dust."

"And I suppose the Dillard Freight Company knows about the little extra?"

"They didn't hire it done, so it's none o' their dern business, kinda like it ain't none o' yours. My outfit, not theirs."

"Well, let's git these horses unhooked. Your second swing set looks plumb spent."

"Just one of 'em. He's new. Got him along this trip for trainin'."

The eight sweaty horses soon stood free of their bonds and nosing around in the grass by the creek. One dropped to its knees and then rolled over on its back. Feet folded and held high like a relaxed cat, he shifted his shoulders and rump back and forth, rubbing his back in the earth. And just like a cat, the horse turned over and nimbly got to its feet with agility that surprised Simon.

Thirty minutes later a small fire burned,

and Malm dug around in the box he'd taken from under the driver's seat.

"I'd be happy to cook for us," Simon said. "I've had some experience."

"I ain't never been one to turn down an offer like that. I hate cookin', and some of the stuff ol' Levi throws together'd make your dog retch."

Simon peered into the box, then poked around for what he needed. The coffeepot came first, and was soon wafting steam. The two older men settled down on the ground and watched while he fixed them a meal. An hour later, the dishes had been washed and put away, and Simon was more than ready for a good night's sleep.

His back hurt, from level with his hips to the middle of his shoulders. No matter which way he turned, the dull throb persisted, every heartbeat a thud that reminded him of the long day in the saddle. Unable to relax, he marveled at the beauty of the night sky, the stars clearly visible right down to the horizon. Across the camp, Buck muttered something and rolled over in his bed. Simon tuned to look, the moon so bright he could see the broad red stripes on the teamster's Hudson Bay blanket. Simon had bought one, a double, twice as long as a normal blanket. He slept on one end, and folded the other over himself. Despite the heat of the day, the night was cool and the weight of the wool felt good. With a low groan, he rolled over on his back again and folded both arms behind his head.

Thud . . . thud, snap! Simon's scalp grew tight as he unfolded his arms and turned to stare toward the sound. Spud's head came up and shifted from side to side. Then his ears pricked and he growled, the barely audible throat-rumble private and re-assuring. The dog's nose pointed straight at Malm's wagon.

Simon rolled slowly to his side and felt around for his rifle, his eyes trained on the dark silhouette of the angular rig. Then the source of the sound appeared, two pairs of legs, moving silently toward the rear of the freighter. His groin tightened and the search for the cold steel of the Winchester became more urgent . . . where was it? He looked to where he was groping, caught the glint of metal in the moonlight, and grabbed. The heft of the rifle calmed him.

His gaze went back to the wagon just in time to see the legs disappear behind the rear wheel. Quietly, he rolled over to his belly, and propping his forearms on his saddle, he aimed the long barrel at the tailgate. "Stay." He breathed the single word and the dog went silent.

In a semi-crouch, the two men stepped into plain view and stopped. One leaned his head close to the other for a moment, and then started to move to Simon's left. Long buried memories of a night just like this sprang to life, so fresh and vivid his stomach sickened — an ambush under cover of darkness.

So, too, occurred the chilling thought of what might have happened on that dark riverbank. Tonight would be different. Tonight it would be his decision, his reason to act, now tempered by experience. His will to survive overriding his blind faith in morality. He breathed in short ragged puffs.

Simon's tightly strung nerves needed no more than the unmistakable double-click of shotgun hammers being drawn back. A flood of resolve willed his hand to rotate the lever of the Winchester down and away, then slap back. The tug on the trigger followed as naturally as blinking, and the rifle blasted brilliant light and thunder across the sleeping camp. The lever ratcheted down and back, and Simon, blinded by the flash, fired again. And again. And again.

"What the deuce is goin' on?" Malm hollered across the camp.

"Somebody was about to shoot us in our

beds." Simon, amazed at the evenness of his reply, stood, rifle at the ready.

"Who?" Malm asked. He rose like a specter in the moonlight, his long johns an eerie white.

"I don't know. They were over there by the other end of your wagon."

A horse galloped off to the south.

"Sounds like he's leavin' in a hurry," Malm said.

"You said *they.*" It was Buck. "That's one horse."

"I saw two men. I aimed at the one movin'."

"Let's take a look."

Malm carried a pistol in his hand, and together they walked toward where Simon last saw the man. They found him, a grotesque heap, twisted back on his legs, his pelvis thrust obscenely toward the moon.

Malm leaned over him, then stood up straight. "Hit him twice looks like, both in the chest. Hard to tell for sure." He picked up the man's shotgun.

"Let's see if we know him." Buck carried a lantern and moved close, casting the yellow light on the face of the dead man. Death stared back, the eyes blank and dull, jaw slack, bloody teeth on display in a mouth open for one last breath.

"That's the no-count fella that hangs around the commission store," Malm said. "Where you bought your stuff, Simon. What's he want with us?"

"Maybe he wasn't after us." Buck looked at Malm for a moment, then shifted his gaze to Simon.

"Me?"

"How'd you pay when you bought your pile?" Buck asked

"Uh, I gave him . . . I paid in twenty-dollar gold pieces." Simon let out an exasperated sigh.

"And I'd guess you fetched 'em out of that belt you wore 'round your belly today," Buck said.

Simon glanced down at his waist and winced. "Well . . . that was stupid, wasn't it?"

"That about says it." Malm sighed. "I expect he sent these boys, or they got wind of it somehow."

"How'n hell'd you hear 'em?" Buck asked. "I was dead asleep when that rifle of yours scared the shit outta me."

"I'm so sore from riding, I couldn't sleep."

"Well, might be your sore ass saved itself." Simon nearly missed Buck's wink.

"What do I do about him?" Simon nodded at the corpse.

"We'll put some rocks over him, and send a note back to Corinne with someone we meet goin' that way. I ain't real sure whether we're in Idaho Territory yet, or still in Utah. Let them figger it out."

"Take a look at his shotgun," Buck said. "It loaded?"

Malm dropped the barrels. "Loaded and cocked. Looks like Simon was right." Malm shook the shells from the opened gun and snapped it shut. "We'll leave it here with him."

The dog sniffed the air near the body. "Leave him alone, Spud," Simon ordered.

"How'n blazes did you manage to keep that dog quiet?" Malm asked.

"Just told him to be still. Not the first time we've been in a scrape."

"How so?" Buck asked.

"Maybe over coffee one of these evenings. Not now. I'm suddenly plumb wore out, and my back stopped aching. I'm going to bed."

"Don't expect I can sleep," Malm said, "but it's too early to be up."

"I'm with Simon," Buck said. "See you later."

"C'mon, Spud. Let's get some sleep."

After a short but fierce battle, his self-righteous conscience gave way to the reality

51

of pragmatism, and Simon sagged into the deep sleep of the justified.

CHAPTER 5

Next morning, bootheels scratched parallel tracks marking the dead man's final journey as they dragged him across the road. Well away from the campsite, they covered the body with rocks, and Simon, deep in thought, stared down at the crude cairn.

"You had no choice, young fella," Buck said.

"He's right," Malm added. "Man doesn't come into a sleeping camp with a loaded shotgun 'less he means bad mischief."

"I coulda hollered at him or —"

"And let him shoot me!" Malm said. "Weren't just you he was lookin' at. I was a wagon's length away."

"Hadn't thought about that."

"You did what a good partner does," Buck said. "You was lookin' out for all of us, so don't be frettin' about it." He pointed at the rock pile. "I know that's a man, but that particular man was bound to get it just like he did. If it weren't you, it'd be someone else."

Malm laid his hand on Simon's shoulder and squeezed. "He's right, Simon. You didn't do anything wrong. Now let's get these rigs on the road."

By noon, a note giving their names, the place of Mound Springs, and a short description of what had transpired was on its way back to Corinne and the law. Simon didn't feel all that much better about the whole deal. The very thing he'd left Fort Laramie to avoid had happened. Was trouble going to follow him everywhere?

The day carried them higher, and Simon noted that the temperature didn't seem to drop. In fact, it seemed hotter, and a steady breeze out of the southwest dried his sweat before it could reach the surface. His skin felt like old sun-bleached tarpaper looked. Simon anticipated the next stop, and Spud had taken refuge under the moving wagon, his tongue hanging out, catching dust like a sticky flytrap. Simon slowed his horse until the wagon drew alongside.

"I know, hotter than the bowels of Hades," Malm said. "Don't know what it is about this climb, but it seems to heat up just to vex me."

"Is there some water along here?"

"Yep, fair-size creek. We'll stop there and give 'em a good blow. Don't want to push too hard today; tomorrow we climb to the summit, and that's hard on 'em."

"Will Mr. Buck stop there?"

"He'll most likely just be pullin' out when we arrive. Reason he left half-hour before we did this mornin'."

Simon tilted his hat back and wiped his brow with a forearm. Resetting it, he gigged his horse to move ahead of the team again and started looking for signs of water. Forty minutes later, a copse of cottonwood and aspen offered cool, damp dirt, and a chance to get out of the sun. His horse smelled the moisture, and her stride lengthened as she stepped a bit higher.

"They needed that," Malm said. He held the bucket to the thirsty horse. "Them horse apples are supposed to break apart when they poop 'em out. Couple of 'em actually bounced. Better give 'em two each. Long haul to the next water."

"How much farther to the top?"

"Reckon we'll clear the summit about sundown Sunday. Then, it's fairly level all the way to where you cut off, couple climbs out of the creek bottoms, but nothing like tomorrow."

They stopped for nearly an hour and let

the horses cool in the shade. The air around the trees made Simon reluctant to step into the direct sun. He waited as long as he could before he swung into the saddle and followed the lumbering wagon north again. His horse soon crusted up with dried sweat, and he looked toward the west, willing the sun to drop out of the sky.

They stopped when they caught up with Levi Buck about ten-thirty. Simon made short work of supper: some beans heated up on Buck's fire, and enough of his coffee to soak a few bites off some hardtack. They ate right out of the cans. Any thoughts about the previous night disappeared as soon as his head touched his makeshift pillow. Spud settled down at his feet.

Buck's stirring around the next morning woke Simon, and he sat up as the crippled teamster hobbled around the fire, encouraging it to restart. Simon pulled his boots on, stood, and immediately headed for the privacy of a clump of willows.

"Hard pull today," Buck said when Simon came back into camp.

"That's what Bill said. He up yet?" He glanced toward the wagon.

"Out with the horses. He's got one that's ailing — heard it coughin' last night."

"Right lung's not workin' the way it

should, all rattly." Malm joined them, shaking his head.

"Saw that yesterday." Buck added a few sticks to the growing fire.

"So what do you do?" Simon asked.

"Not much I can do. If we was down, he'd just stand around till he got better. But we ain't, so he'll just have to pull. Six horses can't pull three tons of goods up Malad Summit." He shook his head. "You take it as it comes."

The grade didn't look that steep to Simon, and his horse didn't seem to mind all that much, but the rumps and shoulders of Malm's horses took on the appearance of frosted sugar buns. The stops were more frequent, and the horses took longer to recover each time, especially the third one on the right side. His eyes looked manic, and he blew snot with every breath.

"Hang on there, feller," Malm crooned. "I'll take you out soon's we get to the top. Pull boy." The voice sounded gentle and encouraging.

"Could we harness my mule with them?" offered Simon.

" 'Fraid not." Malm shook his head. "If we was on the level I might try it, but not on this hill. They start fussin' and I got trouble. Good of you to offer though."

57

Simon let his horse slow and the wagon moved past. He fell in behind.

"Hup!" The shout brought Simon out of his traveler's reverie and he looked to Malm. The teamster half-stood in his box. Simon moved his horse right to study the train. The ailing horse's head hung low, and its feet barely cleared the road as it walked. The uneven gait affected the rest of the string, and the steady strain on the traces became halting.

"Hup, stay in there, boy." The edge of urgency made Malm's words sharp.

Then the sick animal stumbled, and its mate slacked off to even the pair. Confusion swept through the train as that pair slowed, and the lead team felt the added strain and pulled harder. The first swing pair slacked to keep their distance and the wheel pair behind them followed suit. Soon all four pairs were snorting and tossing their heads in frustration. Then, the off horse in the third team faltered and fell.

"Whoa!" Malm hauled back on the jerk line and tromped hard on the tall brake handle. "Whoa there."

The fallen horse caused a hard drag on the off rein, and the lead pair turned sharp right, straight toward the side of the road and an impossibly steep incline.

"Whoa, gawdammit!"

The nearside horse of the third pair shied away from its ailing mate, lunging into the lead horse ahead of it. That horse kicked back and its partner tried to rear up.

Crack! . . . Crack! The first salvo split the air to the right of the lead team, the second over their heads. Eighteen feet of deadly looking black whip snaked back over the wagon, paused as the loop straightened out, and then shot forward for another ear-splitting reverse over the struggling horses. Crack!

"Whoa, damn you. Stand still."

The lead pair stopped short, and the second almost ran into them. All four stood stock-still, feet well apart, their massive muscles quivering as they waited the next command. Caught between the steadied pair nearest the wagon and the standing leaders, the frantic third horse quit bucking. The horse on the ground did not move.

"Sonuvabitch." Buck muttered as he climbed off the seat. Sliding his hand over the wheel horse's back, he made his way up the right side to the downed animal.

"Whoa boys, stand easy," he murmured.

He reached down, turned back the upper lip of the downed horse, and let go, shaking his head. Leaning over, he laid his hand on

59

the horse's shoulder and waited a few seconds. "Dead," he said simply, then heaved a sigh as he stood.

"You mean he just died?" Simon looked down at the sweat-encrusted animal. A lump formed in his throat as a thin trickle of blood leaked from the horse's nose.

"Yep. If you ask them to, they'll pull till their hearts break. This one wasn't meant for it, but you never know that by just lookin' at 'em."

Simon swallowed hard twice. The lump remained stuck fast and started to ache. He avoided Malm's eyes.

"We got a real job ahead of us. Find four good-sized rocks and stick 'em behind the wheels." Malm moved to the left side of the road and picked up a big one.

Simon, glad to have something to do, spied another down the road a little and hurried after it.

"Back, easy now, back . . . whoa!" The heavy wagon settled on the rocks. Malm put all his weight onto the brake lever, then dropped the lines loosely into the driver's box.

"Let's sort this mess out," he said as he climbed down.

They unhooked the lead horses and led them up the hill a ways. The nervous mate of the dead horse came away next.

"Now, the hard part," Malm said. He tugged on the round ball atop the hames that went up either side of the horse's neck. "Ain't no easy way to move thirteen hundred pounds of dead horse. We have to get that collar off, and his left side clear. The swing and wheel pair ain't gonna like that much, and if they get frisky, we could yet lose that wagon."

They struggled with buckles not meant to be released under such tension, and tugged at straps lying under the lifeless beast. Simon thought his head would split with exertion, and they did it all with one eye on the uneasy pair who stood over them. The sweat poured off him under the merciless sun until they freed the horse of all the leather straps.

"Let's take a breather," Malm said. He walked over to the wagon, and squatted in the sliver of shade on the right side.

Simon plopped down beside him. "Can the rest of the string pull us over the top?"

"Not without risking another one."

Simon waited for him to continue.

"We'll wait till sundown and then off-load everything we can lift. There's some stuff we can't unload without help. Then we'll" — he paused — "He hears somethin'."

61

Malm pointed at Spud who stared intently uphill.

The teamster stood and peered around the wagon. "Huh, might've known. It's Buck."

The three of them rolled the dead horse off the harness and over the bank. It slid and tumbled all the way to the bottom.

"Sorry, young feller," Malm said as they watched it go.

"You and your damn sentimentality." Buck sniffed. A tight-mouthed grimace marked his face, yet he winced as the big brown animal slid to a stop in the rocks. He looked at Simon and shook his head sadly.

Malm turned away from the edge of the road. "How long did you wait before you started back?"

"Little over an hour, I reckon. Figgered I'd find you unsnarling a dead one."

"I was watchin' real close too." Malm's clamped jaws showed his frustration. "He didn't falter but once or twice."

"Sometimes you can't tell. I'll put my two in there and get you to the top. Six will make it from there, 'cept that haul outta Marsh Valley is gonna take a little longer."

It was nearly full dark before they hauled the team to a stop by Buck's parked wagon. Simon had never been so tired in his life.

The cool morning air crept under the blanket that Simon had snugged tight around his ear. Settling in a little lower, he willed himself to go back to sleep. One eye popped open. Sitting not a foot away, a striped ground squirrel watched him closely as it took bites out of something it held in its front paws. Three more bites and whatever it was nestled securely in the bulging cheeks, which proudly signaled a successful foraging trip. It went down on all fours, and with a flick of its sparsely covered tail, shot under the wagon and out of sight. Simon smiled, let out a soft sigh, and sat up.

"Oh, damn." He flexed his shoulders gingerly, then reached up with his hands to squeeze the muscles in his neck. Buck and Malm, two disheveled lumps a few feet away, showed no signs of life, and Spud peered from under Buck's wagon, his tail moving side to side, questioning. Simon patted the ground beside him one time, and his dog got up and sauntered over.

"Mornin' boy," Simon said quietly. Spud sat down as close as he could and Simon put his arm around him. "Would you look at that."

Parallel ranges of mountains stretched into the north as far as he could see. The road ahead dropped into a valley he thought must be twenty miles wide; a farmer's dream, covered with grass, trees, and low bushes.

"Wish I had my map," he said out loud. Too loud.

Malm stirred, rolled over on his side, and propped himself up on one elbow. He saw the direction of Simon's marveling stare. "Pretty, ain't it?"

"Beautiful." Simon threw the blanket toward his feet and stood. The cool air felt wonderful. He retrieved his boots and pulled them on, hopping on one leg, then the other. Then he grabbed his hat off the wagon wheel and tamed his hair with it.

They had gone to bed the previous night without making a fire, too tired to care. After taking care of the morning's urgency, Simon broke off several dead branches from a gnarled juniper tree and dragged them over to the wagons.

Buck was rolling up his bed when he got there. "Coffee's gonna taste good even with water out of the barrel."

"Won't be but a few minutes. Do you want me to make a hot breakfast?"

"Whatcha think, Bill?" Buck asked.

"I think them horses earned another hour's rest. Go ahead and fry up some bacon."

"You have what I need to make slapjacks, and I saw a can o' molasses in the box."

"My gawd, you kin make a pancake?" Buck looked at Malm, eyes wide.

"Sure. Be happy to." Simon lifted the lid on the kitchen box and started taking out what he needed.

An hour later, full of fried bacon, pancakes, and coffee, the men harnessed the teams and prepared to descend into the valley.

"Would you mind riding up here with me till we get to the bottom?" Malm asked. "We're loaded heavy, and I could use someone's leg on the brake."

A fleeting pause, a momentary hitch in time, took Simon by surprise. *Me and Buell were always "we"* blinked into his mind. The twinge of recognition turned into a knot in his throat; he hurriedly swallowed. "Sure, I'd be glad to," he replied, too hastily.

They sat atop the wagon until Buck had been gone twenty minutes, Simon absorbing the sheer size of the scene below.

"Okay, kick off that brake, but keep your foot on it. Watch the traces on the wheel pair. If they go slack, gimme a little brake.

Ready?"

Simon leaned his weight into the wooden handle and slipped it free of the cog.

"Git up." Malm shrugged his shoulders and settled his butt into the seat, his right foot firmly planted on the edge of the driver's box. The wagon moved easily toward the slope.

They had an uneventful descent to the bottom, even though in some places the grade became steep enough to smoke the wooden brake blocks. Then the road leveled out, and both men relaxed as the horses took up a steady fast walk.

"How far until we get to the big river?" Simon had shown Malm the map.

"You're talkin' about the Snake. We're all day today and half a day tomorrow to the Portneuf. Pretty good climb outta there and once on top you'll be able to see it."

"Those mountains I'm going into, they as tall as these?" Simon swept his hand toward the range on their right.

"Those are just hills. Too bad it was night when you approached the mountains on your train ride. You coulda seen some real ones there. Nope, wait till we get past the other end of this valley and through what's called the Portneuf Gap. You'll see 'em, stretched out like a string of pearls."

For the rest of the day and a good part of the next, they traversed the gently rolling ground on the bottom of the valley. A couple of times, a steep grade caused the horses to strain, but for the most part Simon sat in his saddle and enjoyed the scenery. Twice they saw herds of deer, one that numbered over forty.

The view opened up as they crested a rise at the north end of the valley. Distant snow-capped mountains on the far side of the immense river plain took Simon's breath away.

"Whoa . . . whoa now." Malm set the brake and slacked off the lines.

"So that's what Walks Fast was talking about." Simon said it more to himself than to Malm.

"If he was talking about big country, yep, that's it. From up here, you can see into next week."

"Those three buttes there." Simon pointed to the northwest. "They the ones shown on my map?"

"The same. Folks've been usin' 'em as landmarks forever. Now's a good time to get the lay of the land. You see that darker lookin' country in the middlin' distance."

"Looks . . . I don't know — unfriendly?"

"It does, and for a reason. That's lava fields, and you go around them. Even the wild animals avoid it. Cripple a horse in a hundred yards."

"Then it's possible those buttes are extinct volcanoes?"

Malm looked him up and down. "Did you go to one of them eastern schools?"

"Nope. But I had a teacher who did, and I've read a lot."

"Humph. Well yer right, and that's what ya got. The stuff is so ragged and sharp and piled up, you can't get over it. And there's no water. A wagon road goes 'round the north side of 'em and a cutoff from the Oregon Trail called the Goodale Route skirts the south. You may run onto the Goodale when you head west from the river, I'm not sure. Both ways will take you past the nasty part." He stood and pointed into the distance. "Now, you see that range running off to the north, the one that seems to start at that biggest butte?"

"I think so."

"Well, you're gonna go up the valley on the west side of that range. Buck and me will go up the east side of the mountains, a range over, almost straight north of here."

"How long to get to the buttes?"

"We got two long days once we git down from here. And then we part company. You go west for a couple of days and then north

68

for three or four. Buck and I'll go on north for 'bout a week."

Simon stared at the white-tipped mountains to the northwest, hazy in the heat of the afternoon. Though he'd been raised on the Nebraska prairie, those snowcapped peaks seemed somehow familiar, the distance minimized by his desire to reach them.

"You got that look in your eye, young feller," Malm said. "Seen it before. You can already feel 'em closing in around you, can't ya?"

"What is it that draws a person, Bill?"

"Usually the feelin' that you can forget yourself in there. I'd'a thought you were a little young to be thinkin' thoughts like that, but I reckon it ain't the years, it's the miles."

Simon recognized curiosity in the teamster's look. "Did some hard living the last five years, and had a couple disappointments just before that. It's not so much that I want to forget something as it is I want to understand some of it."

"Saw you was a thinker right off. Well, that's a place you can do some serious contemplatin'. Yes'ir, some serious lone time."

Malm kicked the brake loose. "You had your rest, now get us to the bottom." He shot an indifferent ripple down the lines. "Git up now. Hup."

The ground on the flat river-plain was a stark contrast between verdant green and a dusty gray-brown. Gangly cottonwood trees and thickets of willow huddled together near any water, creating welcome shadows in whose cool depths dandelions and bunch-grass grew. The road they traveled ran through a continuous carpet of chest-high sagebrush. Silver-gray and aromatic, it covered the ground in every direction. A rabbit, wiry looking with ridiculously long ears, sat stoically in the meager shade of a low bush as they passed. Simon spotted it just as Spud did, and the dog bolted into the brush.

"Jackrabbit," Malm said when Simon urged his horse alongside the wagon. "He'll find them a little faster than the small ones he's been eating so far."

"But he will catch it." The dog zigzagged across the ground until Simon lost track of him. "Many of those around? That critter's big enough to last Spud all day and then some."

"Some years you see hundreds of 'em. This year not so many, but more than enough."

Simon wiped his dust-dry lips with the back of his hand. "You'd think with that much water half a mile away, I'd feel it. I've never been so dry."

"No moisture in the air. That fact caused the folks on the Oregon Trail a lot of bother. The wagons shrinked up so bad they'd fall apart, lit'rally. And away from the river, water's scarce, so they couldn't afford to pour it on the wheels to keep the spokes tight. You kin understand why folks ain't bothered to stop here."

"But my Indian friend, Walks Fast, says it's a lot different just a little north."

" 'Tis. For green anyway, but wait till you spend a winter there. Nope. Folks's wise to keep on goin', far as I'm concerned."

They camped by the river and Simon wondered again how it could be so dry with a stream that large flowing past a hundred yards away. The next day repeated the previous; the sun, hot as a bread-ready oven, burned through his cotton shirt. At midday, Simon tied his horse to the back of the wagon, then climbed onto the seat with Malm. Now, late afternoon, he was half-asleep, lethargic in the scorching heat.

A nudge in the ribs startled him: "What?"

"Eagle Rock." Malm nodded toward half a dozen buildings, conspicuous in the sagebrush, and a sturdy-looking truss bridge. "And Taylor's Crossing."

Since leaving Portneuf Valley they'd passed

71

several small-settler holdings: cabins and low-lying sheds, but this was the first that looked permanent. Half an hour later Malm pulled up alongside Buck's wagon.

Buck eased himself upright from his spot in the shade of the wagon. "Good to see you made it. I been here almost two hours."

"He raised his prices yet?" Malm asked.

"Nope, still four-fifty."

"I gather we're stayin' the night."

"Figgered we could. Finley has a couple horses you might want to take a squint at. Both of 'em look pretty good."

"Finley's a horse trader," Malm said to Simon. "He got any mules, Buck?"

"Couple. They look kinda rank though."

"Well, let's get across."

Malm headed his team toward an impossibly narrow bridge. A man who had been standing at the approach walked toward the wagon.

"How you doin', Bill?"

"Whoa," Malm ordered. "Stayin' outta jail. You still holdin' us up ta cross Matt's two-bit bridge?"

"Four-fifty for the wagon and four bits each for the saddle horse and pack mule. Course you kin always go around." The man winked.

Simon dug a dollar out of his pocket and

handed it to Malm, who passed it on to the gatekeeper along with a five-dollar bill. Two twenty-five cent pieces came spinning back, glinting in the late sun.

The horses moved deliberately onto the corded surface. The hollow drumroll of their hooves sounded a dirge-like complement to the bridge's unnerving creaks and groans as it took the weight of the wagon. Forty feet below, the huge river squeezed through a crack in the black lava-rock that Simon guessed to be not much wider than the horses and wagon. The vertical sides stood ominously sheer and tombstone smooth. Simon resisted the urge to jump off the wagon and run.

"Easy boys, easy," Malm murmured softly.

Simon caught the quick glance Malm gave him. The quiet, calm demeanor of the teamster dispelled for a moment some of Simon's panic. He tried a smile, and knew he hadn't brought it off when Malm chuckled.

"Tends to rattle you the first time."

Upstream, the four-hundred-foot-wide river cascaded over a series of descending ridges, then narrowed sharply to pass under them. Simon thought for a moment how deep the water had to be, but dismissed that terrifying image and turned to counting the pairs of horses as they crossed to the other side. Just the wheel pair now . . . and . . . there, the front wheels jolted as they dropped off the edge and onto solid ground. His sigh of relief brought another chuckle from Malm.

"Hup. Step out now, git up." The wagon climbed the gentle rise from the edge of the river to a fair-sized parking spot.

"If you hurry, you can run back and ride over with Buck."

"I don't think so. That's got to be the longest hundred feet I've ever traveled. How'd they span that cut? The sides are perfectly straight up and down."

"They did it in the winter when the river froze. It does that around here, thick enough to carry a wagon and team."

Simon turned in his seat and watched Buck move across the bridge and hurry his team up the slight slope.

CHAPTER 6

Early the next morning, Simon stepped forward and took Malm's offered hand.

"Been a real pleasure, young feller. I hope you find what you're lookin' for, and don't let that ambush at Mound Springs hound ya. It wasn't your fault." The openness of Malm's face tightened Simon's chest and made it hard for him to swallow.

"I agree with Bill," Buck said from his wagon seat. "You saved at least one of us, if not both. I think you'll do well, and the way you cook, you'll make someone a good wife."

"Thanks." Heat climbed the back of Simon's neck. "I really appreciate your help. Maybe we'll see you again."

"Like to think so," Malm said. "They's more and more folks movin' 'round up there. There's a small settlement where that big river you're looking for crosses your map. Could be I'll freight some in there one

75

day." Malm grabbed the edge of the driver's box and clambered up the wheel. "Watch that new mule. He sets his ears back, you get outta the way."

"He'll be all right. Have a good trip." Simon raised his hand.

"Haw, git up now. Git." Malm slapped the jerk line and the team, once again eight strong, moved the wagon out and away.

Simon watched until his new friends disappeared in the dusty distance.

His new mule had cost him one hundred and fifty dollars, the packsaddle twenty-five more. Malicious thoughts about the Corinne storekeeper's advice to buy the animal here were allayed when he recalled Bill Malm's quiet voice.

"Expensive animal, but I'd say we got the best of the deal, Spud. Some good company and someone to explain the country for me."

He looked toward his horse and the two mules, standing in the meager shade of a juniper tree. Sonuvabitch, ears turned toward him, shifted his weight, and fluttered his lip. The new mule, ears turned away indifferently, stood as far away as his halter rope would allow.

Simon approached the new mule. "Let's get on the road, boys." He took hold of the halter and had taken three steps toward Sonuvabitch when his arm jerked straight and he nearly fell down. He turned to glare at the mule. "Damn it, don't start." He pulled harder. The mule leaned away. "You gonna make it difficult, aren't you?"

The mule raised its head, its ears half-back, and looked down its nose. Simon tugged again, and the animal set its feet. Ears now flattened, the mule's wide-open eyes gleamed a defiant white.

"We'll do it the hard way, then," Simon muttered to himself.

Simon led his horse out of the shade, grabbed the tag end of the mule's rope, and reached up to secure it to his saddle horn. He'd made one turn around it when the mule exploded.

The rope whipped out of Simon's hands, and the mule went into a frenzy of jumping, bucking, and braying. He took two long hops, then sprang three feet into the air to come down again stiff-legged. Spud shot out of the shade, barking and snapping at the mule's flailing feet.

"Get outta there before you get kicked," Simon hollered.

The mule, with four or five lunging bounds, circled the horse. Shaking his head, he rolled mad eyes at the trailing rope.

Another soaring leap, another earth-shaking return, and his purpose was realized: the first strap broke, and off came the three-gallon can of coal-oil. Then, in quick succession, nearly everything on his back landed on the ground. And then he stopped, packsaddle slung under his belly; pots, pans, groceries, and blankets strewn in the dusty paddock. The mule looked at Simon, shook his head once, and raised his upper lip in a long coughing bray.

"Looks like he's got your number."

Simon hadn't noticed Finley walk up. "Contrary son of a bitch."

"Ain't they all? He's packed before, else he wouldn't know how to unpack like that." The trader chuckled.

Finley's humor rankled. Simon turned to face the horse trader. "Did you know he was gonna be like that?"

"Sure. They all will till you teach 'em it ain't worth it."

Simon's puff of exasperation seemed to set Finley's grin even tighter. "All right. How do I teach him?"

"A twitch."

Simon knew his ignorance was the source of amusement, and that made his inadequacy even more irritating. "Okay, what's a twitch?"

78

Finley reached into his back pocket and took out a fifteen-inch piece of braided leather. Then he picked up a short stick and sauntered over to the mule, which now stood quietly, apparently quite contented. "Come here and I'll show you something."

Simon walked over.

Finley put his arm around the mule's head and hauled it down. "Get over to the other side and do the same."

Simon wrapped his arm around the sweaty ears and clasped his hands under the jaw.

Finley let go, and almost too quickly for Simon to see, grabbed the mule's upper lip and threw a loop around it with the leather thong. One twist, and he had the stick in another loop that allowed him to pinch the mule's lip by turning his hand.

"He so much a' moves a muscle, just give this a twitch." He twisted the loop a little.

The mule's eyelids fluttered, and Simon felt a surge of sympathy. It must have showed.

"You don't need to be mean about it," Finley said. "Just let him know you can hurt him if you want to. Now, you get hold of this."

Simon slipped his fingers around the stick as Finley relaxed his grip.

"Okay, start to walk away, and if he

79

hesitates give 'em a little encouragement."

Simon started to move and the mule followed.

"See there? He's ornery, but he's also smart. I'll let you have that persuader for a buck."

Two hours later Simon had everything repacked except for a half-gallon can of molasses, smashed flat by the recalcitrant mule. Tied head to tail, the short pack train started west toward the distant butte that shimmered dizzily in the mid-July heat of the high desert.

The dreaded black rock he expected did not materialize. The ground rose gently as he rode away from the river, and then turned into rolling hills, sagebrush covered and baked bone-dry in the sun. The well-pounded, dusty, dirt road had Simon constantly reaching for his canteen. Tracks, fresh and numerous, suggested a well-used route, but looking ahead into the haze, he couldn't see any signs of movement, not even a dust cloud.

Several hours of monotonous plodding brought them to the first of the three buttes on his map. A great pimple on the desert floor, it poked its decapitated peak into the sky, blackened slopes littered with chunks and pebbles of broken rocks. The third butte, a brooding monster several times bigger than the first, appeared in the haze. It didn't seem that far away, but Simon had learned estimating distances in the vastness of the high desert could be a humbling exercise. His eyes squinted to slits, he glanced at the sun, and reined his horse to a stop.

"To hell with it, Spud, I've had enough." Simon swung his leg over the saddle and dropped to the ground. "We're staying right here tonight."

Simon pulled the saddle off his horse, relieved the mules of their burdens, and then hobbled all three. They were in the middle of nothing; no movement in the air to relieve the oppressive heat or drive off the persistent flies that swarmed around their heads: a sagebrush Sargasso. Small tufts of leathery grass tempted the animals, and they started foraging. Simon dumped his saddle under a scrubby juniper tree and sat beside it.

"You'd think it would be cooler, Spud. Look around, mountains in every direction, some with patches of snow, and it's gotta be a hundred degrees here." Simon doffed his hat and inspected the soaked sweatband. He took in a deep breath, and puffing his cheeks, exhaled with a long sigh. Scooting around, he leaned back on the saddle, one arm cocked under his head, and shut his eyes.

He woke with a start. A charge of panic shot through him as he sat up straight, and looked for the mules. Gone. He scrambled to his feet and was relieved to see the dog.

"Where's the horse?"

The dog cocked its head and pricked his ears.

"Horse. Where's the horse?"

Spud turned two circles, and answered with a questioning low bark.

"Go git 'em," Simon said hopefully.

Spud spun around and disappeared into the brush. Simon headed in the same general direction, listening, and before he'd gone a hundred yards he heard the bray of an annoyed mule. The sound came from the north, and he carried on to find the horse and mules standing knee deep in the grass at the back of a natural corral, protected on three sides by rugged lava-rock walls eight feet tall. Spud waited at the opening, his tail pumping proudly.

"I'll be damned. Good boy, Spud. I don't reckon they'll be leaving this. Wonder where the moisture's coming from? C'mon, let's git back to our stuff."

When the last flash of crimson disappeared on the western horizon, the temperature started to drop noticeably. Two hours later, his supper of hardtack and beans put away, the evening promised perfection, except for one thing: he was alone. The thought struck him as the individual shapes of the sagebrush blended into one dark shadow and the stars took on clarity seen only in the high country. In the last bit of light, he scampered around for several armloads of dry sagebrush, and built a small fire. The flame's friendly flicker eased the melancholy, and as the fire burned down, his mind drifted back to Nebraska and Sar — He shut her name off, along with the thought. Pulling his blanket up to his hips, he rolled over on his side and willed himself to sleep; the wet that flowed into one ear did not exist.

The next morning they were up and away by sunup. The heat on his back felt good, even though he knew it would be merciless later on. They had been moving about two hours when Sonuvabitch raised his head and brayed. His partner followed suit and both animals picked up their pace, nearly pushing Simon off the road. A small grove of trees appeared, and soon he was standing on the caved-in banks of a creek. Only about three feet wide and barely moving, it

83

was, nonetheless, water in the desert. They hurried down to the shallow stream and drank long and deep.

Simon got out his map and finally understood what one strange line meant. It started somewhere near where he was but it looked like where it ended had to be a pass to the north. That meant it couldn't be a stream unless it ran uphill. But here it was — he stood on its bank. At last had something to navigate by. But where did it end? It couldn't simply disappear into the desert. Or maybe it did. Mulling the thought over, he started refilling the water bags.

They moved past the big butte, and as the late afternoon monotony demanded a stop for the day, they rounded a bluff. Simon saw what he had hoped to see: the long valley heading north into the high mountains. He reined his horse.

"There it is, Spud. Look at 'em, two miles high and as far as you can see. That's where we're going, boy."

Excitement held sleep at bay that evening as Simon imagined the meadows and running water he knew must be in abundance up there. He studied the map again. Seeing nothing new did not dampen the enthusiasm generated by simply looking at it.

The next day they traveled up the valley,

always close to water now. That evening they camped by a small stream with high mountains on either side. The air felt definitely cooler. The fourth day they climbed, nothing severe, just steadily rising, and the pass Walks Fast had marked on the map also marked their campsite.

Morning sunrise came late, the sun blocked by the high mountains. Simon treated himself to a cup of coffee, and as he sat and drank, he studied the valley below. Treeless undulating hills ran to the left, towering snowcapped peaks on the right. The valley extended north and the river he sought came in from the left. His destination almost in sight, a thrill surged through him and he stood.

"Almost home, Spud."

Home. His broad smile withered as Sarah's image drifted into focus.

CHAPTER 7

Smoke meant one thing: people. The blue haze hung over a small collection of cabins, a larger building with a porch, and a blacksmith shop. Several plots of ground, lined with organized rows of green, had several people working in them. His long days on the road made him anxious to see someone. He stopped in front of the porch and dismounted. Three men sat on a long bench to one side of the door.

"Good day to you," Simon said cheerfully. "Does this place have a proper name?"

"Spring Creek. This place is Holverson's. Proper enough for you?" The speaker, a squat, ugly man sitting farthest from the door, spit a ropey brown stream into the dirt at Simon's feet.

"Now that was downright rude, Toad." The man sitting to his right leaned over and jostled the spitter.

"Maybe," Toad said.

"Prospectin'?" the jostler asked.

"Yeah, a little . . . I guess."

The third man eyed him closely. "You from back east?"

"I guess you could say so. Why?"

"Thought so. Jist curious."

Simon tied his horse to the hitch rail, and started for the door.

"Best not be leaving that fancy Winchester where Toad can get his hands on it." It was the third man. He winked.

"Bullshit. I wouldn't steal it," Toad said.

"Not now you won't." The third man nodded toward the rifle and then looked directly at Simon.

Simon walked over and drew the long-barreled rifle from the scabbard. "I appreciate that, sir," he said to the third man.

"Don't mention it."

Simon pointed at the ground by the horse. "Spud, stay there."

Toad muttered something to Simon's benefactor, who simply smiled back, and then leaned against the rough log wall.

The low ceiling of the trading post made the interior seem even darker. The dirt floor felt damp, and the whole place had a musty smell. Simon walked toward the only glimmer of light in the back of the room.

"Whatcha drinkin'?" someone asked.

Simon peered into the gloom to find the man behind the bar. Barely visible in the dim light, a single lamp trimmed to nearly uselessness, he didn't move. "Nothing, thank you," Simon replied. He unfolded a piece of paper. "My name is Simon Steele. I'm looking to find a place upriver. I have a map that —"

The man ignored the greeting as he stepped forward. "Prospectin'?" He took the map and spread it flat on the rough plank bar. Scowling, he leaned over the paper, his eyes squinted.

"Well, not really. I just want to find a quiet place I can —"

He shoved the map across the bar. "You could have snow up to your ass in less than ninety days."

"The Indians can do it."

Holverson snorted. "Another fella said that exact same thing not two years ago. Said he'd be back in the spring. Never saw him again."

Simon picked up the paper, and then dug another piece out of his shirt pocket. "I'm going to need some more things. I have two mules, but there were items too heavy to carry from Utah."

"Utah, ya say." The stench from his mouth forced Simon back a step. "You come all the way from Utah for some privacy?"

"I come because a friend told me of a place where I think I can be comfortable."

"Haw, some friend. What you needin'?"

"Some tarpaper, a few pieces of lumber, some oats . . . I have a list." Simon held up the paper.

"I don't have anything like that here. Stable can get the oats. Salmon City, 'bout fifty miles downriver, would be the only place for the other stuff. Sure you don't wanna drink?"

"Uh, no thanks. I'll go see about the oats."

Simon felt his hair creep on his neck as he turned to leave the dank confines of the trading post and sighed his relief when he stepped into the bright sunlight and over to his horse.

"Don't look like that got you much."

Simon turned to see the third man. "Not really."

"That's Holverson. Not the friendliest type if you're not here to buy his whiskey."

"My name is Simon Steele." Simon offered his hand.

"I'm Justin Reed. Welcome to Spring Creek."

Spud grumbled as Simon took Reed's hand and Simon bumped the dog with his knee. The man's grip felt sure, and his eyes looked sincere. "I'm not actually meaning to stay here. I'm looking for a place upriver a ways. You might think it strange, but I want to build a small place back in the mountains, and spend some time alone."

"Don't sound strange to me."

"I'm relieved to hear that." Simon smiled. "Holverson thought I was insane."

"He was hoping. Misery loves company." Reed flashed a wide smile. "Do you know exactly where this place is?"

"I have a rudimentary map. So far it's been very accurate."

"I'll take a look if you like. I've spent some time back in there."

"I'd appreciate that." Simon jammed his rifle into the scabbard and fished the map out of his pocket.

Reed studied it a moment. "He was very careful about putting the side creeks in. I count ten to the one he has marked. The hot springs are right where he says they are, and near as I can recall, the count to them is right."

"So how does a man get some supplies brought in?"

"There's a fella in Salmon named Shoup who supplies a lot of folks around here. Another in a smaller place called Challis. Both are honest as your own mother. You let them know what you need, and arrange some way to get paid, they'll pack it in."

"But that presents a problem, doesn't it?" Simon studied the man. *What is it about him? So easy, so . . . what's the word? Smooth? Spud doesn't like him.*

"You going to be needing those mules once you decide to stay?"

"I . . . maybe . . . well, of course not, obviously."

"Let me give you an idea, then. I can take you in and trail the mules back out. No doubt in my mind that Shoup would jump at a chance to trade a supply run for them mules, and a good bit besides. You pay the skinner for what he brings in when he gets there."

Simon's tongue explored the inside of his lip where he'd just bitten himself.

"You're thinkin' pretty smart, eh?" Reed said. "Well, I've done the same thing before, several times in fact. I make it my business to take advantage of people's needs."

"It's not that I don't trust you, Mr. Reed, but . . ."

"Of course you don't trust me. Why should you? I'm a total stranger in a strange place. But let me put this to you. All you're risking is a couple mules you admit you're not gonna need anyhow."

91

"And what's in it for you?" Simon could not believe his own rudeness. He felt the blush rise in his face.

"Guess who the skinner's gonna be?" Reed smiled and winked. "I'll get mine, don't you worry about that."

Why do I trust this man? Somehow, I know I can. Then it struck him like a double shot of Navy Rum. *It's his confidence . . . he's totally and supremely confident. Just like Buell, only older.* "I think we have ourselves a deal, Mr. Reed."

"I'm glad. And call me Justin. When were you planning on going upriver?"

"Anytime. Today?"

"No reason why not. Gives us a good head start, and gets us away from the likes of Toad and his friend. I'll pay for what I eat the next three or four days . . . that's if you have it to spare."

"I've got plenty. Let's go."

"You plan on keeping that dog?"

"I hadn't given that a thought. Of course I'm keeping him, he's my best friend."

"Does he find his own food?"

"He chases rabbits, rodents, and the occasional bird, if that's what you mean."

"I'm just suggesting you oughta think about how much he eats."

"He's coming with me."

"Just suggesting, that's all," Reed said with a smile that Simon thought was a little thin.

Reed gathered up his horse, and ten minutes later they rode out of Spring Creek. Simon couldn't believe his good luck.

CHAPTER 8

The floor of the river valley narrowed as they rode upriver, until it was only a long rifle-shot wide. Reed swung his horse sideways in the trail. "It'll be hard to find a wide spot shortly, so I suggest we camp here for tonight."

"Sounds good to me. I'm about done in anyway." Simon turned his horse off the trail and toward the trees a short distance away.

After they'd unloaded the mules, Simon dug the hobbles out of his saddlebags.

"Probably be better if we tied up the animals," Reed said. "More than a few around here who won't hesitate to take what they see unguarded. Got any rope?"

"Yeah, in the packs."

He found what he was looking for in the second pannier, stripped off about sixty feet from each end of one coil, and tied the mules. Reed did the same for the horses with rope from another roll.

Thirty minutes later Simon had a fire going and supper heating up in a skillet. He gave the beans a stir. "Wish I had some fresh stuff. I'm tired of canned beans, tomatoes, and peaches."

"If I understand your intentions, you plan on staying up there awhile. That being the case, you can grow a garden." Reed leaned back against a large rock.

"I would've thought it too cold for that."

"You'd be surprised. I've seen gardens raised by some of the Chinese that are a real sight. Only problem is keeping the critters out of them."

"My mother always had a garden. I remember I sure hated working in it."

"That's because you had other things you thought you needed to do. Different up here. Two things have to be foremost in your mind if you expect to survive, food and fire. You'll probably wind up seeing that garden as a pleasure to work. You're not the first one to come in here and stow themselves away like you intend to. I found two of them dead in the spring, one starved, one dead by his own hand. Couple more just disappeared."

"You make it sound kind of risky."

"It is. Come winter, there isn't anyone

gonna come help even if you could get the word out."

Simon concentrated on the beans for a minute. "You said Chinese? I saw quite a few at the train station in Utah and several at a couple stops between Cheyenne and there. You have some here, too, I gather?"

"Hard to tell how many. I've come up on a cabin or a dugout and got a peek inside . . . guaranteed, I wasn't invited in. I'd find upwards to a dozen of the shifty characters squinting at me from a place barely big enough for two white men."

"What are they doing up here?"

"Started on the railroads mostly, and now they'll do anything, and I mean anything. Mostly, they work at gold digging. They'll go in after we've panned a place out and somehow find enough to make it pay. I've never seen a white man work half as hard as they do."

"Huh, interesting," Simon said. "Here, grab a plate and scoop up some beans. Apologize for the fritters. Sometimes they survive the day intact, sometime they don't. Today they didn't."

Reed settled back with his plate and scooped a spoonful of beans into his mouth. Simon ate his directly out of the pan.

"I'm still curious about your plans," Reed

said. "Don't mean to pry, but we don't get many folks up this way who just want to . . . what? Camp out for a year or two? I'd understand if you find it none of my business."

"Nothing mysterious about it. I had a situation at home in Nebraska that . . . I thought one thing was gonna happen and . . ." Simon studied the beans in the pan for a moment and took a deep breath. "I'm amazed I still can't talk about it."

"Sounds like you had a lady problem," Reed said, his tone even and conciliatory.

"Yeah. The frustrating part is, I didn't see it as a problem."

"Doesn't matter. When it comes to matters of a lady's heart, what you think you know won't get you a lot of play."

"I found that out. Anyhow, I felt it best if I just left, so a friend and I did."

"A friend? He know where you are?"

"No. We had a . . . uh . . . less than agreeable parting in Wyoming. Not his fault." Simon's scalp tightened. "I don't expect I'll see him again," he said quietly.

"So nobody knows you're here?"

"I guess not, except for an old Indian who told me about this place. Never thought about it. I'll write when I get settled in. You can mail it for me when I get my supplies."

"I'd be glad to." Reed scraped the bottom of the tin dish and corralled the last few beans against the rim. "That was good, thank you."

Simon didn't answer immediately, the last of his beans forgotten. It felt good to talk to someone again. How many times had Buell and he done this? "You know, Mr. Reed, you remind me some of my friend. You're quite a bit older but . . . I don't know . . . you're a lot like him."

"Interesting. Exactly how?"

"That, I can't put my finger on." *I can't tell him I think he's smooth.* "Just something that makes me easy around you."

"Well, I'll take that as a compliment. Now, I'm gonna check on the livestock, and then get some shut-eye." He stood and flexed his back. "We'll make the hot springs tomorrow and I'll put you in that canyon you've got marked the next day. You're almost there. And call me Justin."

The mule ahead of Simon broke loose a table-sized rock that then slid about a hundred feet before it started to roll. A low berm three hundred feet farther down the slope shot it into the air to arc lazily for another two hundred feet before smashing to bits in the river channel at the bottom.

Simon leaned to the right and shut his eyes as his horse delicately picked her way around the hole the departed rock had left in the trail. Simon felt his horse relax and opened his eyes to look up the narrow trail at Reed's back. The skinner appeared so nonchalant that Simon felt a rush of shame. They had trailed along the riverbank for part of the morning, and then the canyon had closed in. Reed led the mules up and away from the river to where they were now.

The rest of the day was a succession of heart-stopping climbs along narrow trails, and skidding, half-controlled descents in clouds of dust. The last such descent dropped them into a wide spot by the river. Even in the heat of the day, steam wafted off small pools of water, and the bank displayed a riot of red, orange, and rich browns. The smell left no doubt the water came from Hell. Spud went over and sniffed the nearest pool.

"Here's your hot springs." Reed swung out of his saddle. "We made real good time. You surprised me for a first-timer. That trip usually scares the daylights out of people."

"It wasn't bad," Simon lied. "Did you see that big rock you kicked loose?"

"Heard it. Learned early it's best not to look back."

Simon got off his horse. "Phew, does it always smell like this, or only in the heat of summer?"

"Always. They say you get used to it. I haven't."

"How hot is it?"

Reeds pointed to one crusty-edged pool. "That one will scald you, and quick. If you had an egg, you could cook it. Couple others are just right for washin' up in. Something I'm gonna do soon's we get these animals taken care of."

The nauseating smell of soggy sulfur permeated the camp, and Simon hadn't slept very well. Therefore, Reed's shout came as a shock.

"Better wake up before you ride your horse off the bank." Reed's mount stood ankle-deep in water with the mules lined up behind. Spud sat on the riverbank, his ears pricked forward. "Some of 'em don't take to moving water."

"Guess I was woolgathering." Simon shook his head.

"Nothing wrong with that, just not here." Reed's smile turned the admonishment into a friendly suggestion.

Simon studied the fast-moving water for a few seconds and puffed out his cheeks as he tried to guess the distance to the other side.

"Don't worry about it," Reed said. "Looks farther than it is. We'll be to the other side in two, three minutes. Let your horse make her own way. Just keep her headed generally toward the other side."

"What if one of them goes down?" Simon nodded at the mules.

"I've got the mules. You just stay behind 'em. Not a damn thing anybody can do if one falls. If your horse goes down, try to jump clear . . . upstream. But nobody's going to fall. We'll be across before you know it. Let's go." Reed turned his horse into the river and the mules followed docilely, the first staying in the wake of Reed's bigger horse, the second in the wake of the first.

Simon hesitated, and before he knew it, Reed was halfway across, angling right, into the current, and headed for the mouth of a sizable creek. He urged his horse into the fast water, and his fears evaporated as the horse steadily made her way into the river. The dog ran up and down the bank, barking at the departing train. Simon shouted over his shoulder, "C'mon, Spud, get in here."

The clarity of the water amazed Simon. The rocks on the bottom appeared to be only inches below the surface, their shapes shifting and moving . . . mesmerizing. Then he realized his boots were in the water and the horse had slowed. He looked for Reed, now well upstream, and it became clear Simon would not make the same landing spot as the teamster. His scalp tightened and his heart accelerated. He reined his horse to the right, more into the current. She tossed her head, stumbled with her next step, and turned slightly downstream.

Simon's uneasiness turned to skin-tingling panic, and he gripped the saddle horn with his free hand and sawed her neck with the reins. The horse stumbled again, beating the water with her front hooves as she recovered. And then she lunged forward, more downstream than before. Simon looked to Reed, who now stood onshore, looking back.

Reed cupped his hands over his mouth but "-head" was all Simon could understand, and he tried to turn upstream. His horse lunged again, and Simon, now frantic, grabbed the horn with both hands and hung on. With plunging leaps, the horse bore in on the far bank, now below where the creek dumped into the main river, the bank impossibly steep. With a final lunge, she put her front hooves as far up the bank as she could, and gathered her hindquarters under her belly. Simon felt the balance shift and knew they were going over backwards. He kicked his feet free of the stirrups, let loose of the horn, and slipped over her rear, shoving away as hard as he could.

The horse lurched forward, front feet pawing furiously. Her rising rump caught Simon in mid-slide, and he flipped into the air, head down, his arms and legs churning helplessly. The gulp of air he took the instant before he crashed into the icy water exploded from his lungs as he went under. His elbow smashed against a rock, and fire shot up his arm. He gasped, and icy water slammed into his lungs. Clawing at the water, he burst to the surface, sucking desperately for air. His knees banged against an angular boulder. Then he slid over the top of it, to be dunked headfirst into the swirling water on the lee side. Another gulp of the river went down his throat.

His will to live began to fade along with his vision, when, to his great relief, his feet touched firmly on the bottom. Looking toward the bright light, he shoved toward the bank with all his strength. Then he did it again, as he clawed frantically with his hands. And again, until his fingers found a tree root and grasped it in a death grip. He gulped air, his face resting on the rocky shore, and then he retched.

He was only vaguely aware of the dirt and small rocks sliding down the bank and into his face. "Damn, fella, you all right?" Reed said as he came to a stop beside him. The man grabbed Simon's arm and pulled.

Simon tugged back feebly as he fought to get his knees under him. "I . . . think so." With Reed pulling, Simon climbed out of the water and into the riverbank. He sank to his knees.

"Like I said, some of 'em don't take to swift water. What happened?"

"I could see . . . we weren't going . . . to make . . . the same spot."

"So you turned her?"

"I guess I did. I thought you hollered 'Come ahead.' " Simon wiped his muddy hands on his trousers.

"I said 'Give her her head.' Well, you learned a cold, wet lesson. They can see what's under the water a lot better than we can."

"I like bridges." Simon tried a weak smile.

"Next time you'll be fine. Just remember to let her go. She'll carry you across."

"She all right?"

"Sure. Up there browsing, waiting for you to quit acting like an otter."

"Did you see my rifle?"

"And saddlebags." Reed stuck out his

hand. "Here, stand up and make sure everything works right."

Both of his knees hurt and he looked at the brown-green blotches his trousers had picked up from the mossy boulders. Simon shook his right hand, then squeezed it with his left. "Tingles." He grimaced.

Spud came bounding along the bank from downriver. He barked when he saw Simon and then shook vigorously, the water flying off his head and neck.

"Rough ride when the current has you. All kinds of things get banged up. You'll find some more sore spots in the next couple of days, guaranteed. Let's get up on the level and you can change clothes."

With his wet clothes draped over the panniers, Simon followed the pack train into the canyon. The creek water ran white, smashing to foam as it hurried across the rocks to join the river. Cottonwood, aspen, and willow grew alongside short pointed stumps, evidence of dam-building beavers. They traveled through a narrow entrance that started to open up after a quarter-mile. Soon they were riding through a wide meadow, the creek meandering placidly, tamed by the width of the streambed.

Simon rode silently, in awe of the steep canyon walls rising to impossible heights, the stoic peaks naked to the winds and time-less. "Look at that, Justin."

Reed turned in his saddle and looked back.

"Up there." Simon pointed to the jagged skyline at the end of the valley.

The ridge broke perfectly to form the shape of a gun sight. Reed reined the train to a stop and Simon rode past the mules.

"That's amazing," Reed said when Simon pulled alongside. "Give you something to admire when you get your place set up."

"You mean we're here? Uh, I mean, this is the place?" A flush of anxiety swept over him as he stared up at the heights of the mountains around him, their sheer majesty pushing down on him.

"The place is anywhere you want to stop. I've never been up here. It is impressive." Reed smiled at him.

"I don't know how to describe it," Simon said.

"Well, you can look it over real good. Pick a spot that suits your fancy. You lead and I'll bring the mules."

Simon moved past Reed and rode slowly up the valley, Spud ranging ahead. Several side canyons cut away, dry beds now, but all showed signs that massive amounts of water ran down them from time to time. One particularly wide one drew his attention.

"Wait a few minutes. I want to ride up this one a ways."

Reed nodded and dropped enough slack in his reins to allow his horse to grab a mouthful of grass.

Simon turned up the creek bed. A few rocks lay mixed in with the dirt, and from bank to bank, the channel spread over sixty feet wide. It wound its way into the side canyon, gradually rising for almost half a mile, then started to narrow abruptly. Dried mud, with some splatters stuck ten or twelve feet above the ground, plastered the uphill sides of the trees. Six-foot-tall tree stumps, bare roots and all, lay jammed against rock outcrops, and standing timber, their tops not sharp and pointy like beaver falls, but broken off, ragged and splintered. Another two hundred yards, and the channel narrowed to the point of being impassable. Going back downstream, the mud marks were even more apparent, and he could see in his mind's eye a torrent of slurry, smashing downhill, carrying rocks heavy enough to crush trees. Again, the sense of being overwhelmed raised the hair on his neck.

"What'd you see?" Reed pulled his horse's head up as Simon rode out of the side canyon.

"I can see I'm going to have to be real careful where I put my place." Simon looked around with new eyes at the wide creek bed of the main stream. The man-high boulders that lay strewn across it took on a chilling significance. "Let's ride on some more."

The canyon angled right, narrowed by half, and then opened up again. The gun sight could no longer be seen, the massive formation lost in the towering peaks that loomed above. The creek bed now contained a confusion of splintered trees and massive blocks of granite. The water twisted and turned, rushing to clear the obstacles and then rest in the slower meanders lower down. They continued on, and another meadow greeted them, this one over a quarter-mile wide and nearly flat. Simon reined his horse in, and took a slow look around at the peaceful setting. Distance muffled the sound of the rushing water at the far end as it tumbled down the rocks of a narrow defile. His gaze continued right to a pair of magnificent spruce trees. They were as alike as any two trees could be, and stood about seventy feet apart and over a hundred feet tall. Twins, rooted at the same time, and raised in the same ground, destined to keep each other company for as long as they lived. Simon had found his place.

CHAPTER 9

The next morning Simon watched Reed make his way out of the canyon, north along the edge of the meadow. Several emotions struggled for supremacy. Still in shadow, his new friend turned and waved from the bend in the valley. Then he was gone.

"Well, Spud, I guess we're here."

The dog looked up at him for a moment and then turned back to stare toward the spot where the man and mules had disappeared. He rumbled a low, almost private, growl and turned away. Simon walked over to the pile of goods unloaded the day before and stared down at what he had to work with. He sat on the folded canvas and grappled with the feeling currently in ascendance: inadequacy. He wasn't scared, though the sharp edge of fear glinted, ready to cut his tenuous hold on peace of mind. How soon would the dreaded snow fly? The crisp morning felt good.

He had plenty of food and he'd seen signs of deer. Or was it elk? What could be so hard about digging a hole, and putting up a few logs for the sides and something to cover the top? He had a stove. Reed had said, "Food and fire." *There's the food and look around . . . wood everywhere. But . . .* He sat down and stared up at the eastern horizon, and the slender wedge of doubt slipped in.

Simon was lost in thought, the random kind where nothing lingers for more than a moment and one idea has no relationship to the next, when the sun crested the ridge and took him by surprise. An overwhelming emotion exploded in his consciousness and awe banished his disquiet. The jagged rock edges of the sheer cliffs soaring into the eastern sky melted in the dazzling brilliance of the rising sun. The memory of a similar experience flooded back, and he raised his face to meet the light. A feeling of warmth spread through his body, a heat that came from within, the source deep and guarded jealously, exposed rarely.

Simon sank into himself, the sensation warm and fluid. He closed his eyes and absorbed the energy he felt streaming across space; took it, fed on it, and lifted from the earth. Euphoria drafted him up, and he drifted, gently rocked in a cradle of bright light. All sense of the flesh left him, and he became as mist, shifting and spiraling through the treetops, sighing with pleasure. Simon dissolved into thin air, a part of everything . . . and nothing. Time stopped.

His head snapped forward and his teeth clicked together. Spud lay beside him asleep, and the sun now stood well off the horizon. Simon shook his head, slightly confused, then stood. His eyes were drawn to the east side of the meadow by a vague feeling of being watched. He studied the shadows and saw nothing. But still . . . he shook his head in dismissal.

"Time I looked this place over, Spud. Got a lot of work to do, and I don't think I have a lot of time to do it in."

He saddled the horse and headed out the way he'd come in. The day before he'd noticed a curious stand of trees on the eastern side of the valley and cantered the mile to reach them. Tall, slender, and perfectly straight, their clean, branch-free trunks begged to be used. Once into the closely packed grove, he realized he'd seen something like them before, only in a different setting. Walks Fast's teepee. These were the trees used to create that structure.

"Perfect for building a roof," he muttered.

"Lay these side-by-each, and it'd be better than sawn boards."

He wrapped his hands around one, and then another. There were many the same size, and he felt pleased with himself for having solved one problem already. Leaving the copse, he rode back toward his meadow, his eyes on the larger trees covering the hillside. By the time he'd made his way back to the twin spruces, he'd identified enough trees to supply the logs needed for his dugout. Spud, anticipating Simon's intentions, bounded on past the pile of supplies, and they headed toward the narrow end of the canyon.

First the smell hit him, and then he saw the ocher side hill; the hot springs, exactly as Walks Fast had described. A steady seep of water flowed from the bank, across the grass, down a gentle slope and into the creek some two hundred yards away. Simon dismounted and hunkered down by the narrow stream. Cautious, he felt the water. It was warm. His horse browsed the grass eagerly.

"Perfect pasture, don't you think, Spud?"

The dog wagged a mute response, and padded over to the sodden bank.

"I bet this'll stay clear of snow in the winter."

Spud ignored him and sniffed the rusty mud.

"And I bet we could grow stuff here. Look at the grass and those bushes. Got to remember to order some seeds when Justin comes back."

Simon poked around in the mud below the bank and stuffed twigs into the streaming fissures in the rock. Then, he scratched a skillet-sized hole and watched it fill. A short distance away, he dug another reservoir, then created a channel to connect the two. And watched the second one fill.

"You know, Spud, a little work and I could have a bathtub with warm running water. What do you think of that?"

The dog, sound asleep in the sun, ignored him.

"Humph, some company you are." He went back to expanding his miniature canal system.

Simon glanced up at the sun and winced at its high angle. Hurriedly, he cleaned the mud off his hands and started the trek back toward his campsite, leading his horse. The air smelled heavily of pine and the indefinable something that belongs to the mountains. Do rocks have a smell? He stopped and took a deep breath, eyes shut to enhance the sense. He heaved a sigh of pleasure, and opened his eyes to look directly at a small deer, not forty yards away.

She looked back, ears turned fully in his direction. Torn between the desire to simply admire the beautiful creature and the primal urge to kill it, he studied it for several seconds. Then he made a move toward his horse and the deer snorted once, took five or six stiff-legged hops toward the shelter of the trees, and stopped. Simon had his rifle to his shoulder when the animal started walking away and he pulled the trigger. The tawny-red creature dropped to her knees, then toppled sideways, her sleek side marred by the perfectly placed shot. Simon's charge of elation chilled almost instantly as the deer raised its head, and then lowered it slowly to the ground. It didn't move again.

Spud took off, heading straight for the fallen animal.

"Hey! You get back here."

The dog nearly piled up getting stopped. He turned to look at Simon, confused.

"Leave it alone. Sit!"

Simon walked past his dog and approached the deer. A small hole just above its elbow seeped crimson. He poked the deer in the side, the hide soft and pliable.

"Now we get to see how much attention I paid when Dad butchered a steer." He

115

puffed his cheeks and sighed. "And me without a knife." He mounted his horse, and galloped to his campsite.

The chore of eviscerating the small deer was not that bad, but it wasn't that tidy either. By the time he'd finished, he had blood everywhere, had managed to cut through the hide in a dozen places, and had a lot more hair on the meat than he would have liked. Flies materialized out of nowhere and swarmed all over; on him, the deer, the gut pile, and the ragged hide. Simon got tired of swatting at them. He stepped back and surveyed his work. Drawn, hung, and skinned, the small deer presented a spirit-damping sight swinging aimlessly in the light breeze. He went over and laid his hand on the shiny muscles of the shoulder.

"Damn it!" The heat he felt came as a surprise. "Looks like I didn't think this out, Spud." He shook his head in disgust, and started to cut a haunch from the purple and white carcass.

He scooped the last shovelful of dirt over the wasted deer. What would have been an easy task in Nebraska had turned into a two-hour job in the rocky soil of the mountains. Finished, he leaned on the short-handled shovel.

"Makes me wonder if I can make a dugout

in the next week or so," he mused.

Spud went over and sniffed the burial site.

"Come on, let's go cut a few roof poles before the sun goes down. Then we'll have liver for supper. Sound good?"

Simon found that cutting the slender trees down was more easily done with the bucksaw than an ax, and it left a finished end. In the last four hours of the day, he laid down nearly twenty trees, each three to four inches at the butt. That was over half as many as he thought he'd need. He threw a rope around six, and dragged them back to camp. The sun had been gone nearly an hour when he turned the horse into the rope corral. Busting up firewood used up about all the energy he had left.

The liver came cold from the creek, and the strips of red-brown flesh seeped pink fluid as he sliced them off. He floured each piece before he dropped it into the eighteen-inch black skillet, and soon the whole pan steamed with a muted sizzle. Spud sat across the fire, tongue lashing out to catch his drool.

"Smells good, huh?" Simon poked absently at the strips a couple of times, then started to mold his fritters. The extra skillet sputtered grease as he coated the bottom with a piece of bacon end. He laid the cakes in the glistening pan, put a lid on, and scooped some hot coals over the top. "There, fifteen minutes, and we can eat."

Hungry as he was, he found no pleasure in the meal. Every bite brought the sight of the pitiful carcass to mind, squandered and lying in the dirt. The food in his mouth turned to a tasteless lump, and he scooped his plate clean on the ground. Spud looked at him, head cocked, hesitant.

"Go ahead. I can't eat it," Simon said. "Or that either." He threw the rest of the meat to the dog and looked at the single deer leg hanging from a nearby tree.

The dog pounced on the meat, wolfed the strips down in a few hasty gulps, and sat back down. He studied his master and licked his chops.

Simon went to his saddlebags and came back to the fire with a small book. He sat down, steadied the opened journal on his knee, and wrote on the first page.

July 24, 1873. I am Simon Steele. I arrived here in the White Cloud Mountains on July 23, 1873. It is my desire to live here in peace. Today I killed without thinking. That will not happen again.

He closed the book and stared at the fire

118

for a long time before he got up and went to his bed to lie down.

He found the blackness of the forest that covered both sides of his canyon disconcerting. He rolled over on his right side, eyes wide open. His gaze sought the peaks and the solace of something he could center on. All he could see was more black, the peaks simply an absence of stars.

"Spud?" he whispered. "Come over here." Then, he cleared his throat self-consciously, and said in a normal voice, "Spud. Come here." The vague outline of his dog rose from a spot by the supply pile and came toward him. "Lie down."

The pressure of the dog as he settled by his legs and the animal's warmth raised his spirits, and Simon's body gave up to fatigue.

CHAPTER 10

He paced off fourteen feet along the hillside, set the last rock down, and stepped back. With his eyes closed, he tried to imagine what his new house would look like. He couldn't. The two rocks that marked the corners of the back wall were set up the hillside, and for the life of him, the image of a square box sitting level wouldn't form. The size of the wedge of dirt he had to move did.

"That's a lot of dirt, Spud. And if the ground here is like it is where I buried that little doe, I've got my work cut out."

Simon figured eight logs' high would be enough. The trees he had mentally marked the day before were all about a foot in diameter, and he thought a twelve-inch log, fourteen feet long, was about all he could manage by himself. That made thirty-two logs. Simon wished he had Zahn there to help. The solid timberman had made it look so simple back at Fort Laramie. Simon strapped his ax to the back of the saddle, and got on the horse.

"C'mon. Let's get started."

Stripping branches from its neighbors, the first tree fell heavily to the forest floor, showering Simon with pine cones. There was something satisfying about the heavy dull thud, a certain finality. Simon sat on his butt for a minute to catch his breath and grinned at the dog. "See? Nothing to it."

The trees were so straight and even, he was going to be able to get two logs out of each tree. With his ax, he measured off fourteen feet, the three-foot handle perfect for the task. He chopped a small notch and measured the second log. There were very few branches to swamp, and in an hour he had the two logs lying end to end. He sat on the ground, and drank long from the canvas bag. A steady chittering drew his gaze to squirrel-tail semaphore; the agitated twitch telling him he wasn't welcome.

He smiled at the little animal. "Someone told me I'm supposed to listen to you fellas. Tell you what, let me finish here, and I promise I'll be a good neighbor."

Spud padded over and sat down, his head cocked.

"Just talking to the neighbors, boy." He ruffled the dog's ears and stood.

He picked up his ax, and immediately put it down again to stare at the palms of his hands. Two enormous blisters had formed, one in the center of his left hand, the other in the web of his right. Now what? He poked at the soft squishy skin of his left one, thin and vulnerable. He'd had blisters before, but never this big. And he'd always pointed them out to his father who would let him stop for the day. Simon dropped his hands to his sides, his shoulders stooped, and slowly shook his head from side to side. Then he took a deep breath, picked up his ax, and attacked the next tree.

The left blister burst first, a sudden sticky-wet feeling in the palm of his hand followed by a swing-stopping sting. He glanced at it, clamped his teeth together, and continued. The second one ruptured as he made the final chop and stepped back from the toppling tree. By the time he had the logs separated and clear of branches, his ax handle was slick with blood. He stood and looked at them.

"It hurts, Spud. And I don't know what to do." A hot flash of tense nerves rippled through his head and shoulders.

Simon sat down again and poured water

from the bag over his sticky hands. The blisters were now open wounds with ragged flaps of skin attached to one side. He caught an edge of one and tore the dead flesh away, teeth bared in a grimace as live skin came away with the dead.

"I can't do it, boy. I've got to have something to cover these."

Simon went to his horse, tightened the cinch, and got on.

A few minutes later, he was at camp with a butcher knife in his hand and a pair of long underwear in his lap. He cut them off at the knee and then cut two loops off the bottoms where his ankles would have gone. Doubling one loop over with a twist, he slipped his left hand into the hole. It made a snug, fingerless glove. He then cut strips from the rest of the leg and wrapped his hands, securing the makeshift protection.

He breathed an audible sigh as he quit working his hands and settled them on his legs. Spud put his head on his arm and looked up at him. Simon saw the sympathy in his eyes and, with a wince, patted his dog. "I'll be okay. Wish I had some of Ma's salve."

The next day, pain sapped his strength with every swing of the ax, and he only managed to down one tree. That evening, he went to the creek to soak the bandage-glove off. Crusty and stiff, it stuck to the new flesh, and both arms ached to his shoulder from the cold before the cloth came loose. He managed to open a can of beans for himself, and fed the dog some leftover fritters. His journal entry noted the day he'd missed and today's date with one word, "tired." He then collapsed into his bed, asleep in a minute.

Sarah's eyes screamed at him to help, her lips somehow silenced. David stood behind her, his whiskered face buried in the creamy skin of her neck, his eyes mocking his cousin's inability to raise his arms and defend her.

"Turn her loose, you bastard," Simon raged.

"Or what? Nothin' you kin do without askin' your pa."

"Leave her alone!" Simon could not scream loud enough. His whole being shook with fury as David's callused hand cupped Sarah's breast. Simon tried to reach out, but he couldn't force his hands from his side. Sarah, her face now twisted in fear or shame, suddenly shut her eyes and turned her head away.

"No! No, noooo." Simon bolted upright in bed, struggling for breath, his hands trembling with pain. The stars, cold and impersonal, looked down and the black forest offered his tormented brain no solace. Spud whimpered and moved closer to Simon's legs

Next morning by the campfire, he slowly opened his partially closed hand. The flesh, red and angry, cracked in places and seeped a little blood. Bad, he thought, but not as raw as the night before.

"Maybe I ought to keep 'em out in the air. Let 'em dry. What do you think?"

Spud listened intently and wrinkled his eyebrows, willing but unable to help.

"Well, I'm not gonna use the ax today. What say we tackle some roof poles with the bucksaw? Might be able to do that."

Simon stood and went to the supply pile. He picked up the saw and gripped the handle gingerly, then put it back. "Nope." He shook his head. "Looks like we have another day off."

Simon and the dog relaxed in the shade by the supplies, the midafternoon air warm and nearly still. The mesmerizing sound of unseen flies buzzing back and forth emptied Simon's head of all useful thoughts. Then Spud jumped to his feet, and Simon's eyes popped open, his mind instantly alert. The dog stood tensed, his hackles up, his nostrils flared as he tested the air. He was looking at the far side of the meadow.

"What did you hear?"

Simon tried to see into the dark shadows. In the shifting light of the active treetops everything moved — yet nothing would claim an identity. A low grumble from Spud's chest made Simon look even harder. There! Something moved, then stopped, then moved again. Simon concentrated on the place he last saw something change, and Spud's hackles rose to full height. Simon grabbed a handful of neck fur and winced in pain. Again, move and stop. Tree to tree? A man! One more flicker of movement and then nothing. Simon stared at the last spot until his eyes rebelled in tears. He reached for his Winchester.

"Now what the hell was that?" Simon stood. "Sit," he ordered.

He continued to look across the meadow for several minutes, scanning along the tree line. Then, he started for the far side. "C'mon." The dog got up and followed, right at his heels.

He rock-hopped across the creek and into trees where he stopped. *Listen. Listen and they will tell you.* Walks Fast's words came to him. He sat at the base of a tree on the thick mat of pine needles. The breathy sigh of the breeze in the treetops slowly tuned his ears to the background noises: the ever-present flies, the steady mumble of the water in the creek, the chatter of a squirrel — an agitated and excited squirrel! Simon jumped to his feet and splashed across the water to look toward the southern end of the meadow. He saw the flicker of movement as several birds took flight near the creek. And then another squirrel took up the alarm. Someone or something was making its way out of the meadow. *Should I go look? For what? And do what?* A cool dampness settled over him.

"C'mon, Spud. Let's get back to camp. Good boy."

He looked over his shoulder repeatedly on the way back and glanced at the tree line many times more before the light was gone that evening and he pulled his blanket over his hips. He wrote:

July 27, 1873. Had someone or something visit today. Hands too sore to work.

Simon spent three more days treating his hands, and then went back to work with the bucksaw, cutting the rest of the roof poles. It hurt, but with summer half gone, he gritted his teeth against the pain. Twice more over the next three weeks, Simon felt someone, or something, watching, until the last of the trees he needed lay prone. He cut them to the length he needed and notched them to create the lock at the corners, tightening the gaps on the overlapped logs. Laid out side by side, the trimmed lengths were an impressive sight and he felt proud. He'd also built a pole corral with the tall slim trees.

"Now that wasn't so tough after all, was it, boy?"

Spud had just returned from one of his daily adventures. Tired, he had flopped down in the shade and now lifted his tail once in acknowledgment, and shut his eyes again.

"Humph," Simon said. "What do you get into out there?" *Visiting? With what — or who? I wonder if my ghost is one of those Sheep Indians Walks Fast talked about?*

"Get up, you lazy slug. We're gonna leave a present for someone."

Simon dug around in the panniers for several minutes and came up with a knife and a pair of red wool socks. Then, he found in his saddlebags the short leather "twitch" he'd bought at Taylor's Bridge. He smooched his lips and the dog got up, slowly. Together they hiked the hundred yards across the meadow and stopped just inside the trees. Simon looked back to make sure he could see his camp clearly and then swung the knife in an arc and stuck its point deep in a tree. He wrapped the long socks around the hilt, and tied them with the braided leather thong. Stepping back, he looked at his handiwork and smiled. "That'll get their attention. C'mon."

From camp, Simon looked across the meadow, and as he considered his act of good faith, a warm feeling of satisfaction spread through him. The natural beauty of the magnificent setting struck him. He studied the rugged skyline for a few minutes, then dropped his gaze from the jagged crest and back to the forest.

His euphoria vanished at the sight of the wool socks, a jarring discordance, the unnatural red an affront. His mind filled with a vision of the wasted doe, lying in the shallow hole, the flesh dirt-fouled. And he pictured all the wood left on the forest floor, so much scrap, left as he extracted what he wanted, as he wanted it. He was a white man intruding on the peaceful valley.

August 19, 1873. Today I left a gift for my unknown visitor. Also, I saw what waste is. I will live here and not disturb my neighbors.

"I promise," he muttered to himself as he closed the book.

CHAPTER 11

Next morning Simon scrambled out of bed, and looked across the meadow. Against the sun, he couldn't tell if the red socks were there or not. He set about making breakfast, glancing over from time to time, not wanting to see it, but a little afraid, as well, to find it missing. Today, he was going to start the dugout, and he was anxious to begin.

He forked the sizzling bacon out of the fat while Spud licked his chops and watched every move. Dropped into the smoking pan, the cornmeal balls gathered little halos of glistening grease bubbles. A few minutes later, he had his plate full and sat back to enjoy his meal — a glance at the forest and a glimpse of red ruined it.

The shovel point bit into the earth about four inches, and grated to an ankle-jarring halt. Simon pulled the tool back slightly, and tromped down again. A nerve-rattling

131

sound of metal grinding on naked rock stopped him again. He used the shovel point to scrape away the dirt, found an edge, and pried the angular chunk of rock out of the ground. It landed outside the dig with a grudging thud.

"I guess we have our answer, Spud. This isn't going to be easy." Simon reached for the pickax.

The work was slow, frustrating, and extremely tiring. Sparks flew as he struck unseen rocks, and they were everywhere in the soil. He worked along the front edge of the dig, using the pick to loosen the rocky soil. By noon he had no energy left, and had made only two passes between the two marker rocks. After eating something, he leaned back against the folded canvas he'd propped against a tree, and tried to ignore the incessant tingling in his hands. He dozed off.

A smell like nothing he'd ever experienced woke him out of a sound sleep. Blowing air out through pursed lips, he shook his head and turned away from the light breeze. It didn't do any good. Spud, head held high, gathered the information that floated on the wind. He didn't seem to be upset and continued to sniff.

Simon got up. "What in hell is that?"

He stepped out of the shade and looked up the valley. "Phew, that's worse than any skunk I ever smelled." He stood for several minutes, and just as he turned to go back into the shade, he caught a glimpse of something dark moving low to the ground. It was there and gone before Simon could make out size, shape, or color. The smell lingered, and took on a slightly more familiar odor — rotten meat.

"Let's go take a look, Spud," Simon said, and reached for his rifle.

He found the rotten meat, and the source of the other smell. Both were strong. The place where he'd buried the deer was a welter of torn-up ground, scattered bones, and slimy-rotten scraps of flesh. His stomach turned over and his gorge rose.

"What would want to get at that?" He held his free hand over his nose and breathed through his mouth. Then, he spotted the crushed deer's head, the top of the skull gone with remnants of the soupy brain still evident. Simon puked.

The picture of the savaged burial site stayed with him all afternoon as he continued to work on his dugout. Spud stood alert, but showed no sign of hearing or seeing anything unusual. Simon struggled to make progress in the unforgiving ground, but by the end of the day had barely made an impression on the hillside. As tired as he'd been in his life, he threw the shovel down in disgust. That evening he noted his visitor in his journal.

August 20, 1873. Visited today by some foul animal. Started to dig for my cabin. Very hard work.

By the end of the fourth day digging, he felt a little happier with his progress. The corners at the back of the hole were now nearly two feet high, and he had accumulated enough large rocks to set a good foundation along one side. He put his shovel down, and walked over to his fire ring. Kneeling, he gently scraped back the ashes, and laid a few wood chips over the invisible coals. A couple of the chips turned brown and started to smoke. He blew a few puffs of air under them, and they burst into flame. Broken branches followed some twigs, and soon his campfire was going. He settled back on his haunches, dusted his hands together — and noticed how absolutely filthy they were. *Is my face that dirty?* He rolled up a sleeve and winced.

After a glance to check on the red socks the next morning, he grabbed the pick and shovel and headed up the valley to the hot spring. A survey of the ground below the soggy bank showed him a good spot, and he started digging. By midmorning he had dug a hip-deep hole. Three feet wide and almost five feet long, he'd kept a clean grassy edge by throwing the dirt well clear. He gathered all the rocks with at least a rudimentary flat side and threw them back into the hole. There, he fit them together on the bottom in a crude tile arrangement. By noon, he had his bathtub. He cut a channel in the heavy soil back to the spring, then sat down by the basin to watch it fill. It was a disappointing vigil, the water muddy, and the surface of his bath covered with a red-brown scum of foam. Spud walked over to the edge of the pool, sniffed once, and turned away. Disgusted, Simon rolled up his sleeves and washed his hands and forearms.

"They look better, but I don't feel any cleaner. Enough fooling around, Mutt, let's get back at it."

The work on the dugout took on a more methodical pace, and he labored on the vertical face of the back wall. Pulled free with the point of the pick, the earth busted up naturally and exposed the bigger rocks. Those he pitched out by hand, leaving nothing but dirt easily shoveled out of the cut.

The progress over the next week had

Simon in high spirits until, midafternoon one day, Spud suddenly stood and looked down the valley.

"See something?" Simon leaned his shovel against the side of the hole, and flexed his back. He stepped into the open and looked north. Shortly, he saw what the dog had heard or sensed, a rider . . . no. A rider and two pack animals. He watched for several minutes and finally confirmed what he had hoped.

"Got company, Spud, and our supplies."

The dog grumbled and paced back and forth.

Reed climbed off his horse. "Well, haven't we been the busy beaver?"

"Hello, Mr. Reed." Simon stuck out his hand.

Reed eyed the extended hand, then moved to one side before he took it. Simon saw the quick scan and Reed's moving a little further into the light breeze. "I must look a mess," Simon said.

"I've seen worse . . . I think." Reed burst out laughing. "Have you even thought about what you might look like, or smell like?"

"I guess not." Simon felt his face getting hot. "It isn't exactly the Cheyenne Hotel up here."

"I'm sorry, didn't mean to offend. But you

"are a sight."

"That's all right. In fact, I did see I was gettin' pretty ripe and tried to make a bath up at the hot springs. Wound up with a pool of muck-water. And bathing in the creek is not an option. It's colder than the river was, and that damn near froze me."

"I got you the mirror and the shaving stuff. You'll figger something out."

"Were you able to find everything I had on the list?" Simon looked past Reed.

"Yup, except for the fish hooks and line." Reed followed Simon to the mules.

"Where's Sonuvabitch?" Simon asked.

"Salmon City, I suppose. Shoup was pleased to have him, and he knows mules."

"Ah, some boards . . . good. And the tar-paper."

"Let's get if off of 'em. I expect they're tired."

The two men soon had the mules unloaded and put away in the corral. They walked over to Simon's digging site.

"How long've you been at that?"

"Little over a week." Simon couldn't suppress a satisfied smile.

Reed said nothing, and walked over to the raft of logs lying in the sun.

"Where'd you learn to chop like that?"

"Watched a Wisconsin timberman. He'd

knock out a notch like that in eight strokes. Took me a sight longer. Trick is to keep the ax sharp."

"Looks good to me, and I've seen plenty."

"My pa said 'If you can't find time to do it right, when do you think you'll find time to do it over?' I took that to heart."

"Can you lift one of those by yourself?"

"One end. Haven't tried to lift the whole thing. I thought the slope would help me."

"It will, except for the front."

"I've thought about that. If I tie off the rope on the inside, throw the loose end over the top, around the log in a sling, and then back over the top and under the wall, I can —"

"Whoa, you lost me."

Simon hunkered down, smoothed a patch of dirt, and scratched a diagram.

"I tie one end here." Simon pointed to the inside of the wall. "Go over the top with the other and loop it under the log. Then, put the rope back over the wall and pull the end back outside, under the wall. When I pull on the loose end, the loop will close and pull the log all the way to the top."

"If you could do that and keep it level, you'd have it done. But one man can't do that."

"I don't need to keep it level. First I'll

138

lean two or three poles against the top tier of logs. Then I'll work one end at a time, prop the high end up with a notched-end pole."

"You know, it might work."

"I think so, too. I've gone over it a hundred times in my head."

"And you have to get your dugout finished and level before you start. I've got my doubts."

"I've done some figuring, and I can have the hole finished in two weeks. It's about the first of September isn't it?"

"It is the first."

"Can I count on good weather in September?"

"You can't count on anything up here. It could snow tomorrow."

"But it doesn't usually, does it? Snow in September?"

"Not much if it does. You can figger on September, but we usually get a freeze. It'll snow in October, guaranteed, give us a short break after, we call it Indian summer, and then five months of deep snow and cold. But nothing surprises me anymore."

"I think I can get it done."

"Not one to interfere, but you have the option of coming out with me if you want."

"Naw, we'll stay."

139

That evening, Reed leaned back against the stack of logs, put aside the stick he was whittling on, and built a cigarette. The dog watched every move, and when Reed leaned forward to fetch a light from the fire, Spud growled.

"Spud! What in hell gets into you sometimes?" Simon shoved the dog in the shoulder. "Now shut up and lie there." Simon got up and stepped around the fire to Reed. "Let me have your plate."

"He never has taken to me."

"It isn't you. He's been nervous since we got here." Simon dropped their plates and forks into the dishpan heating by the fire.

"Might be the full moon too."

"Could be. Lots of stuff moves around up here when the moon is bright. I've had Indian visitors."

"You have? Did you see 'em or just some sign?"

"Neither and both. I saw something move the other side of the meadow. Saw it two or three times. We went over to see, and I watched birds get flushed and heard squirrels make a racket upstream. I never did actually see anybody, but I'm sure someone was there."

"That's not a good thing."

"The Indian who told me about this place

said there were people here who lived high in the mountains and hunted the sheep."

"Sheepeaters, Dogeaters, Snakes, Blackfeet. Call 'em what you want to, they're Indians, and I don't like 'em, none of 'em. They're diseased, ignorant, and heathen. I'll shoot every one I see."

"Shoot 'em!"

"I would and figger I was doing you a favor."

"Well, you never met Walks Fast. He's as smart as either one of us and saved my life. I damn near died in the snow but for him."

"Maybe the rare exception. Makes me all the more sure you should come out with me tomorrow."

"I don't think I fear them. I left a knife and a pair of socks over there to tell them I mean no harm."

"A knife! Good Lord man, you're asking for it."

"If they wanted what I have here, I think they would have taken it by now. They haven't. Matter of fact, they haven't even taken the knife. It's still stuck in the tree."

"You wake up dead one morning, don't say you weren't warned."

Simon slapped his hand over his mouth.

"You know what I mean, dammit." Reed tossed his cigarette butt into the fire.

141

"I'm sorry. Just struck me funny." Simon swallowed hard and clamped his lips together.

"Well, it isn't."

"I know it." Simon paused, a silent apology. "I also had a run-in with what Walks Fast called a Devil Bear."

"You're having all kinds of bad visitors. He means a wolverine. That is one nasty creature. It'll take on a bear and make it turn tail. Did you see it?"

"Nope. I — he was digging — I killed a young deer and —"

"At this time of the year?"

"I know that now. I buried it, and the wolverine dug it up. Do they stink? The wolverines I mean?"

"Something terrible, and they deliberately put it on everything. Miserable beast, and you're in his territory. He isn't going to like that."

Simon shrugged his shoulders and leaned forward to catch hold of the coffeepot. "Want some more of this?"

"Sure, never turn down a cup of coffee. Never can be sure when you'll see your next one."

"That's strange you say that. I had a friend — a Texas trail boss — who used to say exactly the same thing." Simon poured both

142

cups full.

The air settled in on them, cool, still, and full of the fragrance of the mountains. The silence of the evening fell on their conversation. Simon watched Reed carve on a long, narrow piece of wood, shaping perfect little diamonds; one after another, each attached to the next. The full moon opened the forest with its deceptive light, tantalizing the imagination with distorted details and fabricated images. Spirits roamed at will, as delusive as they were real.

The next morning Simon pointed across the meadow with his coffee cup. "It's to the right of the largest boulder on the far bank of the creek. The tree kind of stands by itself in that clear spot."

"I can see the tree, but I'm telling you, there's no red sock on it."

"It was there yesterday, dammit." Simon shaded his eyes and studied the spot.

Reed drained his cup and set it down. "Let's go see."

The knife was gone, the scar in the tree fresh. A chill scrambled up Simon's back and lifted his neck hair. Reed puffed out a breath of air.

"Well, you can see where it was," Simon said.

"I didn't doubt it was there. I just don't

like the thought of a stinking Indian prowling around my bed at night."

"It is kinda . . . I don't know. Uncomfortable?"

"It's more than that. Unless you have a powerful reason to stay up here, I'd seriously consider spending the winter in Challis or Salmon."

"For some reason, I don't fear them. I want to stay."

"Must be something real powerful holding you here. I'd hate to see you get killed, Simon."

That was the first time he'd called Simon by his first name, and it jarred him for a split second. "I don't know about powerful, but I feel at home here, more than I have in a long time."

"Well, I'm on my way. Offer still stands, regardless."

They walked back across the meadow, and Reed saddled his horse. A few minutes later, he tossed Simon a salute and led the mules north. "See you in the spring. I hope."

I hope so too, Simon thought. He watched a few minutes and saw a puff of blue-white smoke waft over Reed's shoulder; a leisurely cigarette to see him out of the meadow.

CHAPTER 12

Simon admired the new six-foot crosscut saw, its perfectly even teeth long and menacing. "Got everything we need now, Spud." He touched the tip of one tooth and yanked back in surprise. "I hope I can keep it as sharp as that." He put it back with the other new supplies.

His start that morning had been delayed by Reed's departure, but he felt completely relaxed and unhurried, almost lighthearted. The midmorning sun warmed his back as he worked on the rear wall of the dugout. Spud lay in the sun, sprawled on his side, feet extended, a dog in bliss.

Simon stooped to shift a large rock that he'd worked loose with his pick. He couldn't get a firm grip on it, and when he tried to lift one side to roll it out of the hole, the weight of the rock surprised him.

"Huh. Guess I'll find out how the horse reacts to being used like a mule."

145

He'd anticipated using her and had made a makeshift collar out of four strands of rope, tied in a circle, and wrapped in a long strip of canvas. He slipped the hoop over the horse's head, and led her out of the corral. With the rope tied around the rock, he fastened the loose end to the collar, and tugged on her halter. The mare moved forward until she felt the resistance, then stopped with a snort.

"C'mon girl, lean into it." Simon increased pressure on the halter, and the horse jerked her head up. "I know it's not what you're used to, but you're going to learn. Come on now."

She flattened her ears and rolled her eyes. Simon tugged again. The mare leaned forward and the rope tightened. Simon gave the halter another gentle tug and she leaned more. The rock moved, and Spud barked at it.

"Good girl . . . c'mon, pull."

Simon kept pressure on the lead rope and she took a step, leaned into the weight, then took another step, and another, and dragged the rock out of the hillside. She turned to look at what had been holding her back, and fluttered her lips.

"See there, you can do it." Simon backed her up a step and untied the rope.

Four more times that day Simon used the horse to drag an oversized rock free. Each time she proved more willing and savvy. When the sun dropped below the ridge, he led the horse into her corral, took off the collar, and poured half a gallon of oats onto a piece of canvas. She started to snuffle through them as soon as he stepped out of the way; the dual-purpose snorts showing her pleasure and blowing away the dust. He walked back to the campfire.

"I need some hot water, Spud." Simon put his shirt on, grabbed the bar of brown soap, and headed for the hot springs.

Simon stood on the edge of the bathing pool and shook his head. "Will you look at that?" He could see the silt-blurred mosaic of rocks on the bottom of the pool. "I guess I wasn't patient enough, Spud."

He sat, undressed, and then climbed into the pool. After a furtive look around, his hands held low in front, he knelt and eased himself into the warm water. Crouching on the bottom, he shut his eyes and let his arms dangle beside his hips.

He sighed with pleasure as the warm water loosened some of the grime. Spud let out a bark, and Simon looked up at the dog standing on the edge of the pool. "Oh, boy, you have no idea. I think I'm going to spend the night here." He reached for the soap and shifted his weight, straightened one leg, then the other, and sat on the semi-smooth bottom.

A full hour later Simon strode back to camp, naked except for his shoes. He dumped his filthy clothes in a heap and found fresh ones in one of the panniers. Shivering, he donned the clean clothes, then knelt by the fire ring and teased a flame from the waiting coals.

"Next time I'll bring a towel, that's for sure. But that was worth it. I never imagined it would be this good, Spud. I have a house well on its way, plenty to eat, and now a hot bath whenever I want it. I can see why Walks Fast wanted me to come here."

Simon took his time making supper and set his meal on an improvised table made up of sawn sections of log and two of the boards Reed had packed in. The irregular ridge to the west stood in sharp silhouette as the coral glow on the horizon faded to a uniform dusty rose. He picked up his dishes, dropped them into the dishpan, and washed them. A trip to the creek for a bucket of water saw the last of the faltering light, and he sat down on the ground, his back against a rock he'd dragged in. Several bright points of light pulsed in the clear night sky, and he completely relaxed for the first time since he'd arrived in the valley.

September 6, 1873. I think I have found my peace. My body and spirit feel clean tonight. Work goes well.

The next morning Simon lay with his arms folded across his chest, both hands tucked close to his body. Only vaguely aware of the sounds or smell of morning as yet, his sense of feeling focused on the top of his head. It was cold. He slipped a little lower into his nest and pulled the covers tighter around his ears. It didn't help, his slumber permanently interrupted for the day. He opened one eye a fraction and peered across camp at ground level. The reason for his cold head became apparent and stark — frost covered everything. Simon let loose his grip on the covers, thought about his options for a minute or two, and sat up. A thin wisp of smoke lifted from the last remnant of wood on the outside edge of the campfire.

"Wish Buell was here. He could make coffee."

Spud uncurled, stood, and stretched.

"And aren't you a sight? You're covered in frost."

The dog padded over to him and he dusted the icy powder from the dog's shoulder.

Simon pushed the two blankets down, stood up, and fetched his pants and shirt from under the dew cover. Boots stomped on, he soon had a fire going, and the coffeepot set to boil. The meadow displayed a sparkling mixture of green, red, and yellow, the vibrancy of fall muted by the white promise of winter. At the far end of the valley, a cloud of steam marked the location of the springs.

The dog sat patiently as Simon made them something to eat, then they both wolfed it down and went to work. The sunlight, advancing down the western slope, banished the frost as it invaded, and as Simon swung his pick, he felt its first warm caress. Ten minutes with the pick, ten more moving the rocks, and another fifteen with the shovel completed a cycle of excavating. By noon, Simon's spirits were high, and after a short meal of corn cakes and cold ham, he got back to digging.

After nine days of steady progress, each starting with a frosty morning, followed by a glorious, sunny day, he'd finished half of what he wanted to dig. Simon dropped his shovel, leaned his hands against the ever-higher wall, and arched his back before turning to look at his dog, sound asleep in the dirt. "Time for a break, you lazy slug."

He shuffled out of the hole to stand in front of the dugout, and took a long drink from the water bag. He hoped the blue sky was a promise of more fair weather. Even though his muscles burned with exertion, it was a good feeling.

"At this rate we'll have this done in another week, eh, dog?" Spud thumped his tail in agreement.

Simon stretched once more before entering the cut and grabbing his pick. He aimed at the spot where he'd stopped working, centered two-thirds of the way up the wall, and struck. The pick shot a brilliant spark out of the dirt and the head wrenched viciously sideways. A shock coursed through the handle and shot all the way to his neck.

"Damn!"

He took a shorter grip on the handle and poked at the shallow hole in the dirt. He hit solid rock. With tentative pecks, he cleared away at the dirt around the first strike, and found more rock. Two feet to the right, he finally found the curve in the boulder.

"Got a big one, Spud."

He continued to pick around the rock, and the left side only served to raise his anxiety.

With dirt up to his knees, he exposed enough of the obstacle to at last reveal its apparent size, five feet wide and almost as tall. Simon moved the entire pile of dirt he'd knocked loose and stepped back to gauge his challenge. He shook his head. The left side of the rock face was flat and inclined about thirty degrees, the top sloped sharply back and down into the hillside.

"Looks like we get to see how much the horse has learned, eh boy?"

Simon led the mare out of the corral and slipped the collar over her head. He uncoiled a hundred-foot length of rope and fashioned a loop in one end. With his pick, he cleared away the dirt behind the rock until he could get a firm grip on the top, then slipped the loop over the rough peak. With his heels set, he hauled hard on the rope. It held. Playing out the entire length, he tied the rope to the crude harness and urged the horse to slowly take up the slack. Taut, the rope began to stretch, and the horse leaned into the resistance. Further and further she leaned, the collar turning her sideways. Trembling with exertion, she shifted her hind feet and lunged forward. The rope jerked her back and sideways.

"Whoa. Stand easy, girl." Simon patted the horse on the neck. "Easy." He walked into the dugout. The rock showed no signs of having been affected by the efforts of the horse.

"Shit."

Simon slipped the rope loose and put the horse back in the corral. The sun sank into the mountain and took his exuberance with it. Perched on one of the countless rocks in front of the hole, he stared at the obstinate boulder.

"Right smack in the middle, Spud, can you believe that? I couldn't have planned that any worse if I knew it was there."

The air flashed cool with the setting sun, and a chill rippled through his sweaty body. He stood and examined the rock again, picking at the edges with the point of his shovel. The right-hand curve continued around the back and the left side terminated abruptly.

"I think it depends on how deep it's set. What do you think? Reckon we find out tomorrow."

Supper was quiet, and his journal entry that evening was short — *hit a snag today.* Visions of never-ending shafts of rock troubled his sleep.

Simon worked the dirt and smaller rocks loose from around the boulder. By noon he had over two feet exposed down the back and worked into the late afternoon to clear as much on the sides as he could. The sun was dipping low toward the ridge when he led the mare to the dugout. Both lengths of rope were looped through the collar this time, one on either side of the horse, the four ends tied around the tip of the rock. After evenly adjusting the lengths, he took the horse by the halter and eased her into the ropes. The two strands on either side kept her straight.

"We have to do this, girl, we just have to." Simon tugged on the halter and the horse leaned hard, then backed.

"Again, girl. Haw!" Simon jerked hard on the halter.

The mare plunged into the load, rear hooves dug into the ground, and she reached forward with her front feet. Dust rose around them and settled on his sweaty body. Clumps of dirt flew from her churning hooves. Simon watched the rock for any sign of movement, the four strands of hemp pulled straight as a drill bit.

"Haw! Pull, girl! You gotta pull."

Belly down, the horse tore the earth, her open mouth blowing gouts of hot, wet air. Simon pulled with all his might on the halter, his eyes squeezed shut against the effort. Suddenly, he heard the horse gasp and she faltered. His eyes snapped open and he looked up at the struggling mare. Her ears lay flat against her head, her neck out-stretched.

"Until their hearts burst if you ask 'em." Bill Malm's words flashed into his head.

"Whoa." Simon slacked up on the halter rope and the horse jerked back.

"Oh, God, what am I doing?"

The horse stood still and her chest bellowed in and out, her eyes blinking slowly.

Simon stroked her neck. "I'm sorry, girl. I don't know what I was thinking."

With shoulders slumped, he went into the dugout and slipped the loops free of the rock. The mare's head hung low as he led her into the corral and slipped the collar off. She ignored the oats Simon poured on the ground.

That evening, Simon stared into the flickering red and yellow of the fire, his spirit as beaten as his body.

"What are we gonna do, dog? I don't think that rock is gonna move, and I'll be damned if I'll let that poor horse kill herself trying to move it. Already wasted one animal without thinking, and it isn't going to happen again."

Simon got up and walked into the dugout.

The intruding rock, shaped like a mountain peak, mocked him in the flickering light.

"Stopped me cold. Probably hooked up in hell aren't you? Just when I had it going right you have to show up. Been hiding there forever, waiting for some poor pilgrim like me. Well, I'm not done yet. We'll see who wins this one, you sonuvabitch."

Simon spit on the rock and turned back to the campfire.

September 16, 1873. Getting harder and harder. Nearly killed the horse working a big rock. Missed my birthday.

It was over an hour to sunup when Simon stepped into the dugout to confront the immutable rock. He grasped the edge of the cold granite and tugged, then kicked the dirt wall.

"Shit!" He wasted another kick, then picked up a rock, and stepped to the front of the dugout directly in line with the left side of his nemesis. Turning, he started to pace. "One, two, three," he counted off until he set the rock down where his fourteenth step landed, picked up another one, and marked out the relocated square on the hillside. With his lips set in a firm line, he grabbed his pick and started chipping away at the new dig; over nine feet of virgin soil, another ten or twelve days of brutal hard work. After six or seven furious strokes with the pick, he threw down the tool and sat on the pile of dirt. The first tear took him by surprise.

"I'm sorry, Spud," Simon said. He wrapped his arm around his dog's neck when the animal came over to him, whining. He leaned his face into the dog's furry scruff and Simon's sobs of frustration shook them both.

For a week, Simon worked from early light until he could no longer see. Twice his heart had sunk with the sight of another spike of granite sticking out of the ground, and twice his horse had forced it free. Yesterday, the clouds had moved in, and today he felt the cold when he stopped to rest.

Dogged, he kept at it until finally, he set the point of his shovel in the ground and rested his foot on it. "We've done it, boy. That's the last shovelful." Simon slumped to the ground, pulled the cork on the water bag, and drank deeply. "I can get the foundation rocks set in the next couple days, and then we'll start to shift logs into place." He glanced up at the heavy clouds. "We're gonna make it, Spud, I can feel it."

September 25, 1873. Finished hole today. Hit a big rock and had to move over. Getting colder.

CHAPTER 13

The logs fell into place one after another; one level became two, two became three, and long before he thought it possible, Simon was contemplating the fourth tier. He'd used three poles resting atop the wall to ramp the third log into place, but his body was rapidly succumbing to the ravages of long hours of brutal hard work and poor sleep. Twice today, he'd lifted until a dazzling display of bright spots behind his eyes blazed a warning.

"Looks like we try my rope sling idea, Spud."

Simon and the mare dragged a log to the base of the three-pole ramp. Then, inside the walls, he drove two big nails into the bottom log of the front, one on the right side, the other on the left. With the rope tied off to the left-side nail, he threw the rope over the wall. Outside, he looped it under the log and threw the end back inside the cabin. Now, by pulling on the rope, he could draw the loop closed and roll the end of the log up the ramp. To let the horse do the work, he stuffed the rope under the wall and tied the end to her collar.

"Looks like a spider's web, Spud." Simon chuckled and took hold of the horse's halter. She leaned gently into the strain as he urged her forward.

"Gittup," he said quietly.

The rope tightened and the loop started to close, dragging the left-hand end of the log up the ramp.

"It's gonna work, Spud. You see that? It's gonna work like I thought." He released the strain on the halter. "Whoa, now." Simon patted the horse on the neck. "Stand still, girl." He stroked her again and then walked to the angled log, one end now halfway up the ramp.

He'd cut four poles to use as props and laid them along either side of the ramp. He picked up a short one. With one end jammed against the log, he dug out a shallow divot in the ground for the other and set the short pole in place. He eased the horse back and the prop held the log solidly.

His spirits soaring, he leaped over the low wall and tied off the other rope. Soon, he stood by the horse, looking back at his spider's web, and eased the horse forward, his heart racing. The log slipped up the ramp and was soon three-quarters of the way to the top.

"Slick as butter, Spud."

Simon selected a longer prop and wedged it against the canted log. Five minutes later he'd dragged the left end of the log all the way to the top of the wall and propped it up. Switching ropes again, he eased the horse away, and the right-hand end of the log rose to the top and stopped. The first log of the fourth tier was safely perched atop the low wall.

"That's it, Spud. Can you believe it? We're gonna have this done in no time."

Simon put his shoulder into the log and slid it along the side wall. Back and forth, first one end, then the other, he maneuvered the log to the back, then rolled it into place, the notches matching perfectly as the timber settled with a thud. The mare was learning, as was Simon, and each log went up a little easier. Once the prop slipped, and the timber came back down the ramp, both man and horse scrambling to get out of its way. After that, Simon tied off the rope on the free end as he switched back and forth.

Day three came and went, then four and five. Simon's body slowly began to break down. Leg cramps shot him out of bed in the middle of the night, and his stomach rebelled at the fare of cold ham and mouthfuls of raw cornmeal that sufficed for supper. Finally, on the eighth day, the thirty-second log settled into place and Simon collapsed against the end of the cabin, his muscles trembling with fatigue and excitement. Spud came over and sat beside him, his paw on Simon's leg.

"There it is, Spud. No door or window, but we got our house. The roof'll seem easy after the walls. And tonight, I'm gonna have a hot bath and we're gonna cook us something real good for supper." Simon leaned back against the wall and shut his eyes.

The grouse he'd killed by the creek looked a little tough. On his way back from his bath, he'd come up on five of them. They'd stood, unafraid, black eyes watching stupidly, and he'd whacked two of them with a stick. They were smaller than the prairie chickens he remembered from home, but he'd never been able to get within a hundred feet of those. The dog watched intently as Simon cut the second bird up and rolled it in the cornmeal. With the biggest skillet full of meat, he set the heavy lid on and covered it with red-hot embers. He peeled four potatoes from the sack Reed had brought and sliced them into the second pan. He winced as spatters of bacon grease lit on the backs of his hands. He looked over at the finished walls of his cabin and smiled.

"Wish Pa could see that. And Tay . . . and Sarah." The knife poised motionless over the potato as her image floated into focus. He studied her face for a moment. Then, with a deep sigh, he finished the potato, sprinkled on some salt, and put the lid on.

The aroma of coffee blended with the spicy scent of burning pine and set Simon's mind adrift. Relaxed and at ease for the first time in weeks, he glanced at the saddlebags lying by the spruce tree. He went to them and came back with Sarah's letter to sit a bit by the fire. The envelope showed the effects of countless inspections, and he carefully extracted the single sheet of paper. He put it to his nose and imagined, then read it again.

July 14, 1872

Dear Simon,
I take pen in hand with some trepidation. I knew one day your letter would come, and I have thought often about what I would do. Even now I can feel the panic. I am in school studying to be a teacher. It is so satisfying. I know now what Miss Ever-

ett felt. I so look forward to a room full of my own students. I have come to terms with what happened in the past, and I am much relieved that you know the truth. At times it seems so long ago and faded, yet at other times, some of the memories are very fresh and still very much alive.

Please understand that I am happy, both with my life and with what I am doing. If you wish me happiness, wish me success here. Sometimes I weep when I think of what could have been. The beauty of our time together comes clear in my dreams, and I wish for things that seem denied. For now, dear Simon, you must leave us as we are, knowing some things cannot be changed except with time. And knowing those things to be true, I hope you understand why I cry.

Sarah

Simon dropped his hands into his lap and shut his eyes against the sting.

The morning dawned cool and cloudy, a heavy, gray canopy misting the treetops. Simon heated up some of the previous night's potatoes, and with that and a fried slice of ham, he settled next to the fire and studied the angular structure on the hillside. "Got to admit, I had my doubts a time or

164

two, Spud, but there it is."

He chewed and admired his new home, a twelve-foot rust-brown square, set in the hard-won hole. It was during many sleepless nights that he'd worked out the details of how he was going to build the roof, and he felt ready. He speared the last piece of ham on his plate, put the dish down, and got to his feet.

Simon slipped the collar in place and led the horse to the three extra-long poles that would go on top to create the roof supports. The extra length would allow him to fashion a porch cover. Frivolous, he knew, but he couldn't resist the urge to do it just the same.

He led the horse out of the corral. "C'mon, girl, just a little bit more." With the rope double looped around the end of the log, Simon tied the free ends to the collar and took hold of the halter. Together he and the horse stepped off, out of the trees, and toward the new cabin.

The fiery cold shock of a huge snowflake snapped his head to one side and he put his hand to the spot where it had hit him. He looked up to see the entire sky descending on him; countless individual pieces of white, each followed by another in an endless stream. In a matter of seconds, the ground was white, and complete silence fell over the camp. Spud hunkered down under the trees, and the horse, her head down, ears drooping, waited for a command. Simon, dumbstruck, saw his visible world close in to nothing. A tremor of panic chilled his body. The snow came down at an incredible rate, huge globs of white that weren't flakes at all, more like clumps of cotton, and they all fell at precisely the same angle.

Shoulders hunched against the onslaught, he shook off the snow, lifted the horse's head, and started toward the cabin again. The log slid easily over the fresh fall, and Simon started up the slope to the right of the dugout. Without warning, the mare slipped, then lunged forward to catch herself. Caught in the back by the horse's shoulder, Simon went sprawling into the space between the log wall and the hole he'd dug. His head smacked hard against the timber and he fetched up on the bottom with a jolt.

"Oh, damn, hurts," he muttered and tasted blood.

The logs pressed against his back and shoulders. The side of his face pressed into the dirt at the bottom of the hole. He sucked in as much air as his compressed lungs would allow and choked on something. He retched, and the spasm wedged him even tighter. With his left hand, he tried to push away from the bottom, while scratching with his other for some purchase on the rough bark. He barely moved. His head pounded, and he could feel every beat of his heart.

"Spud," he tried to shout, and retched again.

He pushed down harder and kicked his legs as high as he could, hoping against hope that he could catch the top of the wall with his toe. Bright spots appeared. He closed his eyes tightly against them, and struggled harder. Then a narrow halo of blackness gathered around the bright spots and started to grow thicker. The cluster of spots became smaller and smaller, until there was nothing but black. Simon heard someone screaming, "Spuuuud!"

Damp and cold, he lay on his stomach, an angular rock caving in the ribs on his right side. He made one feeble attempt to move, and his will slipped away into the distance and he drifted. The vague sense of daylight came to him once, along with the feeling that he was under shelter. But again, he couldn't make sense of any of it, and sank back into his hazy sanctuary.

Hands touched his arm, and strong fingers tested and probed. They went to his head and gently pressured a sore spot, then felt along his jawline. He willed his eyes open, and the glare of white snapped them shut. The hands left him as the person rose, and then stepped over him. He forced his eyes open again and caught a glimpse of someone's lower leg. Ankle-deep in snow, it was sheathed in a red wool sock. With a shuddering gasp, Simon passed back to the other side, once again comfortable on his bed of stone.

Weight pressed down on him, and he resisted with a shrug. A spasm of pain blasted his eyes open. The weight shifted and Simon felt warm breath on his cheek.

"Spud?" The dog nuzzled his jaw, and another sharp pain shot through his head. "Sit down, boy. Sit." Simon moved his arms and felt the rock under his chest. "Oh, shit," he moaned.

Gathering his arms under him, he pushed away from the ground and rolled to his side. He was lying under the edge of the canvas that covered his supplies, and a soft, white-haired animal skin lay over his torso and legs. Simon eased himself into a sitting position and tried to get up. His vision faded to black for a moment, and he sat back down.

Snow had been tromped down around his bed for a short distance, and that small area gave way to an unbroken field of white, nearly three feet of snow rounding every surface. The trees bent low under the weight of huge mounds piled on the branches. Halfway to his cabin, an almost smokeless fire burned.

His back stiffened and he searched left and right. For what? Tracks? Some sign he wasn't alone. Reed? Nothing greeted him but the brilliant, stark white. His right hand had two fingers with severely torn nails. *I fell into the hole by the wall. The horse?* Peering intently though the covered trees, he located her, safe in the corral. With a shudder, the memory of being trapped came to him, and he bowed his head and shut his eyes against the sight.

Red — I saw red socks. He remembered the Indian's ministrations, and Simon struggled to his feet to search the forest behind him, almost panicked. Nothing moved, not a bird, not a squirrel — nothing. A snap from the fire drew his attention, and he turned to look. Suspended low and well away from the glowing coals were two birds. Skewered on willow branches, they beckoned to his stomach. It grumbled a response.

He devoured the first bird with barely a pause for breath, tossing the stripped bones to the dog, who snapped them up. Simon reached for the second bird, and then stopped.

"How did that Indian get past you?"

Spud gobbled a couple more bites, swallowed, and sat down. He cocked his head and waited.

"Well, how?" Simon studied the dog. "Is that where you've been going every day since we got here? Huh? Is that why you turn up your nose at my fritters from time to time? You raise hell when Reed shows up, and he's a white man. Some guard you are."

The dog cocked his head the other way and licked his chops.

"And that's all you got to say? You're hungry?"

Simon lifted the rock off the butt end of the roasting stick and gingerly pulled a leg off the bird. Sucking generous amounts of cold air around the steaming meat, he bit a piece off and savored the greasy morsel.

October 5, 1873? Had an accident but someone helped me. I think it was an Indian. All's well.

CHAPTER 14

Simon woke the next day to clear skies, and by noon the forest around him hissed constantly as branches slipped their loads of snow. After a struggle, he managed to get up the slope by the cabin. It was apparent the horse couldn't work in such conditions, so Simon spent the day staring at the fire and listening to the snow flop to the ground. For three days, he sat in the wet snow. The sun shone bright, but without a lot of heat. Slowly, the soggy blanket of snow deteriorated to leave only patches in the shade, and the pristine white changed to glistening brown. Simon wished the snow were back.

On the fourth day, the morning showed a meadow of frosty white, and Simon tried several times to burrow deeper into his bed. Finally, he gave up and threw back the buffalo hide cover. Clouds of steam puffed out with every breath, and he hurried to get his boots on. The ground was rough and uneven with frozen mud. He looked up at the sky and felt the presence of winter.

"We're not ready, dog. We got a lot of things to do, and building that cabin is not one of them."

Simon coaxed the fire back to life and went to the water bucket to fill the coffeepot. It was nearly solid ice. With a sigh, he clomped to the creek to fill it.

He considered his situation over a breakfast of bacon and oatmeal mush. Finished, he went to the raft of long poles he'd cut his roof materials from and selected six short and one long. Cut to the right lengths, he fashioned a tent frame, lashed together with wire, and sank the ends into the frosty ground. There was more than enough canvas to cover the structure and the supplies, and he set about arranging the tough cloth over the frame. By noon, he'd finished that task, picked up his ax, and led the horse down the meadow to a patch of dead timber. The sound of the first chop echoed through the valley, followed for the rest of the day by the same steady beat. The sun dropped and with it, the temperature. Simon dragged one full-length tree into camp, ate a hurried meal, and went to bed.

It could have been the cold or his sore muscles or the dog searching for a warmer spot, but Simon woke the next morning tired and irritable. He knelt by the fire ring and puffed at the tiny flame in the smoky pile of wood chips. His mood matched the frosty scene, and the fire's reluctance to gather strength added to his ire.

Suddenly Simon stood. "What the hell am I doing here?"

He picked up a short length of wood and threw it into the fire. Ashes, sparks, and bits of charred wood flew and the small flame went out.

"Damn it!" A well-placed kick scattered what was left of the morning fire. "C'mon, let's get to work." Simon scowled at the piece of timber lying fifteen feet away.

The new and sharp crosscut saw soon reduced the log to short lengths. The steady work wore off his irritation, and he heaved a sigh when he finished. He ran his arm over his brow.

"I think I'll cut all the splitting blocks we'll need before we chop any up. Let's get something to eat, Spud, and then see if we can't be back here by noon with another log."

He was, and had that one cut up and another one back in camp before it was too dark to see. The pile of blocks had grown to an impressive heap by the end of the second day. He sat by the fire and admired his work.

"Seems I remember Pa said a family needed between three and four cords of wood for a winter. Never occurred to me when I was cutting wood with him back home that I'd be doing it for myself one day. I wonder if I'll need more or less. What do you think?" He thumped the dog on the side. "I bought it for the hotel, ten cords at the time, but we were heating — well, there isn't any comparison. And looks like we'll be spending the winter in the tent. I wonder if it'll snow enough to cover us. Maybe I better put some more supports under the canvas."

Simon got up and poured himself another cup of coffee. *Four by four by eight is a cord. The logs are twelve inches average diameter, five four-foot lengths per log and I need thirty-two lengths.* Simon screwed his face up and, with his eyes shut, finished the mental arithmetic. "We have to cut about twenty trees for the three cords we're going to need, and it looks like we can do two a day." Simon looked up at the sky. The cold clear air sharpened the stars, the waning moon a stark mosaic of white and gray. He remembered sitting in the prairie with Buell, sharing young-boy talk of living in the mountains and fighting Indians. The dog looked up at Simon's chuckle. "I got what I wanted. Just wish he were here with me. What was it Ma always said, 'Wish for a shower, live with the rainstorm.'"

Simon opened his journal and sat thinking for a few minutes before he wrote.

October 11, 1873. Today I have doubts. I pray for good weather. I miss Buell.

Simon swigged the last bit of coffee and dashed the dregs into the glowing embers. Then he laid down two of his freshly won blocks on the outside of the fire and went to bed.

For the next three days Simon cut, swamped, and blocked timber. The third day the wind picked up and clouds settled in. Fearing the worst, he increased his efforts. On the fourth day, the force of the gale grew so strong that Simon didn't dare cut a tree, but stayed in camp, splitting wood. As quickly as it arrived, the bad weather moved on, without developing so much as a short snow flurry.

Simon led the horse north toward the timber and smiled at the clear sky. By the time he'd dropped the first tree, he was so warm his coat had come off, and he rolled up his sleeves. Wood chips flew from the log, and the cut separating the heavy trunk from the skinny top was nearly done when Spud barked. Simon put down his ax and followed the dog's gaze north.

"I don't see anything, boy." Simon looked up the mountainside and then south, up the valley.

The dog "woofed" and continued to look north. He ears switched from tipped forward — listening — to back — warning, his tail curled up defiantly.

"You seem sure. I'll take a breather, and we'll watch for a few minutes."

The dog looked up at him, and then sat, his nose pointed down the valley. Less than fifteen minutes later, Simon caught a glimpse of movement, and then the pack train crossed the creek and moved into plain sight. The dog stood, and his hackles rose.

"It's Reed, Spud. I'll be damned, he's made another trip."

Simon picked up his ax, finished chopping the top off the log, and tied the rope around the butt. He arrived in camp well ahead of the packer.

Reed rode in his shirtsleeves, and the horse and mules were well lathered when he swung out of his saddle.

"Wondered what I'd find." He nodded at the tent. "Figgered that storm would've

176

slowed you done a mite."

"Hell of a story," Simon said. "Let's get the mules unloaded, and we can talk. Sure good to see you." He stuck out his hand. "Didn't think I'd see a white man till spring. I'm sick of the snow and even sicker of the mud. And then that last mess blew through, and I thought for sure I was going to be stuck. Got knocked into the hole by the horse and . . . sorry. Guess I'm talking a lot."

Reed chuckled and let go of Simon's hand. "Thought I'd give you one more chance to get out of here. This is that late summer I told you about. Could last two or three weeks, or four or five days. Like you said, let's get the mules unloaded."

Reed held up a long, dark-brown, woolly coat. "If you don't want this I'll take it back with me. And those too." He pointed at a bundle. The curved ends of a pair of snow-shoes poked out from between the folds of a heavy buffalo robe. "It's up to you."

"No, I'll keep 'em. I really appreciate it."

"I thought you might end up in a tent, and looks like I'm right. You're going to be glad you have the robe."

"So you don't think I'll be able to finish the cabin?"

"Nope, and neither do you. I haven't

177

known you long, but I know you're one who thinks things out. Have you calculated how much more time you need to cut your wood?"

"Six more days."

"See what I mean? Calculated." Reed pointed at the cabin. "And there. You have to put up at least three rafters, cut and frame a doorway and make a door for it, and then put the roof on. And that means the poles and the tarpaper with enough dirt over it to keep the first blizzard from taking it to the Salmon River. How long for one man to do all that?"

"I was thinking —"

"I know what you're thinking, but I can't stay even two days. I'm not prepared to live here all winter, and you're not prepared to have a visitor for that long. I'll stick around tomorrow, but the day after that, I've got to leave."

"Yeah, I guess I knew that." Simon pitched a twig he'd been fiddling with toward the cabin.

"Have you seen any elk yet? That storm should have given them the hint."

"I have. Twice, a group has moved past me. I guess they're headed toward the river."

"Might want to think about knocking one down with the next snow."

178

"Will it keep?"

"Oh, yeah. All you have to worry about is keeping the vermin out of it."

"Vermin? You mean worms and such?"

"I mean your wolverine friend, and bears and cats and wolves."

"There're wolves up here? And bears?"

"Sure."

"What kind of cats?"

"Bobcats and mountain cats."

"I haven't heard anything, and I know what a wolf sounds like. Wyoming was full of them."

"They won't be where you are unless they have no choice. All but the bobcats get out of the high country in the winter. It's easier hunting and not so much snow. Why can't you take a lesson from them?"

"Because I'm here to find something."

Reed's manner changed; where before, he'd been looking right at him, the packer now averted his eyes. "Everybody's looking for something," Reed said, and walked toward the dugout. "Let's go take a look at your cabin."

"I fell in there," said Simon. He pointed to the space outside the left wall.

"Tight fit," Reed replied with a grin.

"I fell in head first."

Reed's grin evaporated. "How far back?"

"Almost to the rear. I couldn't get out."

"Then how come you're standing here?"

"Remember those red socks I told you about?"

"Stuck to the tree?"

"Yup. I woke up the next day, near as I can tell, to someone feeling my arms. To see if they were broke, I suppose. I was on my belly." Simon reached up and pushed on his ribs. "Lying on a rock." He chuckled. "Kind of funny now. Anyhow, all I could see was snow and somebody's legs from the knees down. That somebody was wearing red socks."

"You're joshing me."

"Nope, gospel. That Indian pulled me out of the hole and took care of me at least overnight. Left me under an animal skin of some kind, fixed a fire, and cooked two birds."

"Did you see him again?"

"Nope. I didn't actually see him the first time, just the socks, and then I guess I passed out again for a while. He saved my life. I know that."

"Do you think they're watching all the time?"

"I don't know. I think Spud knows them though. He didn't make a sound while that Indian was in camp."

"You're crazy. You can't trust a damn Indian, I'm telling you."

"I don't see where trust comes into it, Justin. I was in no position to make a decision, but I'm sure glad he was there."

Reed wiped his chin with his hand and gazed narrowly at Simon. "I'll say it one more time, and then I'll let it be. An Indian will cut your throat just to see the color of your blood. Either you are the luckiest man I know, or you have some powerful spirit looking after you."

"I think a little of both. Now, let me get some supper going." Simon nodded downstream. "Then you can tell me what's happening down there."

After supper, the two of them sat beside the fire. Simon's ears and the back of his neck were cold in spite of the rapidly burning logs right in front of him. He reached his hands out to the heat and rubbed them together.

"Has that wolverine been back to visit since he tore up your burial site?" Reed's face reflected the ruddy glow of the fire.

"Nope. Maybe we scared him enough he'll stay away."

"That's a laugh. An old boar can have a range of fifty square miles. He's just busy raising hell somewhere else."

"Are they so tough that a .44 won't settle their breakfast?"

"You know, I'm not sure. I've heard of trappers who've caught the same one twice. One day they'd find just a leg in the trap, and the next day a thoroughly agitated wolverine with just three. So yeah, they're tough, and mean."

"But why bother me?"

"Maybe just because you're here, and this is his territory. Hell, I don't know. Ask him next time he visits." Reed spit in the fire. "You are one bull-headed Swede."

"So I've been told."

"Might make a suggestion about your campfire here."

"Sure."

"Build a wide U-shaped berm of logs about four feet high. Leave a space or two in the bottom for air to come through and face the opening toward your tent. Leave enough room so the logs won't catch fire. It'll save on your wood and push the heat into your tent."

"Okay, I can do that. Anything else you can suggest?"

"A hundred things, but I'd be sure to forget the important ones. You're going to learn some lessons. Put your water bucket next to the fire. Hang your meat high. Never leave your rifle in the tent with you at night. A south wind means a weather change in the next couple of days. Eat fat, lots of it, and drink often. The air up here is dry as an old bone. Snowshoes are slow but safe, so wear them."

"I don't know how to use them."

"Then be prepared to kiss the ground a few times till you learn. You'll be tempted to leave them home, but the first time you find yourself ass-deep in snow, you'll wish you hadn't."

"It all makes sense, except the rifle in the tent."

"You take a warm gun outside when it's twenty-five below zero, you'll soon discover where your wet breath settled during the night."

Simon reached over and ruffled Spud's ears. He realized that Reed was doing his best to shake his resolve, and maybe for a good purpose. But exactly why? Simon had lived through winters before, bad ones. One had nearly killed him and his family, so he wasn't afraid of the snow and the isolation. As a matter of fact, the isolation held a strange appeal. "How are things down below? Any news worth repeating?"

"Not a lot. I don't pay any attention to politics and even less to social affairs. Challis is growing and so is Salmon. Holverson got robbed and murdered."

"When?" Simon jerked back the stick he'd been poking in the fire.

"About a month ago. That reminds me, a U.S. marshal is looking for you."

"The law? Looking for me? And you're just now mentioning it?"

"Don't have much use for the law."

"Well, what did he want?"

"You. I didn't talk to him, just heard some stuff in Challis. Seems you killed a man down on the Utah border and then sent a note confessing. You didn't do something as dumb as that, did you? Sorry, but that's how I see it."

"I did. He came into our camp, armed and ready to shoot. I shot him first."

"That's all well and good, but why tell the law?"

"Because — because I don't want them chasing me."

"Well, you went about that the wrong way. He's asking for Simon Steele. Good Lord, man, you signed your real name?"

"Of course. It was self-defense."

Reed shook his head and sighed. "Well, you're safe up here. With Holverson dead, the only other person who knows where you are is me, and like I said, I don't put much store in the law."

"You can tell him I'm here. I don't have anything to hide."

"I'm not about to go looking for the law. He finds you, fine, but he's not going to get any help from me."

The next morning their breath billowed white as they stomped their feet and waited for the fire to build.

"Make the best use of me that you can," Reed said. "I'll stay the day."

"Well, we can either put the rafters on the cabin and a few roof poles, or we can cut firewood. What do you think?"

"Not going to make a commitment one way or the other. You know what I think about you staying up here. You're not going to find what you're looking for if you're froze in your bed."

Simon felt a flush of — something: chagrin, embarrassment, irritation. Could have even been anger. The feeling was gone before he could analyze it.

"Let's cut wood."

"Suits me."

Simon fastened the extra handle onto the six-foot crosscut saw and the sharp tool made short work of the dry twelve-inch logs. Soon, the first tree came crashing through the limbs of its neighbors. Simon chopped off the few side branches, and they bucked the timber into a twenty-foot log. They cut down eight more, and Reed dragged the first one back to camp as Simon started swamping the others. By noon, they had all nine back in camp, and spent the afternoon sawing the logs into blocks, stopping only long enough to sharpen the saw.

"It's amazing how much two men can do," Simon said. He felt the fire in his shoulders, and his hands wouldn't completely straighten out.

"You got some bottom. I haven't worked that hard in years. You might make it, Simon. You just might make it."

Simon's face flushed. "The trees are easy work compared to digging that hole."

"Yeah, I've thought about that. And I see you don't wear gloves. How in hell can your hands take it?"

"They didn't at first, but I can't work with gloves. I sure appreciate your help today. Maybe —"

"Nope. Feel the breeze? Out of the south, and look at the clouds."

The long wispy mare's tails swooped across the sky, thickening over the ridge at the upper end of the valley.

"Those clouds are attached to something," Reed said, "and I'm not sticking around to see what. Make up a list of what you want in the spring, and I'll be out of here early in the morning." Reed flexed his back muscles, pulled off his gloves, and started to build a smoke. "I'd give us two days," he said, looking up at the sky. "Two at most."

The next morning Simon waved as Reed rode off into the gloom of the early light. If Reed waved, he didn't see it. He went over to the campfire and hunkered down. Lying on the ground was one of Reed's carefully carved sticks. Simon picked it up and admired its symmetry.

CHAPTER 15

Reed had been right. Simon was on his way back to camp with his last log two days later when the first pellets of grainy snow hit his face. He ducked his head into it and urged the horse on. By the time he'd reached home, the ground was covered and the wind was blowing steadily.

"This might be it, Spud. I expect we'll know by morning." Simon took the collar off the horse and fed her.

He and Reed had cut the logs for his fire berm and, ignoring the snow flurries, Simon set to work notching and setting the four-foot logs into the arc Reed had suggested. By nightfall, he'd finished the fire shelter, and the effect on the fire he built within its confines was apparent. A steady wind blew through the treetops behind the tent, and the three walls of the berm dampened the swirls that whipped closer to the ground. Sitting in the tent opening, Simon felt the fire's radiance. "Let 'er snow, Spud, we're snug as a cottontail in here." He sopped the grease off his plate with a piece of soda bread, took a big bite, and handed the rest to the dog. He reached inside for his journal.

October 19, 1873. Snow started, maybe winter is here. I'm not ready. Tired.

He was robbed of the rest he badly needed by the slapping canvas, and at the first sign of light he pushed back the flap and looked out. He gasped. The handy berm he'd constructed to dampen the wind had also acted as a perfect snow fence, and the drift it collected filled the receptive "U."

"Oh, shit!" Simon sat and put on his boots, glancing up with irritation at the wintry scene.

The overcast sky grazed the ridgeline, and ranks of lower clouds marched ahead of the blustering wind. They seemed to pause just long enough to spit snow at him before scurrying out of the valley. He stood before what should have been a dormant campfire, hands on hips. "Just what I need."

He stomped through the snow to the cabin and got his shovel. Ten minutes later he poked around in the soggy ashes with a stick for a bit, then started throwing the gray sludge out of the fireplace. With splinters he axed off a split block, he coaxed a fire to life, and then sat on a short log in front of the struggling flames to dry his pants. Spud sat beside him, ears perked.

"How can you be so cheerful? This is a mess. First thing we do today is use some of those roof poles and make something I can put over the fire pit at night. This is bullshit."

All day the flurries continued, and the wind held its strength. Simon worked against the cold by building the cap for his fireplace. With wire, he lashed the skinny poles to three cross-members, and before noon had it finished. After a hurried bite to eat, he set to work sawing block after block of wood; his determined cadence cut the afternoon away. The snow and the wind mocked his efforts. Exhausted, he left the saw halfway through a log as the light failed, and he went to bed cold and hungry.

The morning light didn't faze him. He slept soundly until the sun was just cracking the ridge. Nature urged him back to consciousness and made him hurry into his boots and out of the tent. He stood at his toilet and let the cold air start to untangle the cobwebs in his brain.

It took several heartbeats for the sight of the animals to register. Simon crouched and forced Spud to lie down. A surge of excitement shot through him as he watched, his hand on the dog's back. The five tawny cow elk moved slowly through the snow, stopping frequently to raise their noses. They moved in and out of the trees on the far edge of the meadow, following the stream's meandering path through the valley. Directly across from him, the creek cut back against the hillside, and the five were forced to either climb up into the thick timber, or cross the open ground to the trees on his side of the valley. The lead cow stopped, and the rest bunched up behind her. She puffed her steamy nervousness into the dead calm of the morning.

Simon caught a glimpse of movement back upstream, and he concentrated on the spot. Again, a flicker of motion, and this time Simon was able to track it. Deep in the trees, whatever it was moved stealthily, revealing very little. Simon switched his gaze to the open space where he had left the knife and socks. He stared, barely blinking. Suddenly, a bull elk, his antlers laid back, nose high, burst through the clearing in a single bound. The hair on Simon's neck rose and Spud started to get up. He pushed down on the dog's head. Two hundred yards farther on, the big bull came to the waiting cows and stopped.

The lead cow turned, looked at the bull, then, sniffing the air once more, she stepped into the clearing. The other four followed one at a time, then all five hurried, stiff-legged, across the meadow and disappeared into the trees. Simon felt Spud's urgency again.

"Sit!" He spit the word out and grabbed a handful of hair.

The bull stood and waited, clearly visible in the trees; nose up, his massive head swinging from side to side. On some unseen cue, he stepped out of the trees and trotted across the meadow, looking left and right. When he reached the far side, he snapped his head back, antlers laid on his shoulders, and pushed silently through the aspen trees. Simon stood, shrugged into his suspenders, and buttoned his pants.

"I wonder why they didn't smell us." Simon turned his face back and forth to find the breeze and could not detect it. "Should I go after them?"

The dog whined and ran off a short distance to stop and look back.

"I didn't mean you. I can just imagine how much help you'd be."

Simon hustled to the tent and got his hat, then picked up a butcher knife from his cooking things and stuck it in his waistband behind his back.

"You stay here, boy."

Spud spun around twice, and tried to jump up on Simon, tongue out, tail wagging furiously.

"No. You stay. I know you want to go, but you'll just mess things up."

Spud's ears drooped along with his tail, and he sat in front of the tent. His gaze never left Simon's face.

"Look all you want. You're not going."

The dog lay down, put his chin on his front leg, and sighed.

Simon picked up his rifle, jacked a shell into the chamber, slid the cover into place, and lowered the hammer. With one last look at the dog, he headed down the valley.

The small herd had left clear tracks where they'd gone into the aspens. While the five cows had angled down the valley, the bull had climbed into the thicker timber. Simon started to stalk the cows, moving a few yards, careful with his feet and avoiding any branches that might drag against his clothes, then stopping to listen. The silence was so complete, he could hear his breath hissing softly though the hair in his nose.

For over two hours he followed them. Twice he found spots where they'd pawed through the snow and grazed on sparse grass, and once, near the creek, they had stripped willows. About a mile from camp, the meadow narrowed sharply and he approached the restriction. They would either have to come out in the open, or climb the side hill and go over a ridge. So far, the tracks had always taken the easiest route around rocky outcrops, and Simon was convinced they would again take the easy way through the narrows. He slowed his pace even more.

A slight puff of air brushed his cheek, and he turned his face into it. The low branches of the big tree he stood under moved ever so slightly and Simon sniffed the air. There! Pungent, like bad cheese, the smell struck him. They were close. He instinctively ducked with his shoulders hunched and searched side to side with his eyes, head immobile. He saw nothing, but remained still quite awhile. The smell kept coming to him, the intensity the same. Slowly, he moved from the shelter of the tree and made his way to the next one. Another few minutes there, and he moved on. Watching his feet and the space ahead, he followed the scent.

Just as he reached another tree, he saw

them. Bedded down in a rough circle, all five cows had their noses pointed to the north, into the gently moving air. Simon's heart beat so hard, he thought for sure that they'd hear him. He breathed long, slow breaths and waited until he felt calm. Holding the trigger back, he silently cocked his rifle, let go of the trigger, and lowered the hammer until it caught on the sear. His eyes went back to the elk. The five worked rhythmically on their cuds, periodically lifting their heads to test the air. Slowly he raised the rifle, then paused anxiously when his selected target stopped chewing to burp up another cud. Finally, he had the long barrel aimed directly at the cow, her upper neck and head nestled in the "V" of the wide rear sight and the blade of the front sight centered just behind her ear.

The peaceful scene exploded when the gun went off. One moment Simon was concentrating on slowly squeezing the trigger and keeping the sights lined up; the next, four elk were on their feet, bolting in four different directions. One cow came right at him, saw him at the last possible moment, and nearly fell as she dug her front hooves in to turn away. The popping sound of snapping branches faded rapidly.

Simon walked into the small clearing and

approached the cow. She had simply turned over on her side, her legs stuck straight out. The brilliant crimson of her life flowed steadily out of the wound at the top of her neck. Simon touched her wide-open eye with his rifle muzzle. Satisfied, he leaned his gun against a tree, and reached for his knife.

The body shape and internal organs of a deer and an elk are nearly identical. The only real difference is size, and Simon was learning the hard way that meant a lot. He knew that ideally the animal should be strung up by its front legs or, failing that, laid head up on an incline. Simon's kill lay on perfectly flat ground, and even getting her paunch open turned into a battle. He could get her turned on her back, but as soon as he let go of her hind leg, she'd flop back onto her side.

With his rifle stuck between her hocks, and a rock stuffed under her hip, he managed to open her up. His wide, long butcher knife proved not to be the best tool for the job, and a vivid memory of his father's reaction when an errant cut had taken its toll on a heifer's gut made the work go even slower. By the time Simon had the elk's innards on the ground, it was well after noon. He'd broken the tip off the knife trying to part the pelvic bone by driving the blade through it with a rock. He had no choice but to go back to camp for another knife, so he decided he'd just as well go get the horse and drag the elk home.

Spud saw him coming and could not resist. He bounded across the meadow, tail high and ears alert. "Good boy. I was afraid you'd give in and come find me." He ruffled the dog's ears. "I got one, Spud. Got her cleaned and ready to skin. Let's get the horse and I'll show you."

With a final tug, the hide came free, and Simon spread it out on the woodpile. He couldn't believe the amount of fat on the animal. It lay in patches. The two on either side of the spine lay four inches thick on the rump. Simon stroked his knife on the stone, then removed the first gleaming white lump and laid it in the snow. The dog walked over and sniffed it. It took Simon an hour to finish, and by then his arms were leaden. He went over to the hide and lifted a corner.

"What am I going to do with that? If I knew how to tan it like the one Red Socks left me, I would." Simon had decided that hide had come off a goat. He glanced across the frozen ground to the trees on the far side of the valley. "Answered my own question, didn't I?"

He rolled up the raw hide and packed it across the snow-covered meadow. With a length of rope, he tied the hide well up in the "gift tree" where he'd left the knife and red wool socks before, and went back to camp. The thought of a hurried trip to the hot springs came to him, followed by the thought of standing naked in the cold. The first thought dissipated. He washed his hands and arms, then set about getting a good fire going.

The fact that the meat would be tough did not deter him. He cut a big piece off the elk, then sat by the fire and listened to it sizzle and pop in the skillet. The evening was not as cold as it had been of late and the clouds, thinning that morning, had thickened up again. A glance into the darkness above, totally absent of stars, sent a chill through him. More snow? He lifted the lid off the pan and flipped the meat over. His mouth flooded with saliva. Just outside the light, the four quarters of the elk hung in a tree, and immediately to the left he knew there was a huge stack of wood, more than the three cords he needed. He pulled his coat tighter against the night air and relaxed.

October 21, 1873. Shot a big elk today. I have meat for winter. Wood is cut. I am happy tonight and ready.

CHAPTER 16

With a belly full of fresh meat, and his food and wood supply seen to, Simon slept like he hadn't in weeks. He woke with a start, the tent fully lit by the daylight, and lay still for a moment and listened. Soon he heard the lip flutter of an anxious horse, followed by the sound of her hooves as she pawed at the ground. He shoved with his feet to dislodge the dog lying against his legs.

"I bet it snowed two feet, Spud. That would get us going, wouldn't it?"

He tossed the elk hide and wool blankets back and sat up. The tent walls billowed in and out like they were breathing. He stood and opened the tent flap. It was cold, but not as it had been. The sky held a high cover of clouds, and a light breeze explained his tent's lifelike movement. He pulled his boots on and stepped out of the tent.

Simon thought he'd probably missed sunrise by an hour or so. He stretched hard

200

until a cramp threatened his shoulder, then went over to his fire. Soon, the coffeepot sat gathering heat, and he went to the horse.

"I think I'm going to take her up to the hot springs later today, Spud. There's lots of willows and shrubs there, and always a little grass showing. I don't think she'll leave the easy grazing."

He fastened a rope to her halter and led her into the snowy meadow. Though tied, the length of the rope gave her plenty of freedom to move around. She immediately went to the creek and drank.

For the first time since he'd arrived, there was nothing going on to make his life difficult, and he enjoyed a leisurely breakfast. His third cup of coffee sat balanced on his knee, and his hand rested on the dog's shoulder. "I can't believe the temperature, boy. The rate it's going, it'll be almost balmy soon. I wonder how long this can last."

He took a sip of coffee and studied first the tent, then the unfinished cabin. His eyes moved to the stacked roof poles, all cut and ready, and his thoughts went back to his original plan to build his roof with three supporting rafters, the center one elevated a little to give the roof some pitch. Two of the eight-inch logs lay beside his stack of roof poles, the third on the hillside where he'd left it after his first aborted attempt to build a roof. He glanced at the horse in the meadow and then back at the three logs.

"Why not? I can't fail if I don't try." He drained his cup and got up.

The horse looked up the snowy slope, then at Simon, and snorted. He tugged on the halter rope and she stretched her neck, her feet firmly planted. "Come on. I remember too." A glance at the gap between the log wall and the dugout sent a shiver through him. "We just have to be careful."

He tugged again, and the horse took a tentative step up the slope — Simon backed up another step. Slowly, he led the horse up until the log was positioned alongside the cabin. An hour later the first rafter lay in place, the front end jutting out over the ground, and by late afternoon, all three were set. He heel-stomped down the slick hillside to stand in front of the cabin. Spud ran back and forth barking, responding to Simon's enthusiasm.

"There it is, boy. That's what I was trying to do the first time. By damn, we might not have to spend the winter in a tent after all."

It was all Simon could do to resist working on into the evening, but when the sun slipped below the western ridge, the temperature followed it down.

The next morning, sun reflecting off the snow-covered mountains hurt his eyes when he looked at them. The clear sky had drawn all the heat out of the air, and Simon didn't even check the thickness of the ice on the water bucket. Instead, he just picked it up and headed for the creek.

Standing sideways to the heat, his wet pants leg steaming, he waited for the coffeepot to boil while he studied the stack of poles. He'd cut them in two and angled the ends that would butt together at the peak of his roof. Mentally, he placed a few on the roof and thought for a minute. Two days, maybe a little more. The sound of water hissing to steam as it boiled over brought him back to the morning. He moved the pot off of the coals and dumped in a handful of Arbuckles. "About time we ground some more coffee, boy," he said, hefting the bag. "Sure will be nice to have the grinder stuck to a wall like it's supposed to be."

His breakfast of elk roast and corn cakes lasted him well, and by noon he'd laid ten rows of poles and nailed them in place. Measured with his ax handle, what he had finished was just shy of three feet. Simon stopped only briefly at midday, then kept at it until he couldn't see to drive a nail.

The next day he worked like a machine,

the routine well-honed, no motion wasted. He nailed the last pole in place with the sun still an hour above the horizon. He dropped his hammer by the supplies and found his cup by the fire. A section of firewood provided a makeshift seat, and he sipped at the bitter dregs of the day-old coffee — and winced. The dog came over and sat beside him.

"Got a house with no way in, Spud. Tomorrow we cut the door and shovel the snow out. Then I can put the stove together and we can . . . Shit!"

The dog's ears went up at the emphasized word. He looked up at Simon.

"I didn't leave a place for the chimney. How stupid can you get?" Simon dashed his tepid coffee into the dirty snow. "That's gonna be a lot of fun, boxing in the hole from underneath."

The weather held for another six days, and with dogged determination, he stayed with the task. First, he cut the door and shoveled the snow out, then framed the chimney hole, and laid the tarpaper down. At last, he carefully spread the last few shovels full of dirt over the roof and walked down the slope to the front of his new home, Spud right on his heels.

"Well, we have a house." Simon leaned his

shovel against the log wall and went in. Light streamed through the cracks between the logs and down the chimney hole. "Look at all the room. Plenty of space to do the rest of the things we need. First, we got to have a door and some shelves. And then a bed and a table, a bench, and a stool or two." He turned and waved his arm at the north wall. "Put the shelves there. I think I can split those skinny poles in quarters and chink the walls real tight. Let 'er snow, Spud, let 'er snow."

He only had to wait sixteen hours. At first, the snow fell lightly, almost gently, but as the morning wore on, it ramped up its intensity as the wind picked up. Straight out of the north it came, the worst kind. Simon managed to get about half of his supplies into the new cabin before the wind made it impossible to walk. The tent justified his fears when it collapsed. Fortunately, it fell right on top of the remaining stuff.

He used the boards meant for building the table, shelves, and the door to close off the hole in the front and cover the chimney opening. The amount of snow sifting through the walls didn't amount to much, almost none in the rear of the cabin. The wind moaned at the defiant pines standing on either side of the dugout.

Simon dug a lantern out of the pile of supplies and filled it from one of the oil cans. It offered very little heat, but he found the warm glow comforting, so he let it burn. Afternoon turned into early evening, and still the storm lashed them. Spud got up, let out a slow whine, and walked to the door. He looked steadily at Simon.

"I got the same problem, boy, and I'm not sure what to do about it. It sounds vicious out there."

The dog whined again and scratched at the bottom board. Simon threw back the elk hide he'd wrapped around himself and stood.

"I think your instincts are right. We got to go out." He pried loose enough of the boards to do it. The draft through the space ruffled the dog's hair, and Spud jumped through the hole, out of sight in an instant.

"Spud!" Simon kneeled to peer into the weak light and saw nothing but swirling snow. Going feet-first through the opening, he ducked outside for a moment, and immediately came back in. He found the buffalo coat and put it on. It was the first time he'd worn it, and the instant warmth surprised him. Through the hole again, not so easily this time in the bulky wrap, he turned his back to the wind, and it pushed him to the lee side of one of the twin spruces. Hurriedly, he fumbled loose the buttons on his pants.

Snow had drifted over the downed tent and looked deep enough to keep the whole thing from blowing away. Satisfied, he stepped out of the shelter of the tree and into the wind to check on his meat cache. If it weren't for the buffeting, he wouldn't have felt anything; the thick coat blocked the frigid air completely.

His breath caught in his throat when he peered through the driving snow at the sparse branches of a yellow pine where he'd hung the four elk quarters. They were gone. He started for the tree, and nearly lost his footing as a gust hit him. Regaining his balance, the storm warned once more by an even stronger blast, and he turned toward the cabin. He could barely make it out through the snow.

Panic shot a surge of paralysis through him and he hollered, "Spud!" He set his tongue against his upper front teeth and issued a piercing whistle. The wind stripped it from his lips and swallowed the sound. "Spuuud!" he screamed.

He leaned into the wind, and wished he had something to hang on to. Swirls of snow whipped around the cabin, and it slipped in and out of view. He started toward it. Once he fell to his knees, and there he tried to crawl, but the big coat tangled his legs. And then the dog was beside him. "Spud. Am I glad to see you!" He grabbed hold of the dog's scruff. "Go, Spud. Go in."

Just hanging on to something made it much easier, and soon they were in the cabin, the boards replaced. Simon shrugged out of the snow-plastered coat. "First thing we do when this blows out is to string some rope to the toilet. And it looks like I better store a good supply of wood against the front of the cabin. That kinda scared me. How about you?" The dog curled up on his piece of canvas and answered with raised eyebrows and a sigh. "All right, so it didn't worry you. You didn't see the tent. We could have been in there when that ridgepole snapped, and then you wouldn't be so smug."

Simon opened a can of beans and broke two squares of hardtack into pieces. They ate and listened in silence, the hammer of the wind beating on the anvil of Simon's confidence as he wrote in his journal.

October 29, 1873. Thankful cabin is done. Storm tonight.

He decided to forgo a drink of water, and

climbed under the blankets. His last thoughts were a prayer of thanks for nine days of good weather in October, and a request that the storm be a short one.

Simon woke to silence, total and complete. His eyes blinked open to white light and Spud standing over him. "Morning, dog." Simon tasted the sleep in his mouth and dug a knuckle into his right eye. "Quiet, huh?"

He pushed back the covers and sat up. A small pile of snow graced the northeast corner of the room, and a white line defined all the cracks along the front of the cabin. He shuddered as he reached for his boots.

The same boards came off, and Spud bounded through the opening. Simon followed a minute later. The roof overhang looked to be a stroke of genius. A three-foot-high drift tapered away from the south corner of the cabin, and the fireplace with its cover had created a drift that completely covered the tent site. The front of the cabin was clear of snow, the ground almost bare. Simon waded through a drift south of one of the spruce trees and stood there to take care of his morning duty. Suddenly, from around a tree and headed straight for him, came an animal. It moved fast and silently in a cloud of snow. A drift exploded out of its way and Simon threw his hands up and fell to one knee. His dog tumbled to a halt a step away, and barked.

Simon stood. "Damn it, Spud, I peed all over myself." He shook his hand, then reached down and pulled his wet trouser leg away. "Look," he shouted. He picked up a handful of snow and with a nod to hygiene, made a couple of perfunctory swipes, one hand against the other, then wiped them dry on his shirtfront.

He scowled at the dog. "All you see is the fun. We could have been in serious trouble with this blizzard."

With his chest to the ground, his rear hoisted to display a wagging tail, Spud uttered a soft huff sound and took off around the tree before Simon could react. The big dog slammed into a drift and burst through the other side, then took off into the meadow, belly down, running as fast as the snow would let him.

Simon started to chuckle as he headed toward the fireplace. He broke into laughter as he stomped through the snow, and the farther he went, the harder he laughed. Finally, he collapsed in a heap by the fireplace, his spasms of mirth making him choke on his own spit. Spud came up and forced his nose under Simon's arm, and together they sat in the snow. At that moment, Simon remembered Walks Fast's counsel: "Listen to the animals and you will learn." He ruffled the dog's ears and for the first time since he'd arrived in the White Cloud Mountains, Simon thought he understood why he was where he was.

Cleared of snow, the fireplace soon crackled with fire and Simon set about making a hot meal. The night in the cabin had been an eye-opener. The sturdy walls that afforded him protection also formed a prison. That thought stirred around in his head as he made up his slapjack batter.

"We'll go check on the horse soon as we're done with breakfast. And then we better dig the meat out of the snow." A glance at the tree where he'd hung the meat solved the mystery of its sudden disappearance; the branch he'd tied it to was now a short stub. The meat would be buried in the three feet of snow around the tree.

Simon put his cup down and stood. "Let's go, boy." Another cup would have tasted good, but he worried about the horse. Maybe he'd indulge himself when they got back. He paused a moment, and looked at the makeshift canvas rifle scabbard leaning against the cabin wall, then shrugged his shoulders, and headed for the hot springs.

About a foot of snow covered the meadow and was light enough not to impede his travel overmuch at first. Or so he thought. By the time he'd reached the springs, the pain in his shins had become nearly unbearable. With a sigh of relief, he stepped onto the bare earth by the rust-colored bank and plopped down on a rock. "Learned a lesson there. Next time I'll try the snowshoes."

Spud padded over to the bath basin and sniffed the water. Hoofprints marked the ground all around, and Simon got up to study them. A well-traveled track led up a draw and into the trees. He followed them and soon spotted the horse standing in a clearing under an outcrop of rock just inside the tree line. She whinnied as they approached.

"Looks like you come through that just fine." Simon patted the mare's neck.

An overreaching cliff of stone explained the lack of snow on the ground. The bare rock wall stretched back into the trees. "Picked a good spot, didn't you? I guess I won't have to worry about you at all."

The mare fluttered her lips and nudged him.

"Didn't bring any oats. You're on your own till spring. There's plenty to eat up here, and this is a nice sheltered spot. You'll be fine." He stroked her muzzle for a minute or so, and then walked out of the shelter. Clearing the trees, he turned to look back at the rock-sheltered cove.

"Wished I'd looked around here before I started building that cabin. This'd be a perfect spot to build one, without all the digging. Actually, we could've gotten by with a tent. Oh well, that crock's busted. Let's get back to camp."

The previously traveled trail made his return trip a lot easier. He stopped and examined a set of deer tracks he'd seen on the way up. It looked like as many as a dozen deer had come out of the trees and gone to the creek for a drink. He looked around for a convenient landmark. Spud barked his impatience from behind.

"What's your hurry? It's all work when we get back. Wish you knew how to carry stuff." He started homeward again, content that his horse was safe and he, the mare, and Spud were ready for winter.

CHAPTER 17

Spud pushed his nose into the back of Simon's legs, a low growl coming from his throat. Simon nearly stumbled and fell. He stopped in the trail and turned. "What the hell's the matter with you? Get off me."

The dog's hackles stood at full rise and his nostrils flared as he drew in the scent that was upsetting him. Simon followed the dog's gaze, his eyes tracing his trail across the snow to the camp a hundred yards away. Nothing moved. He studied the tree line by the cabin and then to the right, across the meadow. He hadn't checked on the elk hide since he'd hung it up, and now couldn't make it out because of the snow. He increased his stride and soon had the cabin in sight between the twin spruces. He was nearly to them when the smell came to him. His scalp contracted and his testicles shrank out of harm's way. The dog crept forward until he stood by Simon's leg.

"It's that animal, Spud. He's been here. Or he still is."

He sought the canvas scabbard and found it before studying the area: the collapsed tent, the cabin, the fireplace. Nothing unusual. One careful step at a time, he edged closer to the rifle. The dog continued with his low rumbling growl, and Simon grabbed him by the scruff of the neck. He was within fifteen feet of the gun when he saw the animal. It stood on an elk haunch just beyond the yellow pine tree. Dark brown with a white chest, the hair on its neck stood up, and a pair of coal black eyes stared at him from under white brows, coolly impassive. Simon, mouth open, licked his lips and cast a sideways glance at the rifle, then looked back at the wolverine. Spud leaned forward and Simon pulled back. The wolverine flashed its teeth and growled.

Spud tried to twist free and Simon shouted, "Sit. Damn it." He tightened his grip until the dog whined out loud and obeyed.

The wolverine climbed over the haunch and moved slowly toward them. Simon stepped back, pulling the dog along. Wolverine forward . . . Simon back. And again. He glanced at the rifle, now even farther away, and mentally cursed his stupidity. The beast slowly turned to show a dingy white stripe that ran from a mangled ear all the way to its tail. It growled again and then shuffled quickly past the scattered meat supply, its body shifting from side to side, headed toward the rocks on the hillside.

Simon waited until the beast was nearly to the trees before he raced to his rifle. Stripping away the scabbard, he levered a shell into the gun, and slapped it to his cheek, searching over the sights for the dark form. One glimpse and it was gone.

"You sonuvabitch," he shouted at the forest. "I get one shot at you and . . ." He looked down at the dog. "Damn it, Spud, when I tell you to sit, I want you to sit." He cuffed the dog on the head, looked toward the spot where the wolverine had disappeared, and slapped the dog again. "You hear me, you dumb bastard? Did you see its ear? That thing *likes* to fight."

The strength suddenly drained from Simon's legs and he sat, his back against the cabin wall. Spud, cowering, raised his eyes and immediately lowered them as he caught Simon's. "I'm sorry. Come here." Simon patted the ground beside his legs. The dog came over and sat down, eyes still averted. "That thing just scared the shit out of me. I've never seen anything so . . . so evil." He couldn't control the shake in his voice. "He was daring me to go for the rifle. I know he was." With a deep sigh, he leaned his head back against the wall and shut his eyes.

After a few minutes, the wet seeped through the seat of his pants and he got up. The smell, still strong, grew stronger as he went to see how much of the elk was left. One front shoulder had been torn to shreds, pieces of meat scattered about, the leg bone splintered as though it had been axed. Simon stooped to pick up a hindquarter and jerked his hand back. "The filthy thing. He's pissed all over it." He went to another one. "And that one too. Dammit, he's ruined it all." Simon shook his head in disgust.

He moved the rest of his supplies into the cabin, and re-pitched the tent with a new ridgepole. His riding tackle went inside it, along with the oats and his tools. Supper that evening was a quiet affair; the dog avoided Simon, content to lie on the far side of the fireplace, baleful eyes watching every move.

October 30, 1873. Snowed two feet. Wolverine got my meat.

We met. It's an evil thing. I'm worried.
Spud is mad at me.

Closing the book, he looked at the dog again. "I said I was sorry."

Spud wrinkled his brow.

"You could have gotten hurt bad."

The dog closed his eyes.

"Fine. I'm going to bed. You can sleep in the tent."

Simon got up and went into the cabin. Five minutes later he had the door boarded shut, and was settled in his bed. Sleep was quick to take him.

Slowly the naked man moved backward until his shoulders bumped into a plain board wall. His hands up in defense, terror showed in his eyes as he stared at the dark man facing him. Simon felt a surge of pity for the man's nakedness. Or was it something else?

"Please, mister, I don't even know you," the naked man said, his voice quavering.

The dark man flashed his teeth and took a quick step forward. "But that didn't stop you from taking what's mine," he said. Simon thought the voice vaguely familiar.

"I didn't know. I just stopped and there it was." The man's lower body shrank into the wall until only his chest, shoulders, and

218

head showed. "You can have it back." He dropped the piece of meat he held in his hands and crossed his arms in front of his face.

"Your mistake, and now you pay me," the dark man said in a voice that wasn't quite human.

Simon tried to shout at the dark man, and wondered why his mouth wouldn't open. He licked his dust-dry lips.

The dark man advanced three or four quick steps to stop directly in front of the terrified thief, and reached out a hand. Simon stared in horror as the bare hand turned into a mass of yellow teeth, red chunks of flesh tangled in them, some pieces still quivering with life. Again Simon tried to shout, and the dark beast slowly turned to look at him.

Lifeless black eyes peered to the center of his brain and warned him to be still. Simon's will to resist started to fade, and it somehow felt right. He knew it shouldn't feel good and turned to argue with the barking dog by his side. The dog? Where had he been? The beast slipped in and out of focus as a low guttural snarl came from its striped head, and Simon noticed the horribly torn ear. A piercing wail came from the thief, and the scene snapped sharply into view.

Simon stopped breathing as the jaws of the enormous head opened. The yellowed teeth settled around the thief's head, cutting off the terrified scream.

"Buell! Don't!"

Simon sat in his bed and stared into the darkness, his sweat-soaked body chilled by the cold air. Outside, Spud barked and growled savagely while scratching at the boarded door. Simon threw off the damp cover, crawled on his hands and knees to the front of the room, and tore two boards loose. The dog charged through, then turned to face the door.

"Oh, Spud. I hope nothing's out there. I got plenty to deal with in here."

He draped his arm around the dog's neck and stared into the night and the snowy ground lit by a sliver of moon. Hurriedly, he put the boards back and climbed into bed. "Come here, Spud. I think it's a long time to morning."

For what seemed like hours, he listened and drifted in and out of a fitful sleep, dark shadows creating secret places in his mind, places where demons could hide. He watched for them, fearful, ready to flee. Then at last, a soft glow lit his misty dream world, and a soft female voice whispered,

"I'm here, Simon . . . when you need me," and he sank into the soft bosom of the light.

"I'm here, Simon . . . when you need me," and he sank into the soft bosom of the light.

CHAPTER 18

Simon stuck his finger in his mouth, sucked the blood off the cut, and held it to the light that streamed through the doorway. The cut proved to be minor, but it bled profusely. He glared at the offending square of flat metal. Three completed sections of stovepipe lay in the dirt of the cabin floor next to the newly assembled sheet-iron stove. He picked up the sheet of blue-black metal and started to roll the tube needed to connect the pre-bent edges. The other three had gone so easily, and the sides of this one were tantalizingly close to connecting up.

"Hook, dammit." He gripped the top of the nearly formed pipe, holding the bottom between his knees. The opposing flanges teased him with several promising clicks, only to slip apart again.

"Hook." He pursed his lips and concentrated on the two edges. "And if you cut me again I'll . . . What the hell you lookin' at?"

Simon glared at the dog. "Go outside." He jerked his head toward the door. "Go on, git."

Spud slunk out the door, and Simon released his hold on the stubborn pipe, jerking his hands out of the way. It flopped open, flat as a pancake, not one bit the worse for wear. Simon slumped against the wall. He stared at the sheet for a while, then reached over for the fifth and last one, and got back to his knees. The tube formed on the first attempt. Simon shook his head slowly, picked up the stubborn one again, then threw it to the floor, got up, and went outside. Spud was lying by the tent and gave him a glance, then closed his eyes again.

"Let's go see if that elk hide is still there."

The dog raised his head, but made no attempt to get up.

"Come on, ninny. I didn't mean nothin' by it. I was cussing the stovepipe." Simon picked up his rifle. "C'mon."

The dog got up and slowly crossed to the cabin. Simon ruffled his ears and finally the dog's tail responded.

"Good boy."

They set out across the meadow, angling away from the path to the water hole and into undisturbed landscape. It was cold, and the powdery snow tired his legs quickly, but it felt good to be out of the dingy cabin and away from the irritation of stovepipe assembly.

He didn't have to cross the creek; from fifty yards away, he could see the rolled-up hide was gone. He scanned the forest, and then chuckled to himself. "As if he was going to wait for me."

His face felt stiff when he wrinkled his brow and his ears burned, so he pulled the hood of his coat over his head. It felt good. He had half a dozen jobs that needed to be done, and they sat on his mind like a toothache, but he couldn't face going back to camp just yet. The perpetual cloud of steam over the hot springs caught his attention, and he started up the creek. About a quarter of a mile up the valley, dozens of hoofprints pockmarked the snow by the creek, and he started across the meadow toward the trees on the other side. The trail forked several times, each new path reducing the numbers of prints in the snow, until he was on a single fresh track that led into the trees. He levered a shell into the chamber and dropped the hammer.

"Can you stay behind me, Spud?"

The dog looked up at him and wagged his tail. It didn't look as if he aimed to oblige.

"Stay there." Simon pointed at the ground.

Spud sat and Simon turned toward the trees. After several steps he looked back. The dog stood where he'd left him, but his posture showed a dog ready to hunt something.

"You stay," Simon commanded in his gruffest voice and stepped into the trees.

The snow there reached almost to his knees. The tracks followed the bottom of a draw that angled up as he followed. He'd gone about a hundred yards, the snow getting deeper as he climbed, until the tracks turned abruptly right and into a four-foot drift, the top notched by the deer's underside. The sign disappeared around a rock outcrop. Simon stood thigh deep in the snow for a moment, heaved a sigh, and turned around.

The dog stood patiently until Simon reached him, then he jumped up and put his paws on Simon's chest.

"You're a good dog. I like having you along, and if you'll mind like that, you can come." He pushed the dog back to the ground. "It's going to be harder to get a deer than I thought. They can go through stuff I can't. That one jumped a drift, landed in three feet of snow, and just climbed right up the side of the hill. I'll have to think about how we're gonna catch them out in the open." He stepped around the dog and started back down the track. "Let's get home."

The last section of pipe snapped together without a hitch. Simon jammed three of them together, shoved the top through the roof, and settled the bottom onto the stove. Outside, he stuck the remaining four feet on top, and fastened four pieces of wire through holes he'd punched in the pipe. He tied the ends to four chunks of rock in the roof. Then he nearly froze his hands trying to arrange some flat rocks around the pipe to separate the metal from the wood of the roof. He daubed the cracks between the rocks and the pipe with mud he'd collected from the hot springs. When he was through, he stood inside and couldn't see any light around the pipe.

An hour later, the stove radiated enough heat to drive Simon out of the cabin. He stood by the tent and watched the trail of thin blue smoke climb straight up into the clear air. He remembered the many times he'd visited his friend, Tay, back at Fort Laramie, and had seen the same sight.

"You might not know it, old man, but I

learned a lot just being around you. Now let's see if I can duplicate that door you built for your place."

Simon went into the tent and came out carrying an armload of boards.

The provisions arranged along the new shelves weren't as many as he would have liked. He needed more meat. It had been a week since he'd tracked the deer into the trees. As he'd closed up cracks in the walls, built and hung a door, and started on his table, he'd thought a lot about a way to get close enough to shoot one. Twice he'd gone back to the animal's watering place and seen plenty of tracks, but no deer. They obviously visited at night. Simon decided to do the same.

Canvas covered his back from the top of his head to the floor. With a piece of rope, he fastened the cloth around his shoulders and hunkered down. Peering around both sides, he checked to see if the heavy cloth completely covered his dark coat. Satisfied, he took off the cover and his coat, then sat and wrapped the barrel of his Winchester with a long strip of canvas.

The frigid air stiffened the hairs in his nose, and the snow crunched dryly under his feet. Spud had wanted to go, and Simon heard him scratching at the door as he angled off across the meadow. The stark white of the winter night, stripped of all color by the false light of the bleak moon, offered no encouragement. He wasted no time crossing to the stand of willows upstream from the water hole. The deer tracks, a clearly visible dark line, meandered very little across the flat ground. Simon knelt down, tucked the hem of his buffalo coat under his knees, and pulled the canvas around his shoulders. He leaned the barrel of his rifle against his chest. Settled back on his heels, he began his vigil.

An hour later a tingle started in his right calf and soon worked its way to his foot. Simon shifted his weight to his left leg, and tried to massage some blood back into the pinched limb. It didn't do any good. He concentrated on the tree line, willing something to move. The minutes jammed against each other as his sense of time slowed.

A sting, like a bug bite, attacked the skin between his shoulder blades, and he tried to ignore it. The itch intensified. Finally, he pushed his arm from under the canvas, leaned his rifle against the willows, and reached over his shoulder to scratch. He couldn't get to the offending spot, and a cramp developed in his extended arm.

Simon grabbed the seizing muscle, struggled to his feet, and fell face-first into the snow, his left leg useless.

"Sonuvabitch."

Simon rolled to his right side and sat up, glancing at the deer trail as he did so. Nothing. He rubbed his leg and banged the heel of his boot into the ground. Suddenly he stopped, and held his leg steady, grimacing. The sole of his foot felt raw in his boot. Gradually, the pain subsided as the blood flowed back into the tortured leg. Then the cold overwhelmed the need to let the leg recover completely. He struggled to his feet, picked up his rifle, and limped back across the meadow.

As he approached the cabin, the ragged growl from the other side of the door took some of the disappointment out of his wasted night. "Spud." Simon dropped the canvas by the wall. The growl stopped, Simon pushed the door open, and entered the blackness of the cabin. "At least I know nothing can sneak up on me with you here." He chucked the dog under the chin, and pushed the door shut. Darkness engulfed him, and he swallowed a tiny surge of panic as he felt his way to the supply of splinters that lay beside the stove. Hurriedly he lifted the lid, lit one splinter on the coals, and transferred the flame to a candle. The soft glow pushed back the gloom, and Simon shrugged out of his coat and sat on his new bench.

"Got skunked, Spud. I have no idea when those critters might come to drink. I thought with a full moon they'd be down before midnight. It's so cold out there, I think a fella might freeze if he weren't careful."

The dog laid his head on Simon's leg, and Simon put his hand on the warm muzzle. "Do dogs worry, Spud? Or are you just trusting old Simon to get us through? I've thought about that a lot. How much do you know?"

Spud shoved his nose into Simon's belly and made a huffing sound.

"You know I'm talking to you, but what do you make of it? I think you're just happy to be right here. And if we was someplace else, you'd be happy there, too, wouldn't you?" The dog wagged his tail. "Are you the smarter one?"

Simon pulled off his boots and shuffled across the dirt floor. He still had no bed and knelt down by the heavy buffalo robe. "I'll try again in a few days."

November 16, 1873. Tried to get a deer today. Not easy. Cabin is snug and infernally dark. It is cold here.

He carefully stowed the book and went to his bed. Dreading the darkness, he shut his eyes before blowing out the candle and lay down. The luxury of the soft robe soon transported him out of the cabin's black confines and into the diffused light of the dreamer. In the night, Simon sensed a presence, and his consciousness lifted just enough to deny it, then sank back again into sound sleep.

It was morning. Light streamed through the cracks in the door and assaulted his one eye, opened in a trial slit. He sat up with a start, both eyes now focused on the glinting lines. Throwing back his covers, he got up, shuffled to the door, and pulled it open. The sun stood well above the eastern crags, and he squinted against its brilliance. Spud pushed past his legs and headed straight for the tent. Once there, he turned around and barked.

Simon frowned at the noise, ran his tongue over his teeth, and grimaced. After another glance at the dog, he went back inside to encourage a fire in the stove. Spud came back in, looked directly at Simon, and left again. A minute later he was back, looking.

"All right, I'm coming." Simon pulled on his boots and followed the dog outside.

Spud went to the tent again and pawed at the front, his tail wagging. Simon threw the flap back and his jaw dropped. Three pieces of meat lay stacked on the ground in a low pyramid. Two hindquarters of some large animal lay with a second piece, the front part of a smaller beast. Tied to the small piece was a leather thong, the twitch from Taylor's Crossing.

Spud went inside the tent to sniff at the meat and Simon turned around to search the tree line across the meadow for a minute. The hair on the back of his neck bristled.

"C'mon, Spud." Simon returned to the cabin and finished getting dressed. He moved the meat into the cabin, then grabbed his rifle and went outside. It wasn't long before he found the tracks he sought. They ran into the trees and headed north. He followed.

Simon strode along, placing his feet precisely in the evenly spaced footprints of his elusive visitor. Spud followed close behind. The trail made a straight line toward a rock bluff over half a mile away. The heat rose under the heavy buffalo coat, and he wondered if he should have worn it. As he hurried, his breath came more quickly, pushing clouds of white ahead of his face. The dog came up on his heels, tried to pass, and nearly took Simon off his feet. He stopped.

"Stay back there, Spud. I don't want you in front. Understand?" Simon pointed at the ground.

The dog's tail drooped, then he sat.

"That's where I want you. There." Simon pointed again and turned. He walked about thirty feet and looked over his shoulder. Spud got up and started to follow.

The tracks angled off to the right long before he reached the rock bluff. "He knows where he's going, Spud." Simon knew from tracking the elk that angling to the left and over the bluff meant a trip back when you came to the sheer cliff at the other side. He shifted his rifle to his other hand and hurried on.

He'd been walking steadily for over an hour when the trail suddenly veered left up a draw. He stopped and studied the trees on either side. Moving more slowly, he followed. The footprints were spaced closer together now, a man walking more carefully. Why? He stopped and looked around at the dog, uneasy. Spud looked back, apparently undisturbed, and sat. "Should we follow him, boy?" Simon found himself whispering.

The dog cocked his head.

"I mean, do you think we can catch him?" This time he spoke out loud, somewhat embarrassed.

Spud let out a soft woof and stood.

Simon turned and started off again. The draw curved to the right and rose steeply. The closely spaced tracks wove a careful thread through the rocky bottom of the ravine. Once his quarry had fallen, the Indian's foot slid down the face of an inclined rock, and two handprints were clearly visible where he'd pushed himself upright. The sight of the tumble made Simon smile, and he felt slightly superior for a moment. It also explained why the Indian was traveling more slowly, and how much danger must lie just beneath the snow.

Then the draw opened up and leveled off into a three-acre meadow visible through the trees. Simon hurried to the edge and stopped inside the tree line. The track led straight across for about a hundred yards to disappear into a steep slope of jumbled rock. He tried to find a track in the broken surface of the scree, scanning it all the way to the top. And there stood the Indian.

Simon swallowed hard and almost choked. "There he is, Spud," he whispered hoarsely and glanced down at his dog. "We'll never catch him up there."

Spud was watching too, his tail swinging slowly from side to side.

Simon stared at the figure on the rocks. He couldn't tell how old he was, but he could see the man wasn't very big. He wore a gray animal-skin cape across his shoulders, his head covered by a brown fur hat. He held a bow in his left hand. Simon wanted to step into the open, but his feet wouldn't shift. This was the man who'd saved his life and now brought him food when he couldn't shoot it himself. But this was also an Indian, a godless, murdering savage. Wasn't that what Reed called them, or something like that? For several minutes he studied the Indian, who never moved. He couldn't tell if the man was looking at him or not.

Slowly Simon moved into the open and the Indian raised a hand. Simon suppressed the urge to wave back. With his hand hoisted head high and palm out, the Indian didn't wave; he just held it there. Then he lowered it sharply toward his body, turned, and in three strides, disappeared from view. Simon caught a glimpse of red and stared at the spot where the Indian had slipped from sight. A lump formed in his throat, and it confused him. Kneeling down, he ruffled Spud's ears and looked in his face. "Do you think he's my friend, boy?" The soft brown eyes gazed back as Simon stood. "I think I might want him to be." Simon looked again at the top of the rockslide, then turned, and started the trip back home.

November 18, 1873. Indian left me meat. God bless the godless. Tracked him but could not get close. He waved.

236

CHAPTER 19

It wasn't the size of the cabin, more the closeness of the walls. He knew that made no sense even as he thought it. He scowled at the rough logs, their coarseness dimly lit by the feeble glow of the single candle on the rough table. He wasn't using the oil lamp. He'd calculated he'd run out of oil in eight weeks if he burned the lamp only four hours a day. He'd tried to leave the door open, but his wood consumption rose dramatically as the frigid air rushed into the warm interior. Better to be in the dark than in the cold. He'd shut the light out again. That had been a month ago. His journal told him it was January the tenth. At least that's what it said. He'd stopped writing every day. Did it really matter what day it was?

The dog had taken to sleeping in the tent. Once in a while he came in during the day, and he went with Simon whenever he left

237

camp, but Simon thought he wasn't as friendly as before. Leastwise, that's how it seemed. He scowled at the feeble flame of the candle. "To hell with it. I've got to get out," he muttered as he got up from the table.

He shrugged into his coat and pulled his hood up over his head. With a tap of his finger, he snuffed the candle, and then pulled the door open. The bitter cold stabbed him instantly, and he slapped his mittened hand over his mouth. The frigid air had been with him for over a week. He had no idea how cold it was, but when he spit, the saliva would crackle in the air. It had never been this cold in either Wyoming or Nebraska, and he'd seen minus thirty in both of those places.

"Spud, you coming?" He pulled the cover off his rifle and leaned the stiff canvas case against the cabin wall. A few seconds later, the dog poked his head under the tent flap, looked left and right, and then pushed out into the clear.

"Keeping all right, are you?"

The dog stretched, then walked over, his tail wagging slowly.

Simon reached down and held the dog's muzzle. "This is getting monotonous, ain't it?"

He stepped onto the snowshoes and kicked into the straps. Then they walked between the twin spruces and headed up the canyon. By now, he was somewhat used to the shoes, his rocking, side-to-side gait getting better and better every time he wore them.

He recalled the first time he'd tried them on. Two feet of accumulated snow had been covered overnight with another foot of fresh fall, and he needed water. He'd slogged ten steps though the fresh powder, every other one breaking through the crust of the original two feet and sinking him up to his crotch. He turned back to get the snowshoes.

At first, it seemed easy. He took one step, then carefully followed with the trailing foot, swinging it wide enough to clear the other shoe. One more step, pause, bring the trailing one up. He'd taken about six steps like that when, confidence building, he quickened his pace a little. One step, next step. One step, next step, one step, and the next step landed on his forward snowshoe. Momentum being what it is, he frantically tried to raise his impeded foot and crashed facedown in the snow.

Spud promptly jumped into the middle of his back, happy to join in the game. He swore and hollered for a full minute before he got the dog to understand he wasn't in the mood to play. By then, he'd packed enough snow down his neck to chase him back to the cabin to dry out. The trip to the creek postponed, he'd made due with flat and tasteless meltwater.

Simon chuckled and turned to find the dog. He was about twenty feet back. Several hunts had taught him that there was where he belonged, and he rarely got closer. As he approached the hot springs, he saw the steam had covered the surrounding trees and brush in frost. His horse stood out dark against it. She raised her head and tipped her ears toward them. The long hair of her winter coat dulled the sleek hide. Simon headed toward her. She stood her ground until he was about fifty feet away, then turned and bolted toward the trees to disappear into the darkness under the rock overhang. Simon was glad to see her, and pleased to see she looked healthy.

The area around the springs was completely clear of snow, and the horse had eaten everything green. Simon stepped out of the snowshoes and slogged over to inspect the bushes. She'd eaten a lot of the dry leaves, and even stripped some of their bark. He felt satisfied she had plenty to eat. By his bath pool, he knelt and swished his hand in the warm water. He immediately wished he hadn't. The wet skin flashed cold. "Now that was dumb," he mumbled. He rubbed his hand on his trouser leg three or four times, then slipped his mitten back on. "C'mon, Spud. Let's see what it looks like up the creek a little."

Away from the spring, the snow took over again and he kicked into the snowshoes. After checking to see where the dog was, he tromped upstream. Lost in the silence, he walked for a time, pumping clouds of breath-steam rhythmically into the still air. He couldn't see a track of any kind, the snow smooth and pristine. Suddenly, he felt compelled to stop, but it wasn't a conscious decision or something he actually thought. It was more like he'd sensed the ground had become unsteady. Frozen in place, he snapped his head one way, then the other. He'd never been very far past the springs and looked back to see Spud snuffling after something well over a hundred yards behind. The uneasy feeling still held him immobile as the cool fingers of fear caressed his heart.

What was it? He looked around some more and saw nothing but smooth, unbroken snow, unmarked by bare rock, tree, or bush. Even the creek was invisible. The cool fingers turned into an icy hand that clamped hard. Where was the water? His emotions jumped from fear to fury. How stupid can one person be? He looked upstream to the narrow defile that marked the end of the valley. The black of wet rock stood stark against the ice on either side of the stream that tumbled down. He tried to trace the path of the creek, but soon lost track of it in the blinding white.

Willing his breathing to slow, he listened, his hood thrown back, his head cocked sideways. Then he heard it. The faint sound of running water — right under his feet! With a gasp, he lost control of his breathing and his bladder tensed. Swallowing hard, he carefully angled his right snowshoe away and eased his weight onto the other one. As he launched off on his left foot, the snow gave way beneath him, and he flung his body full length on the ground. The sound of water was now clear, and his feet hung over open space.

He pressed himself into the snow and tried to think. All that came to mind was how quickly his wet hand had frozen at the springs. He imagined his whole body being soaked. At that moment his body shifted, and he knew he was going to fall into the stream. Simon jammed his chin into the snow as hard as he could, dug his hands into the snow, and shut his eyes tightly.

A violent yank on his hood flashed his eyes open. Spud, teeth locked in the fur of his coat, all four feet dug in, repeatedly jerked back, growling deeply.

"Oh, God. Pull, boy!"

The dog rocked back, his head down, and pulled, then again, his head dipping with every effort. All the while a low, steady growl came from deep within. Simon pulled with his hands, and his body moved ever so slightly away from the brink.

"Pull, Spud. Pull hard."

Simon cocked one leg, and the snowshoe dug into something solid. He pushed once, and then again, and his second foot found purchase. A moment later, he turned on his side and scrambled away from the black hole. He flopped on his back, grabbed a handful of neck fur, and pulled the dog to him. Spud managed to give him a lick before Simon buried his face in the frosty hair, and let loose the sob that was about to choke him.

His journal that night was half a page of closely spaced, carefully printed words.

January 10, 1874. Today I learned what loyalty means. It is not the province of man alone. My dog pulled me from the grasp of the reaper this afternoon. Sure as soap sets, I would be gone but for his lack of regard for his own life. This creature I took for granted as I took others for granted. Walks Fast was right. Listen to everything. A head held too high will miss the warning from under the feet. Today, I am humbled by a dog.

The experience at the creek had shaken Simon, and for several days he sat in the darkness of his cabin and brooded. He was not fully aware of when the cold snap broke, just that one day on a trip to his toilet he noticed that winter's bitter bite had left the air. He went back to the darkness of the log house, gathered up his bed, and took it to the tent. Inside, the extra poles he'd installed held the sides easily against the deep snow. Spud sat on the horse blanket he'd claimed for his bed and watched as his master moved in.

Simon finally managed to kill a deer. On a trip to the creek for water, he spotted a mature doe. Inexplicably, she'd waited while he went back to the cabin for his rifle. She was old and tough, but welcome.

Simon and his dog spent the next two months in close company.

The fifteenth of March brought the first sign that winter's snowy grip might loosen a bit. Simon pushed back the tent flap and stepped into the morning air. Movement by the fireplace startled him, and he reached for his rifle. A scrawny ground squirrel scrambled to the top of the fireplace windbreak and sank back on its hind legs, its creamy belly exposed.

Spud came out of the tent and sat by Simon's leg. The squirrel watched intently for a moment, then scrambled down the back of the logs and raced over the snow to the south spruce tree. There it stopped for a look back, and then disappeared. Simon smiled to himself, went to the fireplace, and started poking around to dredge up some coals. After breakfast, he left a few morsels of fritter on top of the log berm. When he got back from his daily trip to the creek, they were gone.

March turned to April, and the snow started to shrink. The mornings were still cold, but by afternoon, he could sit comfortably without his coat on the bench in front of the cabin. Simon was doing just that, and scratching at a persistent itch under his left arm. He'd twice used his knife to hack at his beard and hair, and once he'd taken a look in the small shaving mirror. He decided that once was enough. He scratched under his arm again, then leaned back against the rough log wall and shifted from side to side.

The squirrel he'd been feeding scurried around the fireplace and up on top. There it sat and preened, first one side of its face, then the other. Carefully the tiny paws smoothed the fur, until, apparently satisfied, it gave Simon a glance, and scampered out of sight. For over a minute he stared at the place where the little creature had sat. Then, with an exasperated gasp, he stood. "C'mon dog, let's go see about a bath."

The snow was still solid enough to carry him, and it was not long before they were at the springs. The horse watched them all the way in, and then stepped back into the safety of the trees. The ground around the springs was thoroughly tromped, and it was apparent by the piles of dung at his bath pool that the horse had decided the bath was a convenient place to drink. Simon looked up at the weak sun, and an involuntary shudder passed through him. He paused for a few seconds, scratching through his beard, then sat down and pulled off his boots. A sock he had been meaning to repair let a pale white toe escape into the cool air. It felt rather nice. Next came his shirt and pants, then his long underwear. Holding them up in front of himself, he screwed up his face in disgust and turned his head. He dropped the filthy garment on the ground, and stood a moment, stark naked, and looked around.

Seconds later, he sank into the warm water while Spud stood on the edge and watched. Simon settled slowly so as not to stir up the fine silt covering the bottom, then leaned back against the end of the pool. He sat, luxuriating in the warm water, until the skin on his fingertips started to pucker. Then he reached for the bar of brown soap and stood. The shock took his breath away. "Good Lord, Spud, it's cold as a widow's kiss. Didn't feel that way when I got in." He gave the sun an accusing look, and started to apply the soap to his stark white skin. He hurried.

Settled back in the warm water, he reached up and scratched his scalp through a mat of ropy hair. He looked at his fingers suspiciously, then bent forward, and dunked his head under. Vigorously, he raked his nails over his head for as long as he could hold his breath, then resurfaced, sputtering. Spud barked and ran around to the end of the pool. "Don't worry." He grinned at his dog. "I'm not going anywhere." Simon got hold of the soap again and rubbed the bar through his hair and beard. Then, he ducked under the water once more. With his head wet, there was no getting away from the cold air.

He scrambled out of the warm water, stood on his pile of dirty clothes, and toweled himself with a meager strip of cotton cloth. He could not control the shivering that overtook his body. Getting his clean underwear over his wet feet proved a struggle, and he fought an even more frustrating battle with the dry socks. With his pants and shirt on, he fumbled with the buttons on his suspenders, then settled for fastening just one side. He shrugged into the heavy coat before he sat down to put on his boots. After sitting a few minutes to wait out the shakes, he wrapped up his dirty pants and underclothes in the equally dirty shirt, and headed for the cabin.

Back at camp, he was aggressive with the knife, cutting the hair on his head as close as he could. That done, he attacked his beard the same way, then stropped his razor and shaved for the first time in months. It felt wonderful.

April 24, 1874. Squirrel said I needed a bath. He was right.

CHAPTER 20

May brought real warmth to the valley. The creek grew to twice the width he was used to seeing, and the spot on the bank where he usually dipped his bucket lay under two feet of fast-moving, icy water. Bare patches showed in the snow-covered meadow and birds reappeared, flitting from tree to ground and back again. The path from the tent to the cabin turned into one long mud-hole, and the floor of the tent developed wet spots that moved Simon from side to side and end to end in search of a dry place. He finally gave up, and on May the tenth, he moved his bed back into the log house. The slightly sloped floor and the shallow trenches he'd dug along the outside of the walls channeled the roof-melt away and left him a firm and dry floor.

The day after his move, the temperature in the valley rose dramatically. Within four days, there was more bare ground than

250

snow, and the area in front of the cabin actually started to show signs of getting dry. A trip to the creek revealed an even stronger torrent of water, so much so that he dared not get close enough to fill his bucket. That evening he washed his dishes in murky snowmelt, wrote a few lines in his journal, and went to bed.

His first feeling was of pressure. Not the kind you relieve by moving something off your body, like a heavy robe, or the dog from your legs. More the kind you have a hard time identifying, or even admitting to, a stuffy-head feeling that pervades the whole body. Had he been awake he might have known its cause, but he still hovered on the edge of consciousness. Until the pressure turned into a trembling that came through his bed. That's what slapped the dark away, and yanked Simon back to the conscious world. His eyes snapped open, his every sense on full alert. He listened.

A low rumble rose out of the bare earth by his bed, and when he put his hand on the log wall, a vibration resonated with the sound. With a rush he threw back the elk hide and sat up. He fumbled the first match when the growling dog started barking at the door. The second flared to life and he lit the lamp. The rumbling was more pronounced now, punctuated occasionally by a solid shudder that shook dirt from the ceiling. He stuffed his feet into his boots and hurried to the door. Spud rushed through as he pushed it back and ran out, barking frantically. Simon reached around the door jamb and grabbed his gun before stepping into the full moonlight.

Spud stood in the clear, barking at the eastern side of the meadow. Simon walked toward him. The scene before him was eerily unfamiliar, somehow flat where he expected it not to be. Then he recognized the reflection of the moon, scattered into a million fragments by the rushing water. The meadow had disappeared, replaced by a sea of surging snowmelt. In the marginal light, he saw what had to be trees roll and turn in the water. The rumbling sound came from up the valley. Thudding tremors, almost subliminal, traveled through his feet and up his body to meet the same sound vaguely registering in his ears. He imagined some giant beating on the ground with a monstrous hammer.

Spud sensed his presence and came back to stand beside him, hard against his leg. "Something upstream let loose, Spud. Thank God I saw signs of that when we first came in here." The vision of mud marks ten feet up the trees came to him and he shuddered. He moved toward the edge of the moving lake and looked back some thirty yards to his camp. He estimated some eight to ten feet of vertical rise — safe enough. "I wonder how the horse is doing." He looked into the night and tried to picture how high above the creek the hot springs were. "Guess we'll find out. C'mon, let's go cook some coffee. Ain't no way I'm going to go back to bed."

Simon, unable to tolerate the cabin, sat by the campfire and listened to the steady rumble of the water. He'd finally deduced what the heavy thumps were. He imagined one of the cabin-sized boulders strewn along the valley floor being undermined to the point of toppling over. Then, one ponderous turn after another, moving farther downstream ahead of the powerful torrent.

The first hint of light appeared in the eastern sky as one star after another gave up its life to the coming day. Simon filled his cup again and settled back on the bench. Spud lay in the open door of the cabin, head down, but ears alert. Simon found he could bear the darkness at night and, with the warming weather, he kept the door open to the light of day. The faint gray on the horizon soon turned to a dusty purple, which gave way to a band of red-tinged yellow. His cup had long gone cold by the time the sun flared the rocks high above him and freed itself from the earth's embrace. "C'mon boy, let's see if we still have a ride out of here. I don't feel like breakfast."

Three side-canyons disgorged their snow catch, the muddy water joining with the swollen stream coursing down the valley. None flowed at a rate that stopped Simon, but by the time he got within sight of the springs, he was soaked to the knees, and his legs burned from walking in mud. The horse let him know she was all right before he saw her. Her musical call came out of the trees, and she soon followed. She looked no worse for wear, though she'd lost a little weight. He started for her, and as before, at about fifty yards away, she turned back into the trees. This time Simon followed.

From the nearly dry ground in front of the overhang, Simon peered into the dimness. He could make her out in the very rear of the shallow hideout. "Hello, horse. Remember us?" Simon advanced slowly, his hand extended. The mare fluttered her lips and shook her head. "Come here. I want to look you over." He turned to the dog. "You sit down." His hand still out, he took a few more cautious steps. When he was almost within arm's reach, her left foot shot out. He felt the air of its passing and he jumped back. "What in hell's wrong with you? You see that, Spud? She damn near got me!" His scalp twitched with a cold flush.

The horse snorted again and pawed at the ground two or three times. Simon backed away a little, then turned and strode into the sunlight. "Damn, Spud, she sure developed a bellyache. I'm going to leave her alone for now. We'll come back when I need her, and I'll have a rope and halter with me. We'll see who's the boss then." Simon had his doubts.

As he stood in the clear, another rumble vibrated through the ground and Simon turned to head upstream again. He stopped by his bath pool and put his hand in the water. Still nice and warm. Another rumbling thud. He stood up and walked south as fast as the mud would let him. The low rumbling got louder.

He rounded the point of rocks where Spud had pulled him from certain death, and nearly fell down at the sight before him. The rocky defile, so clean and fresh looking in his mind, was now a roaring cascade. The narrow passage had been torn asunder, the mountainside across the creek ripped away. As though waiting to show off, a squat block of dark gray rock, half the size of his house, slowly parted from the mountain and dropped twenty feet into the roaring water. The ground shook once, and the force of the surging ice water swept the boulder away. Simon looked up the hillside, and then climbed until he crossed a game trail. He stood there and watched in silence as the water rearranged the mountain below him.

May 14, 1874. Here by the grace of God. Warm today. Creek is in flood.

For over two weeks the flood ravaged the secluded valley. Then, spent, the water receded, and by the first of June, the creek had shrunk back to near normal. Simon decided it was time to see what was up the valley. He stuffed a piece of meat and a few fritters into a used rice bag, picked up his rifle, and set out. The sun had yet to light the valley floor when he came to the hot springs. The horse stood out in the open, grazing at the new grass by the rusty bank. He stopped and put out his hand. "You going to let me touch you this morning?" The horse raised her head and looked at him coldly. He took a few slow steps forward, and she turned and trotted toward her shelter. Simon smiled at the retreating animal. "It's gonna happen soon old girl, so get used to the idea."

He continued up the valley and soon came to the steep defile. The creek ran as before, sparkling clear water that changed to foaming white as it dashed around and over the rocks. The spring flood had cut away the bank on the far side of the creek, exposing two smooth boulders. Side-by-side and nearly six feet high, they straddled the stream, blocking it like a pair of lopsided breasts. The image of the pale white orb he'd seen as a twelve-year-old blossomed, and Simon enjoyed a mental smile. Water, caught on the upstream side of the twins, formed a small pool that emptied between the granite humps. Simon made his way across the bare rocks of last year's streambed. He stood on the edge of the pool and studied it. It was hard to tell precisely, but it appeared to be only about three feet deep next to the boulders. The sandy bottom sloped upstream, tapering to the depth of the creek where the base changed from sand to clay. Simon couldn't resist throwing a couple of rocks into the clear water, then watched Spud dash back and forth across the narrow end and bark at the splashes.

As he climbed, the sun hung over the eastern ridge and the heat eased some of the spring stiffness out of his back. From the top of the steep incline, the pool below looked like a crystalline pear. Simon pitched one last rock, which fell short. His inner boy satisfied, he continued up the creek.

Both sides of the canyon rose steeply away from the waterway, and the game trail he walked hung precariously to the side hill. About a quarter-mile from the pool, the valley opened up and leveled off, much like his own below, only much smaller. He hurried his steps to get a better look. The trail angled up and as he rounded a point, he was stopped dead in his tracks by the sight of a small lake. About five acres of ripple-free water reflected, nearly perfectly, the mountain opposite. "Will you look at that, boy?" Simon sat down on the hillside with his dog and stared.

Naked rock surrounded the alpine lake with not a tree or bush close to the edge except at the far end where the creek dumped in. There, willows and brush grew in abundance and the greenery extended up the valley. He drank in the view for several minutes before he stood and picked his way along the narrow trail, heading farther up the canyon.

Three hours later, he stood above the trees, able to see for miles to the north. His trail angled to the right, just below the ridgeline, and he followed. Thirty minutes later, he rounded an outcrop and spotted what looked like a short pine tree growing out of the bare rock. It was off the trail, and about two hundred feet above him. Looking down, the steep slope with its jumble of ragged rock made his skin crawl, but the strange tree beckoned him. He untied his lunch sack, stuffed it behind a rock, and lay his rifle down beside it. "You stay here, dog. I don't want to worry about you. Sit."

The dog dropped to his hind end and looked back at him.

"Now I mean it, stay there." Simon stroked his dog's shoulder as he mentally laid out a route to the top of the ridge and the little tree. Picking his footholds carefully, Simon climbed the first fifty feet and looked back at the dog. Spud lay on his belly and stared back intently. Simon continued to climb until he pulled himself to the top of the rocky ledge.

There, on an improbable flat spot, stood the strangest tree he'd ever seen. From below, what had looked like a short pine turned out to be a single branch on an otherwise bare tree. A three-foot-wide base supported the nine-foot-tall trunk that twisted like a corkscrew. Incredibly rough bark bore deep linear expansion cracks that spiraled up from the ground. Simon's finger fit second-knuckle deep in the grooves. He stepped back to count the number of times the tree had turned in the wind during its hundreds of years of life. He counted eight. The back side bore charred bark, signs of an old fire, sparked perhaps by a thunderstorm's battle with the earth. And at the very top, jutting defiantly at right angles to the trunk, the single branch with a sprig of dark green needles testified to the tree's tenacity.

Simon backed off a ways and sat down to admire this stumpy, gnarled example of life. It sat firmly on the solid rock and he imagined its roots going deep, turning and bending, seeking any tiny advantage to secure a firm grip. And here it survived, alone, fending for itself, taking only what it needed, and using what it took to best advantage.

June 2, 1874. Visited on high today. The depth of a man's roots will speak to his mettle. Spring is here, glorious.

CHAPTER 21

His visit to the rocky peaks the day before had given Simon a look at the vastness of the country he'd decided to live in. It reminded him again of how isolated he was. He rummaged around in his saddlebags for a minute, then went over to the tent and got the halter and lead rope. "C'mon Spud, let's go see the horse again."

She'd obviously heard them coming, because this time she was nowhere to be seen. Simon walked directly to the shelter. "Hey, girl, you in there? Think you're pretty smart, but you've got yourself in a corner." The horse moved enough to confirm his suspicion. He stepped into the dense shade of her hiding place, and let his eyes adjust to the low light. He soon spotted her; backed to the rear of the cove, she studied him suspiciously. Simon advanced slowly, his hand out, the last close encounter with her fresh in his mind. She nodded her head and pawed once at the ground. "Easy, girl. It's time you came home with us."

Simon watched her shoulder muscles as closely as he could in the dim light. He stopped when he was within her striking distance. She had her head turned slightly with one ear cocked in his direction. He moved forward again, hand out. His heart pounded furiously as he watched her front legs. Then he took three quick steps and threw one arm around her neck. She threw her head back and tried to rear up, but his weight held her. She tossed her head and shoulders back and forth as she tried to back up, but he hung on with clasped hands. His feet lost contact with the ground every time she turned. Then she stopped.

Simon waited a very tense minute for her to buck again. When she simply stood, he fiddled with one hand to get the halter opened up, and showed it to her. She jerked her head, her eyes rolling wildly at this fresh insult, but as soon as the leather dropped onto her nose, she settled again. Simon buckled the strap below her jaw and took his arm from around her neck. "There now, that's not so bad, is it?" He reached into his shirt pocket and took out the braided leather thong. "Didn't even need this." He led her out of the shelter and into the sunlight. Twenty minutes later, they were back at the cabin.

A frustrated Simon picked the saddle and blanket out of the dirt again, and turned to face the horse. Short-tied to the pole corral, her defiant rolling eyes dared him to try again. The trip from the hot springs to camp had been a pleasant walk as the horse had plodded along, showing no signs of being upset. Then he'd thrown the saddle on her, and she'd exploded like he'd set her on fire. He'd been at it for over an hour.

"We're going to get this done," Simon muttered, wiping the side of his nose with his sleeve. He crowded her against the corral poles, put the saddle down, and laid the folded blanket on her back. As soon as he flapped the blanket open, she pushed away from the rails. He put his shoulder into her flank and shoved her back. She stood still, trembling. The saddle slapped onto her back, and she flinched. Simon cautiously drew the cinch tight. He stroked her neck with one hand while he untied the rope with the other, then led her out of the corral and into the meadow.

She started to spin as soon as his second foot left the ground, but he managed to throw his leg over her back. Spud danced around her hooves, barking, delighted to join the fun. Soft dirt and tufts of grass flew as she turned furiously in a tight circle. Then she stopped, jumped straight up twice, landing stiff-legged, and took off toward the hot springs. Simon gave her free rein, leaned over her neck, and kicked her in the flanks. Into the boggy ground along the first feeder spring she flew, almost falling as her hooves sank in. Then through the next, and the next, until she slid to a halt in front of her sanctuary. Simon let her blow, head down, for a few minutes before he reined her around and walked her back to the cabin.

The horse shook after he pulled the blanket off, her big muscles outlined in white foam and gleaming wet with sweat. Simon rubbed her down with a feed sack, then dumped a half gallon of oats onto a piece of canvas. As he slid the gate poles into place, she raised her head and looked at him. Her soft eyes told him all was forgiven, and she went back to snuffling through her treat.

As usual, Spud noticed the visitors first and stood with his nose in the air and his tail curled stiffly over his back. Simon studied the north end of the meadow for several minutes before he saw the familiar sight of Reed and his mules.

"Wondered about you all the way to the mouth of the creek, then I smelled your smoke. How you been, Simon?" Reed climbed off his horse and tied him up.

"Had some times I thought I might not be here come spring. Had some others that made me glad I am. Good to see you." Simon put out his hand.

"Looks like he still holds a grudge for something." Reed pointed at Spud.

The dog sat in the doorway of the cabin, ears up, watching Reed.

"Ignore him. I do." Simon nodded his head at the mules. "You brought three."

"Yup. Couldn't fit it all on two, so I added a few things you might want. No problem if you don't. I'm going on upriver with some of it anyhow. Nice-looking cabin. Sure didn't expect to see that." Reed headed toward the log house. The dog got up and moved away.

"It was close, but we got it done," Simon said. "And the first thing on my list for your next trip is a window."

"Glass?"

"Yup. I couldn't stay in there. Had to move into the tent soon as the bitter cold was over."

"Real glass is hard to come by out here, expensive. Isinglass or vellum will work."

"Ever been in a hole with no light?" Simon pointed into the dark interior.

"Can't say I have."

"I don't recommend it. It really messes with your senses."

Reed glanced at the tent. "Better than freezing."

"Just barely. No, I want glass, about sixteen inches square. It's on my list."

"Okay. It'll come from Boise City or Corinne, so it could take a while."

"Just order it up and pack it in." Simon pointed at the coffeepot sitting by the fireplace. "Want a cup of coffee?"

"Wondering if you was going to ask."

"Want to unpack the mules first?"

"Naw, we had a real easy trip coming in. They're all right for a bit."

Simon went into the cabin and got another cup. Reed was standing by the fireplace when he came out. Simon poured the cups full, and handed one to Reed. "Let's go sit on my new bench."

They both leaned back against the log wall, legs stretched out straight. "How high did the water come up? I had to find a different way in. The old trail's gone."

"I suppose it came within forty feet or so." Simon swept his hand over the ground in front of them. "That whole meadow was a

266

slow-moving lake, except on the far side. There I saw whole trees tumble. Felt the ground shake. Found out what that was in the cut at the south end. Part of the mountain washed away. I was worried about the horse. Needn't have. She found a nice shelter by the springs."

"What do you mean, shelter?" Reed looked at him over his cup.

"Up the draw behind. Nice rocky overhang and lots of trees. She was better off than I was. Glad it was there. I went to get her just today, and if she hadn't been backed in there I don't think I could have caught her."

"So, you gonna put her there again."

"I won't have to. When I rode her, she wasn't too cooperative and took off. I let her go, and that's where she ran. I suppose she thinks it's her second home."

"Those horses are gonna try your patience in the spring." Reed drained his cup and stood. "Let's go unload those mules."

Later they sat by the fireplace and ate. Reed had brought a lot of extra things, canned fruit among them. Simon speared a slice of peach with a fork and laid it on his tongue. The tart-sweet fruit filled his mouth, and eyes closed, he played with it, squishing it from side to side. When he opened his eyes, he found Reed staring at him. He chewed the piece twice and gulped it down as heat climbed up his face. "You want some more?" He offered the can.

"Nope." Reed started to chuckle. "To interrupt what I just saw would've been like knocking on a honeymoon door. Want me to leave for a few minutes?" He covered his mouth, but couldn't stop a burst of laughter.

Simon's face felt on fire. "I . . . it's jus . . . if I . . ." He put the can down as Reed's shoulders shook. Then the infection struck him, and he giggled. The girlish sound took him by surprise, and he burst out laughing. Spud padded over from the tent and pushed his nose under Simon's arm. Simon dissolved into a helpless fit of alternate gasps for air and howls of delight. As one, the men came off their respective stools and sank to the ground, tears streaming down their cheeks. The dog looked from one to the other and whined softly.

Finally, Simon gained enough control to speak. "I haven't done that since I was home. Oh, damn, my side hurts."

"You should have seen your face. I thought you were going to swoon." Reed started to chuckle again.

"I'd forgotten how good a peach tasted." Simon got off the ground and set his log stool upright.

"Well, you made the trip in here worth it." Reed arranged his seat also.

"If Red Socks is watching, I expect he'll think we're crazy."

"Red Socks? You mean that Indian that's been skulking around?"

"Yeah. I had a run-in with that wolverine. He fouled the meat I'd stored. The Indian brought me some more."

Reed's eyes went wide. "Just walked in and give it to you?"

"Well, no. He left it in the tent. I heard him, but I was half-asleep and passed it off as something else. Spud heard too, I think, but he didn't get upset. The next morning I found three meat haunches. Two elk and the other smaller one had to be a sheep or a goat."

"If you didn't see him how'd you know it was your Red Socks?"

"There was lots of snow, and I tracked him."

"You what?" Reed threw his hands up. "You have any idea what could have happened if you'd caught him? They live up here. He could have walked you into a trap and knocked your brains out before you could blink."

Simon looked at his agitated friend. "I did

269

catch him," he said quietly.

Reed looked perplexed and exasperated. "Simple as that? Just walked up and tapped him on the shoulder?"

"No. I caught up with him and saw him. He was across a clearing and quite a ways up the hill on some rocks. He had his hand up."

"Did he see you?"

"No doubt. He didn't put his hand up until I stepped into the open."

"How did he hold his hand?"

"Up."

"No. How high? Palm out or not? Over his head or chest high?"

Simon imitated what he'd seen.

"He was telling you to stay away, and if his hand was above his head, he really meant it."

"But he helped me out. I'm afraid if he hadn't given me all that meat, I might have been in trouble."

"I don't know what to tell you. They don't think like humans. Have you seen him since?"

"Nope."

"Does that dog still go off?"

"All the time."

"You're both crazy." Reed shook his head and reached for the coffeepot. "Have you had a chance to look around you, or has it been all work?"

"I climbed up there." Simon pointed to the narrow end of the valley.

"What for?"

"I went to look at the damage the flood did and just kept going."

"Looking for what?"

"Nothing in particular. Just wanted to see. These mountains go on forever, range after range."

"Yeah, I know. There's a range about thirty-five miles west of here that make these look worn out. And beyond that, still more. Folks've found a lot of gold over there."

"That's Boise City you're talking about, right?"

"That's it. You've heard of it then?"

"Yeah. The freighter who took me to the Snake told me about it."

"He tell you there might be gold around here?"

"He said there were miners by Salmon City, but I don't think he knew about this place. Like I told you, an Indian at Fort Laramie told me about this."

"And he mentioned gold?"

"No." Simon looked up from the fire and found Reed studying him. "Do you think there's some here?"

"I don't know if there is. You can find small amounts all up and down most of these creeks."

"Well, I didn't come here looking for that."

"But I can see it interests you now that I've brought it up."

"Yeah. I knew a prospector who found some in the Dakotas. A person can't help but be taken by it."

"Do you know how to look?"

"Yeah. He showed me a few things. Now you got me going."

"Yeah. It'll work on you." A wry smile formed on Reed's lips.

June 8, 1874. Reed surprised us with supplies. He thinks there is gold here. Maybe we'll look. Good to see him.

Chapter 22

Reed stayed for three days. Simon found his company around the fire at night wonderful as he answered Simon's questions about life downriver and whittled on his sticks. Every day they poked around in the meanders and behind big rocks.

And Reed was right; they found gold everywhere they looked. The only problem was the amount. The specks were tiny, a tenth the size of a grain of salt. But in those three days, Simon became quite proficient at panning. On the fourth day, Reed strung his mules and started out of the valley. He was barely out of sight before Simon picked up his shovel and pan, and headed upstream.

Tay had told him that there was only one way to find the source — look for it; the advice as simple and straightforward as all his many words of wisdom had been. Simon started by digging in the bank directly

273

across from his cabin. Half a dozen pans full of gravel yielded the same minuscule specks he'd found downstream. He walked upstream a hundred yards, and dug another hole. And found more specks. By late afternoon he was opposite the hot springs, and his last hole surprised him by showing ten times as much color. Though still small, Simon convinced himself they were definitely bigger than the last find.

He moved upstream some more, and started another hole. The sun dropped behind the western ridge as he reached the bedrock, shoveled two small samples into his pan, and squatted down by the creek to wash it out. The sharp rocks made a watery grinding sound as he shook the pan vigorously and swirled the sample around in the bottom. With a swipe of his hand, he scraped the top third of the gravel into the creek, dipped the pan for more water, and repeated the action. After doing that three more times, he had about a cup of fine gravel and sand in the pan. His heart beat faster as he carefully scraped the top bit off, and took on some clean water.

The residual now swirled around the outside edge of the pan bottom, and he raised the front edge just slightly as he swished the water over the thin layer of fine grit. Then, a flash. Even without direct sunlight, the unmistakable color of raw gold blinked into reality. A streak, like the tail of a comet, lay across the top edge of the black sand. He sat back on the soggy bank and stared at what he'd found.

The next morning, Simon didn't wait to eat breakfast. After a half-cup of tepid, bitter coffee had shuddered down his throat, he headed for the south end of the valley. Spud padded along behind, and soon they stood over the two-foot-deep hole he'd left. Anxiously, he scraped three samples out of the water-filled bottom and dumped them off the tip of his shovel and into his pan. Five minutes later he stared, transfixed, as the same glorious, bright-yellow stripe revealed itself with the last tipped swirl. He grabbed his shovel and moved upstream some more. He dug five more holes, each showing more and more color, each one closer to the narrow causeway at the end of the valley.

As the sun dropped below the western ridge, he started another hole just below the two granite boulders straddling the creek. He stomped the blade of his shovel into the rocky bank. When he stooped to lift it, his vision blurred, and he staggered back, nearly falling over. He straightened up and shook his head, confused. "What in hell?" He looked at Spud.

A pulsating pressure-sensation filled his ears as he stepped away from the creek and sat. The dog came over, poked its nose under his arm, and nuzzled his hand. "You're hungry aren't you? Ol' Tay told me this could happen. C'mon, let's go back to camp." He left the shovel and pan on the bank and started home.

The walk back seemed longer than usual, and Simon sagged onto the bench in front of the cabin. His back protested as he pulled off the gum boots. Next he peeled off his soggy socks and grimaced at the white, wrinkled skin. Massaging one foot, he looked at Spud, who patiently waited for Simon to be done with his strange human antics. "All right, I'll find us something to eat." Simon shuffled into the cabin, Spud on his heels. "Whatever happened to you rustling up something on your own? Getting lazy?" He took a couple of cans off the shelf and grabbed half a loaf of soda bread from the table. "Come on then, let's eat."

As Simon finished washing his plate and fork, early evening dropped on them like a cool blanket. Spud lay on his side, just out of range of popping sparks, all four legs extended in the posture of security. His tail twitched with excitement as dog dreams played out behind his closed eyes. Simon poured a cup of coffee and settled down on the oat bag full of wood shavings and sawdust he'd put together. It was big enough to keep his rear-end off the cold ground and support his back as well. Most nights Spud slept on it.

The first stars winked at him, and he flexed his tired and sore shoulder muscles. The picture of Tay's cabin came to mind and he was swept back to Fort Laramie.

"Gold. It'll make a man act real strange," Tay had said. "Never had a partner because of that. It's one of the things that'll make you hate prospecting."

Buell's memory slipped into the firelight and hunkered down on his heels, semi-relaxed and wary like he always was. A sigh escaped Simon, surprising him. *I wonder what Buell's doing? He wanted to do this, to look for gold. I bet he went to the place Tay told us about in the Black Hills. I hope he doesn't run into trouble. Listen to me. Buell and trouble. They're the same thing. Wish they'd all come over to visit. Tay and Walks Fast, and maybe Amos too. They'd be surprised at what I've done, bet on it. And Lori. Is the hotel running good with her in charge? Not much doubt about that, she was smart . . .*

and tough. Not like Sar . . . Sarah, so soft and
gentle.

He closed his eyes to see her lying on a blanket beside him, and admired her silky brown hair, wispy tendrils inviting a gentle breeze to tarry. He breathed deeply of the lavender on her creamy skin, and his heart pounded at the stir he felt.

He instinctively looked around. Met with the silence of the night, he slipped back to his reverie, safe to continue.

Her breasts rise and fall as she breathes, and his hand slides up her side to lie, tentative, on her belly. Then, he stirs the cream of her bare skin, so warm and supple.

Would she wake up?

He pinched her flesh, gently at first, so resilient, so full of life. He squeezes harder. His breathing becomes shallow and quick as the intensity of his desire pulses through his body. Sarah. Eyes closed tight, he strains against himself to reach her . . . to feel her . . . to know her. Then he is set free, and only the stars bare witness as the pleasure of his own making is spent, his mind having deceived him to meet his needs.

Sated but unsatisfied, he stared into the night sky, searching for order in the chaos.

The next morning, Simon sat on his

bench and waited for the sun to rise above the ridge. The cool air lifted the steam off his coffee. He blew on the scalding brew, carefully took a sip, and leaned back against the wall. As he gazed absently at the trees across the meadow, the streak of fine gold he'd seen the day before hung on the edge of his mind. The thrill he'd experienced shot through him again. He'd experienced it before when he'd seen for the first time a pistol Buell had *acquired.* Strictly forbidden to both of them, just two years later Buell had used the revolver to kill a man. Many times since Simon had pondered the meaning of such personal signs. Where did they come from? And why? It was as though forbidden things are sought for that very reason. But forbidden by whom, and to what end? Simon shifted his shoulders to get more comfortable, then closed his eyes and listened to the silence.

A couple of hours later than usual, Simon trudged to the site of the previous day's excitement. The pan lay where he'd left it, and even viewed from five feet up, the gold was blatant. He sat beside it and carefully scraped the fine dust into a clean peach can. Then, with his shovel on his shoulder, he turned and climbed the trail past the pool behind the twin rocks.

A hundred yards above, he started another test hole. He had to dig down nearly four feet to reach the bedrock. The bottom stayed dry, and he soon had a pan full of sand and gravel. A few minutes later he chucked the final dregs of black sand into the creek and stood. Nothing, not even the fine specks he found down by his cabin. Simon took off his hat and scratched his head.

An hour later and fifty feet up, another three-foot-deep hole produced nothing but a tired back. Simon moved to a spot below the first disappointment and continued to work through the day. By late afternoon, almost evening, he'd worked his way back to the pool. He waded in until the water threatened the tops of his gum boots. When he tromped on the shovel it sank only halfway down to meet the rough grinding feel of solid rock. Surprised, he scooped what he could out of the water and looked at the load. The light gray clay on the tip of the blade made his heart skip.

He dumped the fist-sized dab of aggregate into his pan, and scooped out another sample. At the edge of the creek, he panned it out, then puffed his cheeks in exasperation — nothing. The twin granite boulders were only twenty-five feet away. Slowly he waded back to the middle of the stream, and then moved downstream toward the quartz-streaked granite. He gasped as the icy water flooded down his right leg. He stood still as the boot filled. "Shit."

He took another seven steps toward the rocks and stopped to stand in thigh-deep water. He slid the shovel down the smooth side of the boulder and stepped down. The blade went all the way in, and he levered the handle back to bring up the sample. The shovelhead disappeared as the disturbed bottom fouled the water. He raised the load, careful to not lose too much as it came up. Simon nearly fell over as a bean-sized nugget glinted in the failing light.

Stuck in the mud on the tip of the blade, it winked as Simon's tired arms trembled. His feet no longer cold, he edged to the bank, and carefully put the shovel down. Spud sniffed it once as Simon climbed out of the creek and then sat down to look at his master. Simon sagged onto the bank, boots squishing water, and plucked the cold piece of gold out of the mud. Shaped like the sole of his boot, its weight surprised him. He bounced it in his palm. "There it is, boy. Stuck behind those two big rocks."

He stuck the nugget in his mouth when his feet reminded him of the water temperature. The ache in them had started to climb into his hips. Cocking his knee, he pulled off one boot, then the other, and dumped them out. Next came the socks. The warm rocks in the back brought instant relief to his bare feet, and he sat for a few minutes to admire the treasure he spit into his hand. Finally, he got up and scraped the mud off the tip of his shovel into the pan.

Squatting on a rock, he expertly reduced the small sample to half a cup of sand, and with a final swirl, he tipped back the pan. There, all lined up in the bottom, at least a dozen small pieces of gold gleamed back at him. Not specks, or flakes, but tiny irregular lumps of yellow. Simon nearly dropped the whole thing into the creek.

June 13, 1874. Found gold in pool by twin rocks. Water is so cold I can't work very long. I'm of two minds about finding it.

Early the next morning, Simon stood by the pool and studied the bank. He'd tried to work in the water, but after only five minutes or so, he couldn't feel his feet. His hands ached so much, he had trouble working the shovel. It became obvious that the pool would have to be drained if he was going to see what was in the bottom.

The opposite bank rose steeply and looked

to be solid rock. It didn't appear like the digging would be a whole lot easier where he stood. Several impressive chunks of granite poked out of the ground, the rest of the bank composed of a jumble of rocks and dirt. He sat and shook the few nuggets out of the peach can. The biggest stood proud above the rest, and he picked it up. Hefted in his hand, he thought it might weigh as much as a twenty-dollar gold piece. He figured the rest of the nuggets combined weighed about twice as much, maybe a bit less. That meant he'd dug almost fifty dollars' worth of gold in the same number of minutes. Simon puffed his cheeks when he finished a mental calculation.

He chuckled out loud and looked at his dog. "Whoa, Mr. Steele. You're dreaming with your eyes open. Spud, come over here and bite me on the leg." The dog raised his head and studied Simon for a minute, then lay back down. "That's all you think of it? Hell, dog, we could be rich as Midas." This time, the dog didn't even lift his head. Instead, he raised his eyebrows and sighed. Simon looked at the dog, and then at the small pile of gold in the palm of his hand. The gleam held him for a long time before he dumped the nuggets back into the can. The big one hit the bottom with a solid clank. "C'mon, let's go get the horse. I've got some digging to do."

A little later, Simon stood downstream to study the massive boulders, trying to visualize how deep the water was beyond them. He gritted his teeth when he realized how much he'd have to dig to drain the pool, then picked a spot in the creekside trail about half way up to the bottom of the forbidding rocks. The first strike of his pick rewarded him with a display of sparks as steel struck solid rock. Memories of digging in the hillside for his cabin flooded back.

He moved to the right and swung again. This time he penetrated the ground and heaved a sigh. By late afternoon it looked like he might be able to accomplish what he wanted. The trench he'd dug was by no means straight; it wrapped around two large boulders, one of which he'd tried to move using the horse. She'd struggled for only a minute or so before Simon stopped her, took off the makeshift harness, and tied her up.

For four days, he picked at the cobbled ground, sometimes making such progress that it seemed easy, but mostly, a foot gained meant an hour with the pick, the busted-up soil scraped out with his bare hands. The last few feet were the hardest, the rock packed tight against the shoulder of one of the twin rocks. Early in the afternoon of the fourth day, water started to seep through. He re-doubled his efforts on an irregular piece of granite, probing and prying with his pick. Then the rock shifted, the trickle became a torrent, and the pool drained in a matter of minutes. He glanced at the sun, then back at the creek, which still flowed through the emptied backwater. Simon bent to his second task.

With rocks and some of the meager soil, he created a diversion upstream that carried most of the water along the trailside edge of the now-empty pool. By the time he'd finished building the barrier, his back was so stiff he had difficulty standing up straight. With the sun still well above the ridge, he reluctantly put his shovel down and started for the cabin. He led the horse, his back too sore to ride.

When Spud barked softly, Simon stopped. The dog caught up and stood beside him. "What'd you hear? You see something?" The dog's hackles were up, and his tail arched stiffly over his back. His nose, nostrils flared, pointed directly toward the cabin, some three hundred yards away. "I don't see anything." Simon's skin crawled. He lowered the lever on his rifle, then raised it again, leaving the hammer at full cock. "C'mon, Spud. Let's go slow."

They'd walked about fifty yards when his horse nickered. From the direction of the cabin a horse answered. Shortly, a husky man appeared by the fireplace and raised his hand in greeting. Simon picked up his pace.

"Howdy," the man said as Simon approached.

"Howdy yourself."

The visitor flipped back his vest to reveal, attached to his shirtfront, a silver circle with a star inside. "My name is Hess. I'm the deputy U.S. marshal in these parts. Your name Steele?"

Simon lowered the hammer on his rifle. "It is. Simon." He shook the offered hand. "Make yourself at home while I put my horse away."

The marshal nodded, then offered the dog the back of his fingers. Spud approached warily and sniffed. "Seems friendly enough."

"Usually is. Depends on something only he knows about." Simon smiled and headed left for the corral.

The marshal had taken a seat on the bench, and as Simon came into view, he stood. "Nice place you have here."

"It's home." Simon leaned the rifle against

the cabin wall. "I can offer you a cup of this morning's coffee, or we can wait till I brew some for supper. You will stay for supper, won't you?"

"If you're offering. I don't want to impose."

"No imposition, I guarantee. I don't see much company up here."

"Mind if my horse joins yours in the corral, then?"

"Not at all. Go put him away, and I'll rustle up something to eat."

The marshal disappeared behind the spruce tree on the right, then came back with the biggest and blackest horse Simon had ever seen. Its rump displayed a bluish sheen in the full sun.

An hour later Simon put two skillets on the rough split-log table.

"You eat pretty good for being stuck back here in the sticks." Hess pointed at the steaming dishes.

"Just had supplies delivered. We eat good for a month or so, then it's back to beans, corn fritters, and ham." Simon saw the question in the marshal's eyes. "That's half-baked potatoes, sliced and fried with an onion and some smoked sausage. My ma used to make that with bacon when I was

287

little, except she'd pour whipped eggs over the top and cook it another minute or two. I sure miss eggs. I make a pepper sauce instead. Dig in."

The marshal scooped a mound of gold-edged potatoes onto his plate. "What do you mean half-baked?" He reached for the gravy skillet.

"I lay spuds in the ashes at the edge of the fire. They cook about halfway before the fire dies down. Makes an easy meal, and they'll keep like that for days."

"That's pretty clever. So, what're ya doing up here anyhow? Prospecting?"

"Not originally. I came for the peace and quiet."

"You got that." Hess looked around at the empty meadow.

"How'd you know I was here?"

"I talked to Holverson last fall, before he met with his . . . demise. Told me a young man showed him a map and asked for some directions. Two and two makes you. I try to get out here twice a year." He pointed at his plate with his fork. "That's good."

"Glad you like it." Simon looked pointedly at the marshal. "I've been up here a year now."

"Yeah, well, last year was kinda hectic. Challis is growing fast, and we got some hard cases working the Helena Road." Hess put his fork down. "Bushwhackers like the one you shot down on the Utah border."

Simon swallowed hard. "I thought that's why you were here. Am I in trouble for that?"

"Could have been till I heard more about you. The next time I saw Bill Malm, I asked about you." Hess picked up his fork again and dug into his meal.

Simon did the same. "How is he?"

"He's fine. Still running back and forth. Anyhow, he told me where you'd come from and roughly where you were headed. It's my job to keep up with trouble, and a man carrying four thousand dollars in cash attracts a lot of attention, good and bad."

"The banker in Cheyenne told the law about my business?"

"Nope, your associate, Amos McCaffrey, did. Wired a fella in Ogden and asked him to keep an eye on you. That fella told us. You got some good friends." Hess chewed for a few seconds. "I didn't know about it till you were already gone. I'm a field deputy, so I don't stay in an office much. I expect that news is why you had your visitor. That store clerk in Corinne is in jail for his part. Seems he's fingered several travelers."

"So how did the clerk find out?"

"Don't suppose we'll ever know."

Simon put his fork down and rubbed his face with his hand. "Someone said you was looking for me. It's been in the back of my mind, and I'm pleased to have it cleared up."

"Who said that?"

"Fella named Reed."

"Justin Reed?"

"Yup."

"What's he got to do with you, if ya don't mind my asking?"

"He delivers my supplies."

"Hmmm."

"Something wrong with that?"

"Well, I can't say for sure, but I'd . . . Naw, can't really say anything other than he seems to avoid me. But a lot of people do that. Nature of my business. Forget I said anything." Hess pushed his plate away and set his fork on it.

"He's had every opportunity to cheat me."

"Like I said, forget I said anything. Just a lawman talking."

They both sat silent for a few minutes, until Simon finished with his meal and picked up his cup. The night air lay still and almost warm.

"From the looks of you this afternoon

you're prospecting a little." The marshal took a pipe out of one shirt pocket and a tobacco pouch from the other.

"A little. Justin showed me where to look. We found lots of specks, but nothing worth going after. I don't spend a lot of time at it."

"Hmm. So what else does a man do up here all day?"

"Make things for the cabin. Walk up into the mountains. Cut wood. Always got that to do. Thought about a garden, but there's too many critters around."

"You're the only one I know around here who's living alone. I think I'd go crazy."

"Once in a while the place leans on me a little." Simon put his elbows on the table. "Sometimes I wished I had my friend with me. Got an Indian visitor that drops by every now and then."

Hess got up and picked a piece of wood out of the fireplace. Soon the pipe was glowing and he sat back down. "A woman?" He winked.

"I wish. No, he's a fella about my age, I think. He doesn't actually drop by, just seems to show up when I need something. Brought me meat last winter when I run out. And when I was building the cabin, I fell between the bank and the log wall and stuck there headfirst. Weren't for him I'd still be there."

"That's strange. Only Indians up here are the sheep hunters, and they avoid us like we were death walking."

"He won't come close or let me near him. But he's as close to my friend Buell as I'm going to get."

"Buell? Can't be two men named Buell." Simon leaned forward, his scalp tingling. "Don't tell me you know him too?"

"Don't know him to speak, but I've talked to him. Did he work for Amos as well?"

"Yeah. I've known him all my life. We had a disagreement at Fort Laramie, and I suppose that's why I'm up here alone. Is he wanted by the law?"

"Let's just say we've had reason to talk, and he's clean as far as I know."

"So you know where he is." Simon stood up and moved over to the fireplace.

"Can't never be sure. Last time I saw him was this spring, over in the Boise Basin. Idaho City."

"Any chance of you seeing him again?"

"Hard to tell."

Simon stared at the pulsing embers. Buell's presence was strong, and a wave of melancholy swept over him. "If you see him, tell him . . . tell him I . . . I'm fine and living up here with my dog. Yeah, tell him that."

"Sure will. Sounds like you miss him."

"Yeah, I guess I do."

ing up here with my dog. Yeah, tell him
that.

"Sure will. Sounds like you miss him."

"Yeah, I guess I do."

CHAPTER 23

Marshal Hess left the next morning before
the sun was up. Simon cleaned up the
breakfast dishes and set them on the table.
He put a piece of ham and some fritters in
the cornmeal sack and dropped that in his
empty water bucket. Then he put a plate
over the seven fritters left in the skillet, and
put the skillet on the table as well. "You
ready to go see what's in that hole?" he said
to Spud.

The dog was nearly out of sight before
Simon rode away from the cabin, his water
bucket banging his leg. Twenty minutes
later, he tied the horse to a small tree and
hiked up the trail to the empty pool. The
diversion appeared to be working as he'd
hoped, the entire stream bypassing the two
boulders. He pulled on his gum boots and
walked through the mud to the middle of
the streambed. Almost to the face of the
rocks, he stopped and sank his blade about

four feet to the right of the spot where he'd dug before. The grinding crunch told him he'd hit solid rock just as his foot met the muddy bottom.

He leaned back on the handle, scooped the shovelful into his pan, and squished his way to the running water in the diversion. A few minutes later, he washed the last of a barren sample into the creek and stood. Not a sign of gold. He looked back at the pool bottom, puzzled. The first sample had been taken closer to the trailside bank and right up against the boulders, so he went back into the mud and dug another hole closer to the rocks. Nothing. For the next two hours he dug around in the muck, washing pan after pan of rock, mud, and coarse gravel.

Panting with exertion, he climbed onto the bank again and dumped the sample into his pan. He groaned as he squatted, his knees protesting. Slowly, his tired arms swirled the aggregate as he washed and scraped. Half-heartedly, he tipped the back pan, already committed to calling it a day and going home.

The bottom of the pan flashed alive. Dozens of nuggets winked back at him, four of them the same size as the first one he'd found. His hands trembled as he carefully collected the treasure and dropped the nuggets, one at a time, into the can. Spud sat beside him and watched intently. "It's up against the rock, boy. I'm going to dig a trench all the way across the bed and see what's down there."

Simon spent the rest of the day mucking out a long narrow hole. It soon became apparent that the bedrock followed the bottom of the pool to within about three feet of the rocks. There it rose up, brow-like, to drop off again to form the bottom of his trench. It was a natural trap for anything washing down the mountain. By day's end, he had the overburden removed, thrown upstream, and along the trailside to create a dam until no water at all ran into his works. Mud-covered to his waist, he stepped out of the hole and stretched his tired back. With reins in hand, he slowly walked the horse to the hot springs. There, with a deep sigh, he sank into his bath, clothes and all.

The next morning he arrived at his dig before sunup. He stepped into the bottom of the hole and started to fill his water bucket with the wet gravel, sand, and clay. His shovel scraped along the bottom as he scooped the last shovelful needed to fill the bucket. Hauling the bucket using both hands, he fell twice getting it to the creek.

He wouldn't fill it so full next time. He loaded his pan and started to wash it in the creek. Eager to see, he hurried the process by scraping off over half of the ore in his pan. The second wash went just as fast, and he swirled the water rapidly around the outside edge, then tipped it up.

The gold was everywhere. Simon plopped down in the mud, the pan in his lap, and stared. Spud charged up the trail and sat on the other side of the diversion, his head tilted sideways. "I found it, boy. I wish Tay could see this. It's how he described his Black Hills find, except I don't have to worry about someone coming along and raising my hair." He got off his butt and finished panning the black sand, picking out nuggets as he went. Spud left to find something more interesting to do.

Simon scooped and washed all day. Some pans yielded much more than others, but they all contained enough to scrape into his peach can. When he quit at the end of the day, his back wouldn't straighten completely. Back at the cabin, he ate cold spuds and some sausage to save cooking and washing up. When he finally sagged onto his woodchip-stuffed bag, he figured he'd worked almost fourteen hours. Bone weary, he looked at his journal three times that evening before he relented and opened it.

June 20, 1874. Found the glory hole.
Panned a peach can a quarter full today.
The work is very hard.

The closer Simon got to the far side of the
creek bottom, the more gold he found. By
the end of the fourth day, he understood
why prospectors built sluice boxes. Digging
was the easy part; stooping over the creek
with thirty pounds of sand and gravel in a
pan was taking a toll on his back and knees.
Back in camp later that afternoon, he'd
looked at his supply of boards. He didn't
have enough to make a box, and going to
Challis to order some boards would raise
questions with Reed. It wasn't that he didn't
trust him. Of course he did. After all, Reed
was his friend . . . but. He remembered
what Tay had said about trusting as he
stared at the big nugget he'd retrieved from
the doubled-up bean bag. He'd switched to
a sack after he dropped the peach can once.

The nugget weighed over two ounces and
had a piece of quartz imbedded in one end.
Forty dollars' worth, in one piece, and he
had dozens of them. Not all as big, for sure
— this one was a prize — but still, he was
rich. He'd fashioned a crude balance and

weighed twenty-one gold eagles against the nuggets he'd panned in one day. Close as he could figure, he was panning over three hundred dollars a day. How many men could ever dream of such a thing?

Warily he looked into the shadows around the camp as his hand clapped shut on the chunk of yellow. He put it back in the sack and hurried into the cabin. There he stuffed the sack into one of the several cavities he'd dug under the cabin walls. With the dirt packed down and smoothed with a few swipes of his hand, no one would ever know it was there. He'd buried two smaller sacks under the wood by the stove. If someone came looking, he thought that's where they'd look. At least, it was where he would have looked.

June 24, 1874. I am rich beyond any dream. And cursed that I have no one to share it with. Tay was right.

For a week Simon dug and panned, and the treasure kept building in the hiding places in his cabin. Nearing the end of the trench, he stopped to look at the brazen sun. Sweat stung his eyes, and he wiped his brow with a damp sleeve. The bedrock here rose sharply into the mountainside. The last few buckets had yielded very little, and a slight surge of panic rippled his scalp. Was that the end? All he was going to get? A measly two hundred ounces or so? He looked around for the dog. Where had he run off to again?

He turned his shovel over and dragged the point across the rugged granite of the trench bottom. All the loose material was gone, and he dropped to his knees. The damp soil clinging to the naked rock wouldn't allow a close examination, so he climbed out of the hole with the bucket. Returning with it full, he poured the clear water on the sloping granite, brushing the loose dirt away as he did. He caught sight of a yellow glint, but lost it immediately as the mud ran down the rock. He sloshed more water and saw it again.

Carefully he dribbled the water from the bucket onto the site, and the gold sprang into full view. A narrow vein made a ragged and crooked line in the rock, disappearing under his knees. He moved back and washed more dirt away. The thin line continued another two feet, then tapered to nothing in the granite.

His heart pounded in his ears as he scrambled out of the hole to get another bucket of water. Soon the shiny yellow trace lay exposed. It climbed the slope of the trench for over ten feet, then ended, tapering off as it had behind him. He'd found the source. Pounded and eroded away by the annual floods, the heavier pieces had been trapped in the trench, while the lighter flakes and specks spilled over the twin rocks and into the creek below. Could he bust it up with his pick?

Simon swung the heavy tool as hard as he could. The point glanced sideways and he nearly lost his grip. He chipped at the rock all afternoon, but made little progress. Finally, he dropped the tool and leaned against the bare rock of the boulder. His bucket held about thirty pounds of gold-streaked granite and quartz.

He'd need powder or some of the new dynamite to blast the rock loose. And getting that was going to tell a lot of tales in town. He glanced at the sun, now nearly at the ridge, and threw his pick out of the hole. After lifting the bucket to the edge, he stood and looked first at the dig, then downstream at the lush green valley. Would it be worth it? He wished Tay were there. He'd know what to do. With a sharp whistle for the dog, Simon climbed on the horse and rode back to camp, deep in thought.

Simon didn't sleep that night. Instead, thinking and measuring his choices, he'd tossed in his bed till dawn. Then, sitting on the bench in front of his cabin waiting for sunrise, he'd made a decision. Relaxed and content for the first time in a month, he reached down and stroked Spud's ears while appreciating the sight that spread out before him.

To tell anyone about the gold find would ruin what he'd worked so hard to establish. He had more than enough money to do whatever he wanted, now or in the future. He had no idea how much his investment in the roadhouse might be worth, and Amos would have it ready when he wanted it. He had several thousands of dollars' worth of gold stashed in the cabin walls and in the wood by the stove. That, and he still had the lion's share of the money he'd left Cheyenne with.

It felt good to sit and listen to the casual voices of summer in the valley, the exuberant chatter of the rushing creek against the monotone drone of a bumblebee scouting wildflowers. A crow, way down the canyon, did his best to start an argument. Young squirrels in the tall spruce chased each other through the boughs; and his horse, head down, browsed the meadow, her tail swishing constantly at the flies. Spud moved to his favorite place by the woodpile and stretched out to wait for the sun to drive him into the shade.

Simon leaned his head back against the rough wood and looked toward the edge of the clearing. The countless leaves of the aspen trees shimmered in the breathless breeze, flashing light and dark. At first, the organized chaos of the dappled shadows offered no form or substance. Then, slowly, as he examined small pockets of calm, he found the images he sought.

A spotted Appaloosa horse appeared, so strangely colored, its tail flying as Buell urged him on, pounding across the prairie. Then he stood in front of the sod house where he'd been born, and where his character had been shaped. His mother looked out the door, her smile of encouragement so familiar. He recognized the laugh that dwelt in her eyes, waiting to be set free at precisely the moment it would do the most good.

He sensed the strength being offered and looked deeper into the mystery of the dancing leaves. Even as he watched, his thoughts changed to desire, and his heart raced as the memory of Sarah's lilting call came to him. Oh, the sweet sound. He breathed deeply, hoping to catch her scent. And he searched, so hard he searched, but she would not show herself, and soon the dappled dance took the last few faltering steps, and stopped. He shut his eyes and concentrated on his breathing until his heart quit aching.

When he opened them a few minutes later, Spud stood before him, head cocked, his ears turned forward, questioning. "Go back to sleep, dog. I've been visiting spirits, and they've gone home." Spud wagged his tail and walked back to his bed, where he followed his tail for three turns until, satisfied with his nest, he lay down again, asleep in a matter of seconds. Simon smiled at his dog, stood, and stretched in the warm sun. Life was good.

He'd cut wood yesterday, unhurried, a steady eight or nine hours of work. Today he needed to cut up the four logs that he'd dragged back to camp. Saw in hand, he walked over to the crossbucks. The blade, sharp from the last time he'd used it, pulled smooth and even through the dry wood, and soon the heady aroma of pine tar hung in the air. An eighteen-inch-long round fell off as the saw finished the cut, and he straightened his back, arching against tense muscles, his torso wet with sweat.

The sight of the Indian, standing only fifteen feet away, startled Simon so badly he stumbled back three steps. The movement took him out of easy reach of his rifle. The Indian's eyes followed his own to the Winchester leaning against a tree. Simon glanced over his shoulder at the sleeping dog, then looked back to the native. He tried frantically to remember a little bit of the sign language Tay had shown him and drew a blank. Simon swallowed hard and stared at the man.

His visitor stood a couple of inches shorter than he, about five and a half feet tall. Dressed in tan leather, he wore flat moccasins whose tops wrapped around his ankles. Simon could see no red stockings. Set deep in a round face, the man's dark eyes stared back. Shiny black hair, braided and tied, draped on either side of his head to hang down on his wide chest.

A chill ratcheted up Simon's back when the Indian moved. The man, his face impassive, put his right hand in front of his body and touched his chest with an extended thumb. Then Simon remembered. He clasped his hands in front of his belly, the back of his left hand down. Peace. The Indian broke into a bright smile, repeated his first sign, and then held his hands in front with index fingers crossed. Then he pointed both fingers at the ground and then at Simon. Simon could do nothing but smile back and make the peace sign again. He felt like an idiot.

The Indian touched a beaded sheath at his hip, and Simon's neck hair rose. The native held up his hand, palm out. Then he lifted a knife part way out of the scabbard, and Simon recognized it. The man shoved it back in place, then, with both hands held out in front, palms down, he pushed them out and down. Again, he smiled.

"I take that as a thank you." Simon's own voice gave him a start. "I don't know how to say you're welcome." Simon pointed at the knife, nodded his head, and smiled widely.

The Indian's gaze shifted past him and Simon glanced over his shoulder. There stood Spud, his tail moving slowly back and forth.

The Indian pointed at the dog and made the peace sign.

"Yeah, I thought as much. He likes you too." Simon pointed at the dog, then at Red Socks — it had to be Red Socks. He smiled and nodded his head.

The Indian pointed at Simon, closed his right hand into a fist, and then dropped it a few inches.

"You want me to get down? Sit?" He

grimaced in frustration and shook his head.

With his fingers laced, the Indian formed a tent-like shape with his hands.

"Teepee. I remember that." Simon put his hands together in like fashion and pointed at his cabin.

Red Socks nodded. He pointed at Simon again and shaped his hands like he was grasping an imaginary fence post, then moved his hands briskly toward the ground as though he were setting it in the earth. He then signed peace.

Simon shook his head. "I'm sorry, I don't get you." He made the peace sign again and puffed his cheeks in exasperation.

The Indian smiled, pointed to his chest, then at Simon, and made the peace sign.

"That I understand. We are at peace. I understand." Simon nodded his head and smiled as brightly as he could. He made the food-to-mouth sign with his right hand. Another lesson remembered.

Red Socks shook his head and pointed up the valley. He put the first and second fingers of his right hand up and thrust it away from him, then put both hands out in front of his body, palms down, and crossed the right over the left with a wrist movement. He held up three fingers, then pointed at the ground in front of him.

Simon shook his head.

Red Socks smiled and turned away toward the meadow.

"It's nice to know you're around, Red Socks. I owe you a lot."

The Indian looked over his shoulder, raised his hand, and disappeared into the trees.

"What do you think of that, dog? I finally got to meet your friend. Now I've got to try to remember all the signs he made. Weren't that many." He made four or five to set them in his mind. "The peace one he knew, and I knew the teepee sign. He seemed to be saying it was all right for my teepee to be here. Wished he'd stayed a bit longer. Couldn't talk much, but he's sure a lot better company than you." Simon ruffled the dog's ears. "You know what I mean."

For the rest of the day, he paused often and searched the meadow and tree line. That evening Simon thought for a long time before he wrote in his journal.

July 4, 1874. Somehow fitting that I feel free on this day. Met the Indian who watches me. I find he is a friend. Fear and ignorance sleep well together.

CHAPTER 24

The sixteen-inch-long half-round piece of wood split with a satisfying pop, and Simon stooped to set the other half of the block. His ax flashed over his shoulder, struck, and two more pieces of firewood fell to the ground. He picked up the four wedges and stacked them. Movement caught his eye, and he stepped out of the shade to look farther down the valley. A small dust pall hung over Reed and three mules as they moved up the trail. Simon stuck the ax in the top of the chopping block and grabbed his shirt. He stood waiting when the pack train arrived.

Reed knocked the powder off of his hat and stuck his hand out. "How ya keeping, Simon?"

Simon grasped the offered hand. "Just fine. If it's hot up here, what's it like down below?"

"Same, only more."

"Sit." Simon pointed to a spot in the shade.

"I got to get me a drink first." He headed for the water bucket sitting in the shade of the cabin's roof overhang. The metal dipper hung on a nail in the wall. He filled the bowl, drank it, and then filled it again. "What in hell did you do to that bucket? Looks like you've been hauling rocks in it."

"Uh . . . matter of fact, that's exactly it. Used it when I carried the rocks to set the chimney in the roof." The heat of the lie flared in his face.

"Huh, hadn't noticed that before." Reed glanced at the bucket again and re-hung the dipper. "Let's get the mules unloaded. Got a surprise for you."

Simon glanced at the three sweaty animals, grateful for the change of subject. "Surprise?"

"Yeah, c'mon." Reed walked to the lead mule. "Just off-load the panniers. All that stuff is going upriver." He started on the straps and ropes that held the load in place.

Together they lifted the pack off the mule and set it down. The second mule's load came off in pieces: a sack of rice, a box of canned peaches, and all the rest of the things needed to keep a man supplied. With every item, Simon would look at Reed, who'd shake his head. The third mule was nearly unloaded when Reed unstrapped a square wooden box.

"There it is." He handed it to Simon.

Simon hefted it. "What is it?"

"Your glass."

"Already? I thought —"

"I did too, but I found it in Salmon City. Place is growing. That will cost you though."

"Don't care." Simon studied the box, thin slats for the top and bottom attached using tiny nails to an inch-thick frame. "Looks sturdy enough."

"Guess we'll find out. That's fourteen dollars' worth right there."

"Damn, they are proud of it, aren't they."

"Back east that would cost you maybe a tenth of that, give or take. It's been through a lot of hands."

"Well, fourteen dollars or no, it's going in tomorrow. I've grown to hate that cabin. Even the dog won't stay in there."

"Where is he?" Reed looked around the camp.

"Off somewhere. He does it all the time. He'll be back."

"Can I help you move that inside?"

"Sure. I don't leave anything edible in the tent anymore."

"The wolverine been back?"

311

"Not a sign. But I don't doubt he's around."

The two men huffed as they brought the supplies inside, then sat in the shade of the cabin. Reed built a smoke and blew a cloud into the air.

"Red Socks finally made a show," Simon said.

"Here?"

"Right over there by the woodpile. Scared the hell out of me." He paused, expecting Reed to say something bad about the Indian.

"Well, go on. He just showed up and said hello?"

"That was a problem. I'm not sure what he said. Tay showed me a few signs, but I'd forgotten them. I finally remembered the sign for friend or peace. I did that one, and it seemed to please him."

"Can you remember the rest?"

"He touched his knife handle and then did this." Simon went through the motions.

"He said thanks. Anything else?"

Simon showed him the two-fingers-to-the-sky move and the two-handed sign that came after it.

"He's told you he's going, but he'll be back here. Did he hold up any fingers before he pointed at the ground?"

"Yeah, now that you mention it. Three."

"He said he'll be back in three months."

"He also made the teepee sign. I knew that one. Then he signed like —" Simon pantomimed grasping a pole and tamping the ground once. He followed that with the peace sign.

"Means your place here is safe. And if you believe that, let me recalculate your supply bill. What else?"

"Almost forgot his first ones. He touched his chest with his right thumb, like this." Simon did it. "Next he crossed his forefingers in front of himself before pointing them at the ground. Then he pointed at me."

"He said you have a good camp. Remember any more?"

"Nope, that's all, and then he left. I offered him food, but he didn't seem to want any. Just turned around and walked away."

"That's not like a stinking Indian. They always want something. Have you noticed anything missing?"

"Of course not. I told you before, he could have done near anything this last year and hasn't. I think you're wrong about this man, dammit. Maybe you know more than I do about Indians in general, but I know this one, and he means no harm."

"All right. You don't need to get hot about

it. I'm speaking from experience. You trust one, you're asking for trouble."

Simon's face got hot and he opened his mouth to speak.

Reed put up his hand. "Okay, okay, we'll leave it. But I'd sooner have no friends at all than a —"

"Just drop it, Justin."

Reed puffed on his cigarette and stared out across the meadow.

At the moment, Simon didn't much like the muleskinner. Maybe being alone out here was better than having people come by all the time. He wondered where Spud had got off to. Probably looking for a chipmunk or a marmot. *Maybe Red Socks didn't leave, and he's with him. What did they do together?*

"Sorry. I just can't abide the bastards."

"Huh? Oh, I . . . well, I'm just . . . my experience has been different than yours. I've known three, and one is the salt of the earth. And Red Socks has been nothing but good to me."

"And the third?" Reed raised his eyebrows

"All right, I admit, he wasn't so good. Matter of fact, he was bad enough to get himself killed in the worst way. But he was a half-breed."

"You make my point." Reed looked satisfied. "What else have you been up to?"

"Had another visitor. The law."

Reed looked at his cigarette, then flicked it toward the fireplace. "That so?"

"Yep. Said he was passing through and decided to stop."

"Likely. Passing through a dead-end valley?" He spit at the fireplace and then looked back. His face had developed an agitated twitch.

"No. He was going up the river." Simon paused for a few seconds.

Reed pursed his lips, then shrugged. "And?"

"Said he did that once or twice a year. That killing I did in seventy-three? He said that's taken care of. He found Bill Malm and talked to him. And guess what else? He knows my friend Buell. Had occasion to talk to him a time or two. He's over around Boise City, I think. I wonder where Spud got off to." Simon looked out over the meadow.

Reed leaned forward. "When was that marshal here?"

"Oh, hell, I don't know. What day is this?"

"Today's July eleven."

"I suppose it's been three, maybe four, weeks." Simon paused. "I could look it up."

"How's that?"

"What? You mean look it up?"

315

"Yeah."

"I keep a journal. You know, about stuff that happens, and things you think about. I write once or twice a week."

"Do you write about me?"

"Well, sure. Not a lot happens up here, Justin. You don't mind, do you?"

"Did you tell the law I come up here?"

"I guess I did."

"He say anything about me?"

"He knew who you were."

"His name Arch Hess?"

"Didn't say his first name, but yeah, Hess. So, you know him?"

"I know of him. I told you, Simon, I don't talk to the law unless they're real adamant about it. What I do and where I go is my business. I'd just as soon you didn't mention my name to folks, if it's all the same."

"Well, sure, Justin. It was casual as all get-out. Not like he was looking for you."

"That's the way they operate. Gather information about everybody. I don't like 'em." Reed pulled his tobacco out and started another smoke.

Simon watched for a minute, then scanned the meadow again. Where was the dog?

"So, what else you been up to?"

"Not a lot. Cutting wood for this winter. I discovered last year that it's a lot more work than a man might think. I'm going to keep at it off and on all summer."

"I thought you'd have looked upstream for some more gold sign."

"Naw. I panned a few spots, but there was never any more than what we found when you were here."

"Huh, you seemed raring to go last time."

"I suppose I was, but after I dug a couple holes, the adventure wore off. That's damn hard work."

"Did you get a look up by the hot springs?"

"No, never got that far."

Reed puffed a cloud of smoke into the air and studied Simon closely.

Simon knew a blush had started to rise on his face. "I wonder where that dog is. Not like him to miss a meal." He stood up and started for the fireplace. "You hungry?"

"I thought you'd quit eating. Hell yes, I'm hungry. I can recommend that sausage I brought in. German fella in Challis makes it." Reed stood, walked to the corner of the cabin, and looked up the valley.

Simon's gaze followed, and a twinge of panic jangled his nerves when he saw the gold-pan, pick and shovel stowed in the shadows between the cabin wall and the dug-out bank. Reed's feet were inches away.

He cussed himself for not pushing them farther back into the cavity.

"I'll peel spuds if you want," Reed said as he looked back at Simon.

"That would be good. Yeah, you can peel. You saw where I keep them."

Reed stepped away from the corner and went into the cabin.

An hour later Simon put the pan of spuds and sausage on the table. Reed had been right. He'd tasted a small piece of the spicy meat as it cooked, and he was ready to have some more.

"That sure smells good." Reed scooped his plate full.

Simon emptied the rest of the skillet onto his plate, then carried the pan to the fireplace. "Coffee?"

"You bet. Thanks."

Simon picked up the pot and headed for the table. He almost dropped it when he saw the dog. He'd caught only a glimpse of him, but there was no doubt.

"Spud!"

"What?" Reed asked around a mouthful of sausage.

Simon dropped the pot on the table and took off running across the meadow. Spud lay on his side in the grass and raised his head as Simon approached.

"W-what's happened to you?" The hair on the dog's chest was matted with dark blood. Simon knelt beside him, and carefully raised a front leg. The animal whined and tried to pull away. "Let me see, Spud. Let me look at it."

"What's wrong?" Reed asked from twenty feet away.

"He's been hurt. I can't see where." Simon put his face closer to the dog's chest and lifted the leg a little more. Fresh blood seeped through the hair.

"Let me look," Reed said. As he put out his hand, the dog growled and tried to lift his head.

"Leave him alone. He doesn't like you."

Simon put one arm under the dog's hind-quarters and the other under his chest and stood. He hurried as fast as he dared back to the cabin, his gait stiff-legged with the weight.

"Get the horse blanket off the corral, Justin. Put it by the tent."

Simon laid the dog on it and hurried into the cabin. He came out with a clean shirt, and grabbed the water bucket and dipper. He poured water over the bloody hair and wiped it away.

"I bet that Indian shot him. Looks like an arrow wound to me." Reed stood well back from the tent.

"It's a long cut, maybe two." Simon poured some more water over the wound and parted the hair. "Right there." He pointed. "About four or five inches long. And there are two."

Reed came closer and looked. "Looks like a cat got him. If it was a bear he'd have lost his shoulder. Or maybe your wolverine's back."

"Will he be all right?"

"Depends on how much blood he's lost. The wound isn't that bad, but he's been moving and making it bleed. I don't know. You'll just have to wait and see."

"Can we put anything on it? Do you have some salve or something?"

"I've heard of people sprinkling flour on a bad cut. Or maybe some liniment. I don't think it heals, but it seems to keep the festering down. He won't like it."

The satisfied tone in Reed's voice almost made Simon stand and run him out of camp. He stroked the dog's shoulder for a moment, and bit the inside of his lip. "Go get it, please. I've got to try something."

CHAPTER 25

After a hurried early morning breakfast, Reed left, the farewell perfunctory. The liniment must have really stung, because the dog howled when he'd poured some over the gashes. Simon had done it only once, and covered the wounds with a cloth cut from the legs of long underwear. He then spent the night in the tent with Spud.

For the next three days the dog simply lay on the blanket and panted. It made Simon heartsick to touch the fevered head. He tried to get the dog to drink, but Spud would barely open his eyes. Water dribbled on his muzzle and ran off, untasted.

The morning of the fourth day, Simon was brought from a fitful sleep by movement in the tent. He sat up and saw Spud try to rise.

"Lie still, boy. You're too weak to be moving around." Simon knelt by his friend.

Spud would not be kept down. With a soft whine, he turned onto his stomach and got

321

his legs under his chest, then, after two attempts with Simon trying to help, managed to stand. Tail down and his ears drooping, he looked at Simon.

"What do you want? Are you ready to eat? Shit! Water."

Simon came back into the tent with his biggest skillet, full to the brim. He set it down and Spud, moaning as he lowered his head, drank for a full minute, paused for a bit, then drank some more. He lay back down, feet extended, and looked up.

"That's what you needed, ain't it? Now rest and maybe you'll eat a little later." A thrill shot through him as Spud's tail lifted one time in a languid wag.

July 9, 1874. Spud was wounded. Down for five days. Feels better tonight. Reed was here. I'm kind of glad he's gone.

Spud left the tent the next morning, and slowly moved across the camp to his favorite bush to lift his leg. Simon stood beside the table until the dog, finished, moved over to his usual spot by the fireplace and lay down. There he watched closely while Simon cooked two slices of ham and then fried two skillets full of pan bread. He offered the dog a piece of meat. Spud ate it in two gulps and eyed the remaining one. Simon forked half of it over and the dog ate it. Half a skillet of pan bread followed, and he put up his hand. "You better stop, or you're going to get sick. I ain't gonna let you starve. Not after what you went through."

For the next few days, Simon made the dog stay in camp in the morning while he went down the valley and cut timber. In the afternoon, Simon sweated over the bow saw while the dog lay in the shade, watching. By the middle of the next week, he followed Simon to the creek for a bucket of water. On the way back, Simon let the dog lead, and his heart sang as the dog's tail wagged.

Simon stood a piece of wood on end and stepped back. The early afternoon sun glinted on the finely honed bit of the big ax as it flashed into the pine. He had cut a lot of wood over the past week, and it felt good to see the size of the stack. His tongue stuck in his mouth, and his lips felt crusty dry, so he stuck the ax in the chopping block and walked over to the cabin. Spud followed him with his eyes, but remained in the shade of the spruce tree.

Simon drank three dippers of tepid water, then sat down on the bench to blow a little. Reed's attitude during the last visit weighed on his mind. And what the marshal had said, or more correctly, not said, added to his unease. His own attitude about the precious metal reinforced his decision not to tell anyone about it, and not try to get explosives to blast the rock. Thousands sought that streak in the naked rock. He could be wealthy, really wealthy. But, lingering in the back of his mind, a danger signal chimed at the oddest of times.

Like now. He was happy. Sure, lonely once in a while, but happy. So did he really need more than he had? Did he want hundreds of others swarming into this beautiful place? Was he being an idealistic dreamer? The thought raised a chuckle as he admired his meadow. So calm and tranquil, it made him drowsy to look at it. It also answered his question. Reed had left without a list of supplies. Did that mean he wasn't coming back or had he learned in the past year what Simon needed?

Boy, the air was hot. Sweat, running down his spine, tickled and he gingerly scratched his bare back on the rough logs. He glanced over at the sleeping dog. His gaze wandered back to the chopping block and the handle of the ax, stuck in the block, angled out, poised and ready for him. He puffed his cheeks in resignation and stood.

The dark-brown body blended into the

shade, and were it not for the shiny eyes, he would have missed it. Stock-still, the wolverine stood in the aspens, and appeared to have its eyes fixed on the sleeping dog. Simon took his eyes off the animal for an instant to gauge the distance to his rifle. It leaned against a small tree by the woodpile. From where he stood, the thirty-five feet to the rifle, and the distance from it to the wolverine, formed a roughly equal triangle.

Simon took off without another thought. Spud woke with a start as Simon thundered by, heavy boots stomping the ground. The rifle came to his shoulder as he turned and he searched for the dark-brown form of his nemesis. The second spruce tree blocked his view, and he sprinted into the open in front of the cabin. A glimpse of the running form drew a snap shot from his Winchester. Shit. Clean miss. He ran toward the spot where the animal had disappeared, racking another cartridge in as he went. Another glimpse and another shot, then, as fast as he could work the lever, another. It was like shooting at a shadow.

For such a short-legged animal, the wolverine moved with startling speed. Simon ran out into the open ground of the meadow and searched the tree line. There! Seventy-five yards away at the edge of the forest, the odd gait of the wolverine, rump swaying from side to side, carried it away. Simon stopped and tried desperately to draw a bead, but his breath came in huge gulps, the rifle muzzle swinging wildly. He fired. Dirt flew behind. He fired again, closer this time. He levered another round and stared down the barrel, his eye burning with sweat. He swiped at it with his thumb and squinted again. The blade settled just over the animal's back and he pulled the trigger.

The wolverine spun sideways, reached around as though to bite its own rear, then turned sharp right into the trees and disappeared. *Got you, you filthy bastard.* Simon charged across the distance, never taking his eye off the spot where the animal had turned. Twice, he nearly fell for not looking at the ground, but his discipline brought him unerringly to the spot. A satisfying blotch of blood greeted him. It wasn't much, but it was enough to throw a charge of delight through Simon's scalp. He stooped and pinched a bloody leaf. His fingers came away red and slick with dark blood. He stared into the dark shadows for several seconds, then turned to look for the dog.

Limping slightly, Spud walked up and sniffed the spoor.

"There." Simon held out his bloody fingers to the dog. "That's what his soul smells like, boy. I put a bullet in him. The blood's too dark for a lung shot, and there's not enough for liver or anything vital inside." Simon stroked the dog's head. "I want you to stay here. I'm going after him." Simon pointed toward the cabin. "Go home, Spud. Go on." Tail down, the dog headed for the cabin. Simon watched for a minute, then turned and stepped into the shade.

He had a hard time finding the next sign, but casting back and forth, he finally did. And the next one. The beast was staying out of the heavy timber and making its way toward the hot springs. Simon hurried his pace. At the first small stream that flowed into the valley floor, Simon found another small spot of blood, smeared on a rock the wolverine had used as a stepping-stone over the rivulet. Encouraged, Simon stepped into the meadow and broke into an easy jog. He was soon within sight of the springs. There, the animal had to cross one of two open spaces: the first, into the draw that sloped up to the right; then the second, past his bathing pool and the trail toward the outcrop of rocks upstream. Simon angled away toward the creek and sat down in the grass fifty yards from the rust-colored hillside.

Knees up, he rested his elbows on them, peered down the long barrel, and waited.

Blatant against the dark shadows, the wolverine's dirty-yellow stripes gave him away. He stopped at the edge of the first opening for the briefest time, then ran full speed up the bottom of the gully. Simon was on him in an instant, the slender blade of the front sight tracking the wide rear-end of the animal as it made a beeline for the trees at the end of the draw. A rush of elation swarmed over Simon, and he blinked furiously as a stinging drop of sweat seeped into his eye.

The fuzzy image cleared and Simon stopped breathing as the animal came to a hillock at the draw's mouth. He held the sight picture as the beast slowed, then it crested and stopped for a final look back. He squeezed the trigger. The sound, as resounding as a thunderclap, stunned him — the sharp metallic click of a hammer strike. Misfire!

Knowing it was already too late, Simon rammed the lever down and back and fired into the trees. "Dirty piece of shit!" he screamed at the empty view. "You filthy thing. What keeps you alive?" He stood and threw the gun to the ground. Heaving for air, he spun around twice, his hands clasped over his head, then gave the rifle a vicious kick.

July 16, 1874. The beast came by today. I shot it once but rifle wouldn't fire the second time. Spud is much better.

Sleep would not come to Simon that night, so he got up and fed a few pieces of wood to the fireplace. He sat and stared into the fire as the tongues of orange and yellow painted their pictures like an artist's brush. The fiery shape of a small squirrel appeared in the side of a piece of wood. Its head dipped in the heat eddies. And then the critter's tail blossomed for a moment before disappearing, along with the squirrel. He glanced over at the dog. He lay away from the heat, head propped on his front paws, ever alert. The sharp pop of a buried spot of pitch cracked the night, exploding sparks into the air. He watched as they struggled valiantly to remain alive, to enjoy the night for the brief time they existed.

The shiny black eyes of the wolverine appeared in his mind, and a sudden cool sensation swept over his shoulders. He picked up a stick and poked at the coals, incongruously stoking against the warmth of the July night. A shower of tiny embers, excited by the attention, lifted in a crescendo, then shrank back again, and the darkness crept closer around him.

He stared at the fire, searching for . . . what? His back started to ache and he leaned back against a log. Feet outstretched, he folded his arms across his chest and willed his body to relax. The wrinkled face of his old friend, Walks Fast, flickered into form, his sad eyes and furrowed brow dampening the joy of the unexpected visit. The Indian's long gray hair swirled, then lifted into the air and disappeared as smoke.

The Indian's lips moved and Simon heard the words of a conversation they'd had at Fort Laramie. "Man is born with all kinds of spirits inside. When a man grows, a good family will push out the bad spirits. The spirit of the Devil Bear is strong in Buell. Devil Bear is a crazy spirit. Sometimes he will bite his own leg in anger."

"How will we get this thing out of Buell?"

"Maybe that will not happen."

"What can I do to help? He's like a brother."

"Love him like a brother."

"Can he ever be rid of this evil?"

"When the Devil Bear dies, his spirit will leave Buell."

"How do we kill this thing? How do we find it?"

"Walks Fast does not know that, but I think the Devil Bear will find you one day."

The image of the old Indian faded, then re-formed for a moment, long enough for Simon to see eyes that were no longer sad, but sharp, almost challenging. A chill took him and he glanced into the darkness. Nothing. He reached for another piece of wood and threw it in the fire. Soon, new flames pushed back the edge of night. Spud rose from his place and padded over. His nose found its way under Simon's arm, and he lay down close to his troubled master.

"I'm beginning to understand, Spud. I think I'm bound for a fight, no choice, win or lose."

He sensed the unwavering support the dog offered, and the anxiety melted from his mind. Laying his hand on the prone dog's shoulder, he willed his spirit to search for the one person who always gave him comfort. Soon, Simon, lost in the embrace of Sarah's memory, dozed off, his dog and the fire sentries protecting him against further intruders.

The next morning he woke to a cloudy sky. A breeze carried the fine ash off of last night's fire, and the air smelled like rain. He hated the rain; it meant either time in a damp tent or a dark cabin. He hurried his breakfast, then gathered his tools, and marked out the section of logs he'd have to cut to put his window in. He'd soon chiseled two holes through the wall, sufficient to accept the detached bucksaw blade. Half an hour later, the twelve-inch log thumped to the ground, and he peered, voyeur-like, through the hole. Cutting, then chiseling a six-inch notch in the second log took longer, and a grumbling stomach interrupted his work briefly. Late afternoon had brought heavier skies when, at last, he was able to step back and admire his work.

A raindrop that felt as big as his palm struck his sweaty back and made his heart skip a beat. He bolted for the cabin door. An ear-splitting clap of thunder rent the air and rumbled up the valley, the dull boom bouncing off the high ridges, then fading. Spud had instantly headed for the tent and now sat inside it, looking across the camp at Simon. Soon the ground had taken all it could and puddles formed, creating pools for the raindrops to dance on. The rain fell straight down at a furious pace for fifteen minutes, then quit as suddenly as it had started.

Simon stepped out of the cabin, into the cooled air, now thick with moisture. The line of clouds that bred the brief storm marched east, and the sun, low in the sky, lit the luminous green of the meadow. Steam lifted from the wet grass to hang waist-high over the ground; and the rain-washed air above the mist, now crystal clear, gave the trees and bushes on the hillside such definition that each one drew special attention as he stared.

Alone in the world, unobserved, he looked in awe at the rocky crags, the meandering stream, and the lushness of his valley. A feeling of ownership came to him, a responsibility for the pristine, and in that moment he knew he had another job to do.

CHAPTER 26

Simon bent to his task. Shoveling like a machine, he tore at the rocks and dirt of the low dam that diverted the creek. Slowly the trench in front of the big rocks filled, and at last, a small trickle of water came through the breach. He continued to dig, determined to restore the creek bottom, knowing full well the folly. The spring flood would erase any sign of his presence soon enough, but his responsibility for the wound bore heavily on him, and he was going to see it put right. At last, the dike was leveled, and he set to work removing the small diversion ditch by scraping with his shovel point. He filled the shallow depression, and then moved to work below the twin boulders, shifting some rocks by hand.

A vague feeling of another presence settled over his wandering thoughts. He stopped, slowly stood, and waited for some clue. Spud had taken off some time ago, prancing along the creekside, heading for higher ground. He glanced upstream, then started to turn around.

They were atop the rocky outcrop. Reed stood with his arms folded. Toad, squatted beside him, looked every bit his namesake.

At the sight of Toad, Simon's groin seized. "Uh . . . hello, Justin. Mister —" He chanced a look at his rifle, lying by a small bush at the base of the rocks they were standing on.

"Hello, Simon. Forgot to get your last order, with the dog's problem and all. Where is the mutt? Didn't see him in camp."

"Uh. I guess he's . . . uh, I don't really know." Simon couldn't resist another look upstream. "In camp? You stopped there?"

"Sure. Wanted to make sure you weren't napping or something. Right, Toad?"

Toad grimaced. A smile? Or bad stomach?

"Let me gather up my things, and we can go back to the cabin. I'm done here, any-how." Simon made a move to step out of the creek.

"Stay right there." Reed put his hand on his pistol butt. "Done with what? We've been watching for forty minutes, and all you've done is mess around in the creek bed."

"I don't know what to say." Simon feigned

335

fidgeting in the water with his foot. He shot another glance at the rifle. "Little embarrassed, I guess. Truth is, I've been playing in the water."

"I suspect you've been covering something up." Reed glanced at Toad, who stood. "I think I'll come and take a closer look." He started to pick his way down the rocky slope.

Simon assessed his chances of reaching the rifle before Reed did. He looked at it and then up at the ugly man standing alertly on top of the rocks. He dismissed the attempt, and was then amazed and relieved when Reed moved right past the Winchester. Eyes directly on Simon, he never looked down.

Toad stood where he was until Reed reached the bottom, then followed, taking a wider, more gentle, slope to the right. His short legs made his trip over the rough ground a trial.

"We saw all the test holes you've dug below. Thought you said you hadn't looked." Reed stood eight feet away, facing Simon with Toad a little to Simon's left and a step behind Reed.

"I didn't say I hadn't looked. I said I hadn't looked much. I didn't find anything down there."

"But you did here? Right? Ain't no sense

336

denying it. We found your little hiding place by the stove. They always hide it in the woodpile, or under the stove, don't they, Toad?" He grinned at his partner. "Now, I want to know where you got it." Reed lifted his pistol out of his waistband and leveled it at Simon. Toad took one step forward. "We can do this easy, or I'll let Toad carve you a little."

The tongue tip that flicked out between Toad's cracked lips was an uncommon pink, like a baby's tongue. It ran across his mouth, then disappeared again as a crooked smile exposed scum-encrusted teeth. His eyes narrowed and he chuckled. "I'd like that. I'd like that a lot."

Simon's mind weighed through a dozen options in the space of a heartbeat. Toad didn't appear to have a pistol, and the knife he alluded to was not visible. Reed's gun now pointed at Simon's feet, Reed apparently feeling secure with the distance. Simon glanced at the shovel lying on the ground between them.

"C'mon, spill it, Steele. Ain't worth getting busted up over." He raised the barrel of the pistol and the sound of it being cocked made Simon's throat constrict.

"I . . . I'm . . ." His voice would not steady itself, and he half-choked. "I'll —"

Propelled off the rocks above, the dog hurtled silently through the air. Spud's hindquarters caught Toad in the head and his bared teeth clamped onto the side of Reed's face. The pistol flew from Reed's hand and landed with a splash in the creek. The unearthly scream from Reed's mouth stunned Simon into immobility, and the three crashed to the ground. Toad, scrambling to keep his balance, stumbled over the shovel and fell hard, facedown on the rocky path. Reed and the dog landed beside the creek, Reed's hands flailing at the dog, his legs kicking violently. He continued to scream, the sound piercing, almost painful to the ears.

The unearthly screech shook Simon from his paralysis. He dashed across the trail and snatched up his rifle. He turned to see Toad scramble to his feet, snatch a short knife from his boot top, and start toward Reed and the dog. Simon threw the rifle to his shoulder and followed the squat figure for only an instant. As the knife came up to strike, Simon pulled the trigger.

Toad spun around and cried out, his face contorted in pain, his hand clamped to his ribs on the right side. "Ya bastard, ya hit me." He dropped to his knees, then leaned forward on his hands, gasping for breath.

Simon rushed past him to where Spud was savaging Reed's face. Reed, on his knees, had his fingers locked in Spud's lips on both sides of the dog's jaws. His screams were now groans, pitiable, sobbing groans. Spud growled continuously as he twisted his head from side to side, pulling back all the time.

"Spud! Let him go." Simon slapped the dog on the rear. "Spud!" He grabbed him by the scruff of the neck and twisted the fur. "Quit it." The dog let loose and stepped back, hackles raised, still growling.

Reed's right cheek, a ragged, fat, puffy flap of skin, hung down to his chin, exposing his back teeth. Blood streamed through the fingers he pressed against his face. He hunkered, his eyes on Simon.

He looked perplexed at first, then scared. "Ohhh," he moaned. "What has he done to me?" He took his hand away from his face and stared at it. Shiny red, the blood ran all the way to his elbow and dripped onto his leg. "I think I might need a doctor." He said it as simply as asking for another cup of coffee. Reed's eyes suddenly went blank. Settling back on his butt, he started to rock back and forth.

Simon turned around to face Toad. He, too, sat on his heels, looking back with a venomous glare.

"Get on your feet," Simon ordered. He worked the lever on the Winchester. "Now!"

The squat man grunted as he struggled to get up. He stood, one hand clamped to his bloodstained side, his wound obviously not as bad as Reed's. He looked down at his knife and stooped over.

"Leave it where it is."

Toad gave him another menacing look, and slowly stood straight, still clutching his side. "Wasn't s'posed to be no shooting," he mumbled.

"Get him up." Simon pointed at Reed with his rifle.

Simon puffed out his breath and started breathing through his mouth as the man's body odor wafted past. Toad grabbed Reed by the arm, heaved back, and got him on his feet.

"Now, let's go find your horses, and you can get out of here."

"That's it? Just leave?" Toad looked suspicious.

"That's right. Just get out of here. You want to come back and try to get around that dog, well then, I guess you will. He smelled you from a mile upwind."

"He needs doctoring." Toad nodded his head at Reed.

"I'm not one. He reaped what he sowed. Now move."

Simon got his horse and followed the two men as they struggled the quarter-mile to their mounts. Simon relieved Toad of an old musket strapped to his saddle, and then dug the two small linen sacks of gold out of Reed's saddlebags.

"Nobody to bring my supplies in now, so I'll be coming to Challis in a month or so. And when I get there, the first thing I'm gonna do is tell the law about this. If you know what's good for you, you'll get clear of there before I show up. I see you again, I'll shoot you. Understood?"

Toad didn't answer, and Reed simply sat astride his horse, a bloody kerchief pressed against his face. Stoic, he looked straight ahead.

Simon mounted his horse, and with his rifle trained on their backs, followed them for a mile past the cabin. He watched until they disappeared from sight, then went back to his camp.

He pulled open the cabin door. "Shit." The shelves were on the floor, his table overturned, a leg broken off. They'd cut the bed rails clean through with the ax, and had tipped the stove over, ashes and soot everywhere. The thoroughness of the destruction indicated they had taken some kind of pleasure in ransacking his home. "Shoulda killed 'em. Dirty bastards." Simon pushed the toe of his boot through a pile of cornmeal dumped on the dirt floor, the sack shredded. They'd poured molasses over a torn bag of flour, then coal oil on top of that.

Suddenly a pang of panic surged through him and he frantically searched for his saddlebags. They were under the buffalo robe, emptied of everything. Pawing through the pile of clothes in the corner, he found what he was looking for, Sarah's letter. Half of it. Cursing the dim light, he searched some more and finally laid his hand on the other half. It lay crumpled up and ground into the floor, saturated in lamp oil, ruined.

He hurried outside to the oat-sack cushion. Safe under it he found his journal. Slowly, he turned and shuffled back to the cabin where he sagged onto his bench. With his elbows on his knees, he leaned forward and let his head droop. Reed's pistol, pointed at his chest, filled his mind, and he started to shake. His stomach revolted and he puked on his shoes.

July 18, 1874. Reed and another man came to rob and maybe kill me. Spud took

*care of Reed, I shot the other. Nobody
dead. Cabin ransacked. I thought he was
a friend.*

CHAPTER 27

Simon woke to light stealing through the new window. Though not very bright, the moon infused the room with life and drove the dreaded blackness from the cabin. The events of the previous day wouldn't let him sleep. This was at least the third time his eyes had suddenly opened. Night sweat dampened his body, and he threw back the single blanket. He relaxed a little in the cool air.

Reed's betrayal confused him. He remembered well the feelings he'd had when he, Buell, and Jake had sat around the makeshift cracker-barrel table in Jake's father's saloon storeroom. Breaking wind and making crude jokes, they'd talked about things that help turn boys into young men. Some of the information later proved valid and useful, but mostly it was the naïve eagerly taking instruction from the ignorant.

They told secrets, feelings they had about

themselves they felt they couldn't face, but had to. And shared triumphs as well, most small, but large to a boy's limited experience. They were free to bare their souls, free to admit failings, free to admit silly dreams. Free, because they were friends, those young men. Men that he . . . loved? Was that too intimate a word? It didn't seem so, lying there in the dark, alone. He suffered no embarrassment for it.

He loved Sarah too . . . and his family . . . Uncle John. And he felt he could have loved Justin for exactly the same reasons. He'd helped and listened and was loyal. But now the thought of allowing someone close had new meaning; it contained new dangers that were not part of the equation before. Reed had destroyed something . . . something Simon had taken for granted. He couldn't put his finger on it, but that something was gone.

He lay still for a while, then got out of bed. Outside, the half-moon added mystery to the darkness, offering glimpses of things not fully revealed. The gray-white rectangle of the tent glowed dimly against the dark boughs of the spruce tree, and just beyond, Simon saw Spud. He sat on his haunches, nose pointed downstream. Stepping gingerly in his bare feet, Simon made his way to him.

"What you doing, boy? I don't think they'll be back. And you're the reason." Simon squatted by his dog and stroked his head. "They know you're watching."

Simon sat with his dog until the chill in the air drove him back to the cabin. One more look before he pulled the door shut revealed the dog, patiently sitting, watching, and waiting.

Repairing the damage to the cabin turned out to be a lot easier than he'd planned. Probably because he'd already built the things once, he thought. The full week he'd cut firewood when Spud had been laid up took the urgency out of that perpetual task. He worked at a leisurely pace, enjoying the process of using his hands to create something useful. The days passed quickly and before long, Spud resumed sleeping in the tent or by the fireplace at night. What he'd salvaged, he'd returned to the new shelves or stored away otherwise, and Simon got back to enjoying his valley.

Early in the evening, he'd shot a large rabbit he'd caught drinking at the creek. She'd sprinted away in plenty of time, but her curiosity had gotten to her and she'd stopped for one last look. Her last anything. The rabbit had died instantly, but he suffered the same pangs of regret that he felt every time he killed something. Now she lay in pieces, nestled flat in the black skillet, turning a golden brown and making his mouth water. He shook a double handful of ground coffee into the blue-speckled pot and waited for the foam to rise. He knocked it back with a cup of cold water, then went back to tending the cooking rabbit.

Later, with his plate and fork washed and put away, Simon stuffed his knife into the scabbard, went into the cabin, and got his journal. Settling down by the fire, he opened the cover. Before he could turn toward the middle of the book, the first entry caught his eye. *July 24, 1873.* One year? Today was the twenty-fourth, wasn't it? He quickly recalled the last five days and confirmed the date mentally.

In the fading light, he looked around his home. Home. Fort Laramie, in the five years he'd lived there, had never taken on that mantle. Sure, there were times in the hotel when, sitting around a table with his friends, it felt like it, but it never really measured up. And it wasn't a hotel, he chided himself; it was a whorehouse.

But this was home. Why? He took in the squat form of the cabin. Building it had nearly cost him his life. He had his soul tied up in the cabin and in the meadow with the winding stream. It was his meadow. In the dimmest of starlight, he could point out every feature, and walk sure-footed to the creek for water. The twin trees, one on either side of the campfire, towered above him. They were the reason he'd stopped at this spot. They had somehow beckoned and he had responded. A perfect pair, they offered each other protection, and grew strong and tall because of it.

He laid the journal aside and looked into the fire. A pair. Sarah and him. She'd make this place perfect. He imagined her sitting by his side, her soft brown hair catching the flicker of firelight, her creamy skin aglow in the quarter-moon. Then the reality of such an idea dawned on him and he chuckled. "Can you imagine Sarah in that dingy hut we call home?" He flicked a twig at the dog. "I know you never met her, but think of Lori dressed for church. That was Sarah all the time." He sighed, then picked up his journal again.

July 24, 1874. One year. Melancholy tonight. Cabin is back in shape. Feels like I'm home here. I'm going to town soon.

The next morning Simon took inventory and made a list of the things he'd need. Reed and Toad had destroyed all they could, short of burning the place down. And he thought they'd have done that if not for the smoke alerting him to their presence. But they had managed to do a lot. He studied the long list. He didn't have a lot of time.

While he was restoring everything in the cabin, he'd found a spare kettle and a knife. He remembered the kettle coming in on a load, but the knife came as a surprise. He sat looking at the two utensils and thinking of his Indian friend. "C'mon, Spud, let's take a walk."

The dog got up, stretched, and followed Simon toward the open spot in the trees across the meadow. Simon carried the kettle with the knife inside in one hand and his rifle in the other. A pair of red socks poked out of his front pants pocket.

He hung the pot on a branch of the same tree used to deliver his last present, put the socks in with the knife, then crossed the creek again, and headed upstream. He wanted to see if his work had done what he'd wanted it to do. A perfect day for a walk, a light breeze frustrating the heat, and billowing white clouds lifting their skirts to reveal patches of startling blue. Insects darted past, their high-pitched hum telling the world how busy and important they were.

Across the meadow, in a tree containing hundreds of handy perches, four crows struggled to sit on a single branch. Their raucous argument, annoying in any other setting, made Simon stop and smile. "Just like Axel and Abe," he muttered as he continued upstream. He pictured his younger brothers at suppertime, banging elbows over an imaginary boundary line on the kitchen table. Both knew where the line should be, and each encroached on the other. They'd squabble and argue until his mother settled the issue with a wooden spoon, one whack apiece. They'd grudgingly shift a little bit, then sit and glare at each other. Simon glanced up at the crows again, now spread out on other branches, each busily fluffing feathers. He wondered which one had the spoon.

He stood at the edge of the pool and stared into the water. The mud he'd stirred up removing the dam had settled evenly on the bottom, and even knowing where to look, he couldn't see the trench by the twin rocks. The dry, sun-baked ground where he'd filled the diversion looked as natural as the trail above. He was tempted to continue his walk up the canyon, but a look at the clouds gathering over the ridges gave him pause. Some to the southwest were developing dark bottoms, their tops taking on a fuzzy, ill-defined appearance. He tucked his rifle into the crook of his arm, and picked his way down the slope. Moving past the twin rocks, over rubble splashed wet by the rushing water, he soon found himself at the head of the meadow.

A low rumble of thunder bounced back and forth between the high walls of the canyon. Simon looked back just in time to see a jagged line split the air between the dark clouds and the ridge below. A few seconds later the air split with a crackling pop as the sound reached him. He angled off toward the hot springs, his steps hurried. By the time he'd reached the hillside, the blue-gray curtain of the approaching storm blocked his sight of the defile. "C'mon, Spud, let's go see why the mare liked this place." He took off at a run toward the high rock wall.

Under the boughs of the trees that circled the clearing, he heard the rain hit. A heavy swishing sound filtered down through the greenery with a fine mist. He stepped closer to the trunk of the biggest pine. A brilliant burst of light illuminated the cove, followed immediately by an ear-splitting crash. Spud shied and forced his way behind Simon's legs. A strange smell filled the air, one he'd never experienced before, and the hair on his body stood on end.

Another brilliant strobe of pure white light stopped a million raindrops in midair. The flash revealed a low opening in the shadow of the rock overhang, directly across the clearing. The terrific clap of thunder that followed made Simon jump, and he sprinted away from the tree, across the clearing, and into the black hole. He reached the cave at the same instant as the dog and together they sprawled into the interior. Scrambling on his hands and knees, he kept his head down and turned to face the opening. The dead still air had a sweet smell. He sniffed. Spicy sweet, tinged with the smell of old dust. Simon glanced up and sensed more than saw that the cave was rather spacious. Though it was dark and a little unsettling, at least he was out of the rain and away from the storm. He peered toward the opening.

The clearing outside was now a shallow puddle of dancing water, the ferocious downpour creating a spray that blurred the view. Trembling like an aspen leaf, Spud crowded close, leaning so hard that Simon nearly toppled over. Putting his hand out to steady himself, Simon felt a dry stick of wood, then several of them. Turning to look more closely, another flash of lightning lit the interior of the cave.

"Ohhhh, shit!" Simon wailed, his voice cracking in fear. The split second of light was more than enough to reveal a partially exposed rack of ribs, and a man's skull. Patches of long hair clung to the face, dry skin drawn tight across his cheeks. Another flash lit the cave, and Simon saw the far wall. He was there in a single bound. Looking back in horror, he crouched and waited for the next burst of electricity. When it came, the bones of a full-grown human lay loosely together along the rock wall. Pieces of tattered clothes partially covered the remains. His heart gradually slowed as he got his breath under control. Again, nature's light show lit the interior and revealed the dog, standing over the bones. "Spud, get over here!"

The dog came to sit beside him. Simon inspected the cave in the revealing flashes of light. The ceiling above his head would allow him to stand. Along the back wall, some ten feet away, he made out a bed. Immediately to his right stood a rough table and a bench, the top crowded with cans and various-sized boxes. Most of the cartons appeared to have been attacked by rodents. His gaze returned to the man. Just beyond the top of the head lie a floppy felt hat. That and the face hair made him a white man.

Transfixed by the eerie sight in the lightning flashes, Simon stared for several minutes. The strokes occurred less and less frequently as the thunderstorm moved down the valley. Finally he glanced outside at the still pool of water in the clearing. He stooped to exit the cave through the four-foot opening.

The air outside smelled so fresh it surprised him. He breathed to clear the cave smell out of his nose, then turned to look at the entrance. "How did I not see that opening?" He recalled the two times he'd been in the clearing, and it came to him. It both instances, the horse had backed up against the end of the enclosure. The first time he hadn't approached her; the second time, he'd been too busy not getting kicked to look behind her.

He knew he had to go back in there. That was a white man, and white men were buried, not left to be scattered by animals . . . like that damnable wolverine. But moving around in there without some light never got beyond the thought stage. Simon retrieved his rifle and headed for the cabin.

The next morning, Simon strapped his pick and shovel to the horse and stuffed his rifle into the scabbard. He carefully put the

354

lamp chimney in one saddlebag and the fuel bowl in another, then climbed aboard. Twenty minutes later, he stood in front of the cave, gathering his courage. Should he dig the grave first or first go get the . . . what? Bones? The body? He let his breath out with a puff and stooped to enter.

The flare of the match took his sight for a moment, then it returned as he put the chimney on and adjusted the wick. In the glow of the lamp, it became apparent the man had lived in the cave for some time. He moved over to the bed, and touched the soft hides of his covers. A long wool overcoat lay folded across the foot of the narrow bunk. His brief assessment the day before had been correct; the rodents had chewed open everything made of paper or cloth. White flour spilled from a large bag by the table, mixing with the thick layer of fine dirt on the floor. He picked up a can of tomatoes and looked for rust. Finding none, he checked another one, this time applesauce, and found signs on one end. He cracked a piece of sugar off a partially used cone, still dry as could be. The jumble on the table held his attention for several more seconds, and then he sighed, turning slowly to face his task.

The unsteady light gave the corpse a sickly

yellow cast. It looked rotten, and Simon's stomach turned. He swallowed hard and knelt down. The man's right arm was pinned under his back, the left extended. Unable to see the lower part of the right leg, he swung the lamp closer. It was gone from the knee down. The left one was intact and the foot had a shoe on it, the toe turned up by the curling sole. With no excuse left, he moved the lamp back past the exposed ribs, and shined his light on the head. Vacant eye sockets with incongruous eyebrows stared back at him. The dry skin of the lips drew tight across a mouth that had few teeth. Tufts of reddish-brown hair clung to the man's chin and hung in patches on his head. Simon swallowed hard again, then went over to the bed for the tanned elk hide. He laid it on the floor beside the man. Gingerly, he tried to pick up the leg by grabbing hold of the tattered clothes. He lifted, and the rotten threads gave way, dumping the bones back onto the floor.

"Oh, I don't know," Simon muttered. He puffed through pursed lips, subconsciously blowing the foulness away. The shoe now lay on its side, disconnected from the leg. He took hold of the shoe top with two fingers and delivered the gruesome package to the hide. Next, he picked up the two bones of the lower leg, one in each hand. The thighbones were easy. Then he tried to move the pelvis. It came away, dragging a section of the backbone. Simon bolted for the opening.

Outside, he gulped huge mouthfuls of fresh air as he struggled hard to keep his breakfast down. He rushed over to the hot spring and held his hands in the warm water, willing away the corruption he felt. Emotionally drained, he slumped sideways and sat on the damp ground. Spud sat beside him, gazing intently.

"I don't know if I can finish that. The legs were dry but I don't think what's left is gonna be. Will you hold it against me if I can't?" The dog tilted his head. "Naw, I didn't think so. Give me a few minutes, and I'll be okay."

Simon looked into the clear water of his bathing pool, forever refreshing itself from the source in the hillside. So clean it could cleanse his body when this was over. He was once again thankful that he'd dug it. How many times had he let the water soak away his fatigue? "That's what I'm gonna do, Spud," he said, startling the dog. "I'm gonna dig his grave first so he'll have a clean place to go soon as I pull him out of there. Exactly."

Simon got up and went into the trees for his tools. Stepping back into the sunlight, he dropped the shovel, chose a spot far enough from the trees to avoid the roots, and swung his pick. The point sank to the handle with a satisfying thud sound.

Two hours later he stood over the skeleton. While shoveling the dirt out of the grave, he'd had to cut a few small roots with the shovel and had an idea. Now he put the point of the shovel on the shoulder joint and gently bore down. After resisting slightly, it came away clean. He swallowed and rapidly blinked his eyes. "I'm sorry fella, but this is the only way I can see doing it." He did the same to the elbow, then picked up the bones and tatters with the blade, and put them on the hide. Last, he put the point on the man's neck and pushed. The blade went through to the ground. Simon slipped the shovel under the man's back and pinned arm, and hoisted it up. The sickly sweet smell nearly knocked him down. Holding his breath, eyes squinted, he moved the head, threw down the shovel, and skidded everything on the elk hide out of the cave.

He folded the tanned leather over the man, or what used to be a man, then dragged it across the clearing, bumping over exposed roots and around piles of horse manure to the grave. He stood up and stretched his back, then headed back to the cave for the shovel. "Damn." Halfway to the trees lay the head.

Stooped over to scoop up the skull, he suddenly stopped and looked closer at the grisly orb. There was a round little-finger-sized hole in the left side of the man's head and one the size of a chicken egg on the opposite side. Simon shook his head. "Just couldn't take the dark and lonelys, looks like." He hauled the head to the graveside and put it with the rest of the bones. Then, catching both edges of the hide, he lowered the whole thing into the hole.

He stood beside the grave, his hat held in front of him. "I only been to one funeral, and I don't remember much except something about us all returning to the ground. Well, here you are, and you couldn't ask for a nicer piece of ground to lie in. I'm sorry I busted you up some getting you here, but it's all I could manage. I'll poke around in your things, and see if I can get your name, and maybe find out about your kin. Rest easy." He picked up the shovel and started to dig again.

Half an hour later, Simon pounded the back of his shovel on the rounded mound one last time, then wiped his sweating brow on his shirtsleeve. "But where's the gun?" he asked suddenly, and turned to look toward the clearing. "I didn't see a gun of any kind."

He strode to the cave and ducked inside. He turned up the lamp's wick and started to examine the interior again. Two empty panniers lay under the bed. Near the entrance, a skillet and two pots, all bottoms up, waited beside a ring of rocks. He searched through the stuff on the table. Then he held the lamp high and scanned the interior. High along the back wall, an uneven natural rock shelf protruded, but from his angle, he could see nothing on it. He went to the bed below it, stood on the frame, and felt around on top. His hand met cold metal and he retrieved a pocket pistol. Next, he found a box. Nothing else. Anxious to leave the stink, he took another quick look around and left the cave.

The pistol, a break-top single shot, was loaded. He put it aside and laid the box on his lap. The simple clasp wasn't locked, and he swung the lid open. A folded paper lay on top and he spread it out. He recognized the map immediately. *"CHALLIS"* identified the four boxes drawn beside a river. Below that, a rectangle with the word *"TRADER"* written under it would be Spring Creek. Upriver was the word *"HOT"* and beside it, a south-pointing arrow. The meandering line running off in that direction had to be his creek, and there was another *"X"* where the line stopped, but it couldn't be where he sat now. The stream started high in the mountains, high enough that he'd never been there.

Surely, his hot springs would have been indicated. Maybe the person who drew the map had never actually been up the valley. He folded the map, and took out a packet of papers. Letters. The man's name was Lemuel, and the cramped handwriting of his wife told of hardship on the farm and the hope that he'd find work. She mentioned two children. Her name was Clara. Simon sat and read five more, all similar to the first. Three were dated in 1871, two in 1872, and the most recent in February. Next, he took out a pale-blue handkerchief.

Simon gasped. There, in the bottom of the box lay a steel watch, a folding knife, a few dollars, and a three-inch piece of wood, precisely carved in little adjoined diamonds. Justin!

He'd made the trip back to the cabin the day before in a blind rage. Images of Justin

Reed, sitting at the campfire, smiling and talking, taunted him. The innocent questions had taken on their real meaning, and he'd felt sick to his stomach. Then he'd noticed the initials carved in the stock of the rusty musket he'd taken from Toad. "LL." Lemuel something. Justin and Toad had been in it all along. What a fool.

He jerked hard on the cinch and slapped the stirrup down so abruptly his horse jumped. With his rifle jammed in the scabbard, he tied on his saddlebags and the musket, and climbed on the horse. In the dim morning light, he looked around the camp once, then kicked his horse in the flanks. "C'mon, Spud. We're gonna find us a couple of killers and see 'em strung up."

CHAPTER 28

Simon saw very little of the valley as he rode the seven miles to the river. He fixed his thoughts on what he'd do if he saw Justin Reed or Toad. Would the marshal be in town? He plunged into the Salmon River, and crossed without a thought of his last encounter with it. He pushed the horse hard over the trail, now much wider and well-traveled compared to the track of the year before. He camped that evening where a stream half the size of the river drained in from the south. There were half-a-dozen established fire rings, but he spent the night alone.

He broke camp at sunup the next day, and by late afternoon he arrived at Spring Creek, passing the trading post, now a charred heap of rubble smelling of burned pitch pine. The carefully tended three- and four-acre plots of ground he'd seen now shared the wide valley with several more dwellings and fields of grain and corn thirty acres or more in size. The closest one stood right on the riverbank, and he rode up the trail, now more nearly a rough road, toward it. A figure darted from the shore to the back of the house.

"Ma, there's a man here," a young voice shouted from inside.

A few seconds later a woman stepped into the sun. Slim, she nonetheless looked very capable in her long gray dress and sturdy shoes.

Shading her eyes with one hand, she looked up at him. "Hello. Can I help you, sir?" A small head with tousled brown hair peeked around her side, and a pair of intense eyes shifted their gaze back and forth between him and the dog.

"Yes, ma'am. I'm on my way to Challis and I'd like to know about how far it is."

"Not far at all, about two hours, maybe two and a half. Put your mind to it, you'd make it by dark easy enough."

"Do you know Marshal Hess by any chance?"

"Sure do." She cocked her head. "You got trouble?"

"No, ma'am. I just need to see him."

"Well, he come by . . . what's it been now?" She paused. "Little over a week ago,

364

maybe ten days."

"Could you tell me if he was coming or going?"

"Seems to me he was going. Said something about needing to be up north for a while. Didn't say much, only stopped for a drink of water."

"Thank you, ma'am, I'm grateful." He touched the brim of his hat and swung his horse around the end of the house. The child — he could now see it was a boy — waved at him as he urged his horse north.

He smelled the town long before he saw it. Woodsmoke dominated the array of scents, but underlying that, he picked up the smell of something sour, like vinegar, then the unmistakable perfume of fresh cut meadow grass. Just as he crested a low hill, he detected the scent of curing meat, either bacon or ham — maybe both.

Challis lay strung out along a wide central street. He hadn't expected to see so many buildings, and certainly not the three two-story affairs in the middle of town. He found the source of the bacon smell as he passed one of the first businesses, a smoke-house, Solberger's Meat. Probably where his sausage had come from. For being late in the day, the number of people passing back and forth across the street, dodging each other and a steady stream of wagons, surprised him. He rode up to one of the two-story buildings. A glaring white sign in three-foot letters spelled out Hawke's Hotel and Saloon across the front. He tied his horse to the rail where a half-dozen others already stood, dull-eyed, their tails swishing flies. They looked bored. "Sit right there, Spud." Simon pointed to the boardwalk by the door and the dog sat.

He noticed the high ceilings as soon as he stepped inside. Compared to the saloon in Fort Laramie, this one had at least another four feet in height. The smell of tobacco smoke and beer, pleasantly familiar, followed him across the room. At the bar, he caught the bartender's eye.

"Evening, sir. What can I get you?" The barkeep gave him a wide smile.

"I think a small beer."

The man pumped a short glass full, set it down, and leaned both hands on the bar.

Simon took a sip, and dug into his pocket for some money. The beer was cold. "Could you tell me if Marshal Hess is in town?" He put a dollar on the shiny counter.

"I don't rightly know. He comes in when he's around, but I haven't seen him lately. We have a sheriff — constable actually — but he likes to be called the other."

"You've got law right here in town?"

The man squared his shoulders and sniffed. "Sure do. City fathers hired one last winter. His office is a little farther down the street, same side as we are." He put Simon's change down.

"Do you think he'd be in?"

"For sure. The freighters try to get here about this time of day, and that's when it gets noisy."

Simon nodded his head, picked up his change and beer, then turned around. Out of habit, he counted fifteen people in the bar, most roughly dressed in common work clothes. None looked like cowboys, and there wasn't a blue uniform to be seen. A steady low hum of conversation promised not to approach the more boisterous atmosphere of Amos's place. He tipped the glass back, draining it. "Thanks, that was real good. Just curious, how long does your ice last?"

"Another month, maybe."

Simon saw the curiosity in the man's face. "I ran a saloon in Wyoming awhile back, and thought about storing winter ice below the floor. Never did it, and just wondered if it would've worked."

"Works fine. We lay three-foot-thick blocks on a foot or so of sawdust, then cover the ice with another three feet. Customers sure get snarly when it's gone, though." The bartender beamed him another proud smile.

Just friendly, or is he looking to sell me another glass of beer? Simon smiled back as he mentally kicked himself. Been in the hills too long. He pushed his empty glass across the bar. "Thanks, friend."

Spud fell in beside him as he walked down the street, looking for the sheriff's office. It wasn't hard to find, and neither was the man. He was in a chair, leaned back against the front of the building, his long legs stretched over halfway across the boardwalk. The gold-colored six-pointed badge stuck to the shirt pocket looked heavy on his thin chest. His wide felt hat sat tipped forward to cover his eyes.

"Excuse me, sir. My name's Simon Steele, and I'd like to talk to someone about a murder."

The chair settled back on all four legs with a thump and the man unfolded to stand. "A murder, you say?" He pushed the hat back to reveal soft gray eyes. They narrowed as he looked Simon over.

"Yes, sir. I've been living back in the sticks about two days west of here. I came on a man . . . more like the remains of a man. He'd been shot in the head."

"And you think someone done him in? People have been known to do that sort of thing to themselves."

"His gun was a single-shot, and it was still loaded." Simon handed the lawman the box of personal effects and the musket he had draped over his arm. Then he pulled the pistol out of his pocket. "The box and the pistol were his. The musket I took off a man who might have had a hand in the murder."

"Let's get off the street, Mr. Steele." The lawman turned, opened the door, and let Simon pass.

Simon looked at the dog.

"I don't care," the sheriff said. "Bring him in."

"C'mon, Spud."

The man walked around a small desk, leaned the short gun against it, and laid the box and pistol on top. Then he extended his hand. "I'm Joe Hart. Sit down and tell me what you found."

Twenty minutes later Hart rubbed his face with both hands and sighed. "Well, that explains Reed's face and why he seemed to be in a hurry. We don't have a proper doctor here, but the vet looked at him and did what he could before Reed left. Been too long though, or so the vet told me. Said it'd gone septic. Reed said a badger bit him —

369

in his sleep, no less."

"Was that Toad fella with him?"

"Not that I know, just Reed. Puttin' a couple of things together, I'd say your Mr. Toad didn't make it to town."

"That's what I'm thinking."

"Be that as it may, it's still out of my jurisdiction. You're right. You need the marshal, and I don't expect him back before the end of the week. I know he went to Salmon City and sometimes he stays awhile. If you can stick around, I know he'd like to talk to you. He had some suspicions about Justin. We all did."

"He sure fooled me." A blend of anger and sadness welled up, and Simon clenched his teeth.

"He's fooled a lot of folks, Mr. Steele."

Simon found a stable, and after assuring a skeptical liveryman that Spud would stay with the horse, he went back to Hawke's and rented a room. He now stood looking at the bed, four feet wide with two pillows, and a turned back coverlet that revealed stark white sheets. Twice in Hart's office, the sheriff's raised eyebrows had cued him to the fact he'd been scratching himself in the most unseemly places.

He turned to the woman who'd showed him the room. "Can I get a bath and a shave

370

this time of day? And maybe a haircut?"

"Bath and a shave. Haircut will have to wait till tomorrow."

Simon chuckled to himself at her instant response and thought *I must really stink.*

"Just down the hall." She gave a slight nod of her head. "Leave your clothes outside the curtain by the tub, and I'll see they're washed. Soap and razor are in there too." The lady gave him one more glance, and went back down the stairs.

The bath changed his whole demeanor. And a shave, his appearance. When he walked up to the desk an hour later, the clerk looked up and asked if he wanted a room. Somewhat embarrassed, the man answered Simon's question about where to find the barber, and then Simon made his way to the dining room.

The next morning Simon picked up Spud and located the barber. An hour later, he was directed to the mercantile store. The man behind the counter assured him the supplies on his list were readily available and, when Simon asked about a packer, directed him to a cluster of corrals and shacks on the north end of town.

The thick wedge-shaped stump of a man stood beside a mule, his feet set wide apart. With his head craned over his right shoulder, he was looking at the back of his upper arm, which he rubbed vigorously with his left hand. Then he looked at the mule, murder glinting in his eye. "You sonuvabitch, you bit me." Before Simon could figure out what was going on, the man's hand shot out and the heavy gut-wrenching sound of a balled fist smacking into live flesh leapt across the stable-yard.

The mule bolted sideways, its head raised high against the restraining halter and brayed loudly. The short man followed the animal as it turned, and slugged it again, this time missing the soft tissue of the creature's nose and hitting it in the neck. The mule protested again with a long coughing rant of outrage.

Simon was beside him in a second. "Hey, mister, you can't do that."

The man spun around, his face screwed up and red. "What?" His deep-set eyes were hard to see under the heavy brows. "Mind yer own damn business."

The raised fist reminded Simon of a small ham. "You have that packsaddle all wrong." Simon pointed. "Hell's fire, man, it's set too far back. I'd bite you too."

"What in hell's going on out here, Whiff?"

A man in a leather apron stomped across the yard. He looked every inch a blacksmith.

"This young snot-nose is meddling in my business," the man with the mule said.

"He's beating that mule because the packsaddle's on wrong," Simon said. "And it looks like it bit him."

The blacksmith glanced at the gear, then at the man. "Ya dumb bastard. He's right. I showed you how to do that. Gimme that lead." He snatched the rope from the stumpy man. "Let those girth straps loose and shift the saddle."

"And let the sonuvabitch bite me again?" Whiff scowled, first at Simon, then at the mule.

"I hope he does," said the blacksmith. "Now let 'em loose."

Whiff crept up on the mule, his eyes fixed on the animal's head. He caught hold of the thick leather straps and started to undo them.

"Appreciate ya stepping in there, young man. These animals are my livelihood, and I don't want 'em mistreated."

"I hate to see any animal get beat. Are you Mr. Olsen?"

"That's right. Folks call me Jack."

"I've got a place off the river about two days upstream. Man at the store said you pack supplies for miners and such."

"That I do." Olsen turned to the muleskinner. "There, now shift the saddle to the center of his back. Good grief, Whiff, you can see how wrong you have it, can't you?"

The stumpy man tugged at the contraption until Olsen nodded his head.

"Now cinch 'em up again." Olsen shook his head, then turned back to Simon.

"I need some supplies," Simon said. "Fairly soon. Probably two mules."

"How soon's fairly? If Whiff here can get cracking, I'll have a couple free by the end of the week. I've got twenty-one going into the basin about then. I can add yours to the string. Exactly where are you?"

"Do you know the hot springs about a day's ride west of Spring Creek?"

"I do." Olsen looked at the mule when it grunted. "That's tight enough, Whiff. Take him inside and start loading those sacks of feed. I'll be right there." He handed the rope to the man. Whiff gave Simon a dirty look as he turned toward the barn.

"The first stream that comes into the river from the south just past there is my valley," Simon continued.

"I know exactly where you're talking about. That's called Slate Creek. Fella named Red Larsen worked up there a ways. I was told he'd moved on."

"Do you know where he was from?"

"Can't say I do."

"I found his body. Someone killed him."

"Be damned." Olsen's eyes narrowed slightly. "I don't think I caught your name."

"I'm Simon Steele. I built a cabin about seven miles up that canyon."

"Prospecting?"

"No. And there isn't a real good answer for your next question. I needed a place to think, and someone told me it was quiet there."

Olson looked at him with a wry lopsided grin. "Some days I could see myself doin' that. Were they right?"

"That they were." Simon returned the smile. "How much will it cost me for the two mules?"

"It's three days to Red's place. Or where he was." Olsen shook his head and grimaced. "Two dollars a day for a driver, cuz he'll have to leave the main train and come back directly. And four a day for each mule. Reckon that's sixty dollars. I'll load 'em heavy as I think's safe, and charge you for another if need be."

"Two will do it. I've been supplied every couple of months or so. Keeps things fresh and gives me a chance to talk to somebody."

"You say you've been supplied like you aren't now."

"Yeah, the man who packed for me killed Mr. Larsen, and tried to do me in. My dog took him on, and chewed him up pretty good."

"Justin Reed."

"The same."

"I'll be damned. Things kinda go kerplunk when the parts all settle into place. He came into town several days ago, all tore up. Said a —"

"Yeah, I talked to your sheriff already. He told me."

"Wondered where he was going with his string, and I didn't buy that badger story for a minute. Not a man to trifle with, though." Olsen shook his head slowly. "This is hard country, and ya know something — I hate it." He paused for a few seconds. "Anyhow," he shrugged dismissal with his shoulders, "you have Sutton at the mercantile put your name on your stuff, and I'll pick it up there. That'll be sixty dollars, gold, extra if it's green."

Simon handed him the three coins. "How do I handle my next order?"

"When do you want it?"

"Say the first week in September. And another the end of October."

"Make your arrangements at Sutton's, and I'll check with him. Pay the skinner for my mules when he delivers. Same price. Pleasure doing business with you, Mr. Steele." Olsen put out his hand.

"Likewise." Simon winced as the callused fingers crushed down on his own. "C'mon, Spud, let's go to the store."

For the next two days Simon enjoyed sleeping well past sunup in a clean-sheeted bed, eating whatever struck his fancy, and generally doing nothing. Spud had taken up with a wiry terrier at the stable, but true to his canine code, never left the premises — the bitch stayed at his place. Simon explored the town during the day, and during the evening visited every saloon. There were six. He'd even managed to win sixty-one dollars in a poker game.

About two in the afternoon of his fifth day in town, he was sitting on a chair in front of the hotel, burping radishes. He reckoned he'd eaten about a dozen of the fiery red tubers with his lunch. He covered his mouth again, and chin down, let go another burst. Spud raised his eyebrows, and his look of disgust could not have been more apparent if he were human. Simon chuckled at him. "Can't help it. I haven't had those in forever. Ma used to grow 'em. You don't like it, you can always go see your new friend." He tilted his chair back against the wall and folded his hands across his taut stomach.

Some minutes later, he was in that same position with his eyes shut when he heard, "Welcome to Challis, Mr. Steele." His chair thumped forward with a jolt, and his eyes popped open. Standing in the street was Marshal Hess's black gelding, now gray with dust and sweat.

"Hello, Marshal. Been waiting to see you."

"Well, here I am. Come on down to the constable's office." He gigged his horse and walked it away.

Simon got up and followed.

Half an hour later, Hess rocked back in his chair. "The bastard. I'm afraid I'd have shot him."

"Should have done," added Hart. "Save us the problem."

"I don't ever want to do that again," Simon replied, "but I read Mr. Larsen's letters, and I know Reed was there in his camp. And he said he'd never been in the valley before. When Mr. Olsen told me the man's name was Red Larsen, the Lemuel in the letters I read and the 'LL' carved in the stock made sense. I don't think there's much doubt."

"I don't either," Hess said, "and I'm gonna look for Reed, me and a lot of folks.

If he's around, I'll get word, and we'll see what he has to say. I take it you're willing to charge him with ransacking your place?"

"I am."

"And throwing down on you like that is assault and attempted robbery. Are you missing anything? Money?"

"No," Simon said quietly.

"Well, that's enough to get me started. If I were you, I'd be watchin' for a while, though. When we run him down, I'll let you know. Either personal, or I'll send you a note with your supplies. You're going back in there aren't you?" It didn't sound like a question.

Simon nodded. "Yeah, I miss it already. Way too noisy here."

That evening, his last in town, Simon stayed downstairs after supper. Men in calf-high leather boots and wearing coarse cotton trousers with heavy gloves stuffed in the back pockets crowed the saloon. Teamsters. Not seeing a place at a table, Simon went to the bar and ordered a brandy. The young bartender, with a flourish and a wide smile, poured the drink, then set it on the bar. Before Simon had a chance to pick it up, the powerful scent of lilac and sweat wafted over him and he turned to face the woman standing at his elbow.

"I see you drink brandy. Don't get many here that order that stuff." She stood real close to him.

Her low, husky voice made him swallow hard. It had been a long time since he'd been this close to a woman, and he didn't quite know what to look at first. Her dark-green dress creased tight around a thickening waist. Cut low, it offered her bosom to him, pushed up to overflow the ruffles and lace that tried to contain it all. He stared.

His gaze went to her red hair. Pulled back tightly in a bun, it made the sides of her head look burnished, almost ready to burst into flame. There was still light streaming through the front windows, and it played on a few of the gossamer strands of errant hair on the back of her neck, like spider webs drifting on a breeze. Then he saw her eyes. A startling, almost unreal green, and clear as a winter night, they looked calmly back.

"I . . . uh, you are. . . . I. D-damn, you're pretty." His face caught fire and he silently cussed his ineptitude. Some things never change.

"Thank you," she said, and even though he didn't think it possible, she moved closer yet. "You're different from what I usually see in here. You passing through, or looking to stay?" She canted her head ever so slightly, the corners of her painted mouth turned up. Then she fluttered her eyelashes, just like Sarah used to do, and Simon forgot how to speak. He swallowed hard again. Her calm eyes flashed delight, and the curled corners of her lips turned into a beaming smile. "I'd say you've been away for a while. Say, prospecting in the hills?" She laid her hand on his and it felt as hot as a campfire rock.

"Uh . . . right. I . . . we, that is, me and my dog, we come for supplies and to see the law."

"Ooo, the law. Sounds exciting." Somehow, she could make her lower lip quiver and she did it just then . . . when she said "exciting."

Simon felt himself stir and fought the urge to look down. He glanced at the door and wished for an instant that he was on the other side of it.

"You going to drink alone?" she asked. "Alone" brought another quiver, and another rise. The image of Sarah started to fade.

"Uh, no, of course not. What can I get you?"

"I like what you're drinking. But it would taste so much better if we were somewhere quiet."

For lack of a reasonable response, Simon glanced around the room. His eyes came back to hers. They appeared calm again, almost calculating.

"We won't find it here, I'm afraid," she said. "But I know where." Quiver.

The bartender handed him the bottle, and his eyebrows shot up and back down so quickly and slightly that Simon almost missed it. Who was that meant for? Simon smiled stupidly and turned to leave.

A medium-sized man, feet set well apart with his hands planted on his hips, blocked his way. "And where do you think you're going with Martha?"

The smell of whiskey assaulted Simon. Martha. He'd stood there like a dolt and never introduced himself. Martha. It suited her. He looked at her for a second, and then back at the intruder. "We're going some-place quiet." The steadiness of his voice surprised him.

"I've driven four days to see her," the man almost shouted. "And I reckon that gives me some kind of claim."

Good sign, thought Simon, he's talking louder than he needs to. Buell said that people did that when they weren't sure of themselves. Why was he feeling so calm? The man looked tough as an axle nut. "That's what you think," said Simon, "and you're entitled to that. I see it different."

Awareness rippled across the room as heads turned and eyes lifted off hands full of cards. The squawk of several chairs being pushed back grated on the silence as occupants stood to get a better look at the upcoming melee.

"Well, if you like that thought, think about this one. You're gonna have to go through me, cuz I ain't gonna let you around." The man's hands left his hips and bunched into fists.

Simon looked him over for a pistol or a knife. He saw neither. His calmness remained a mystery as he glanced at Martha. She stood a single step away, somehow managing to seem completely neutral. Then he saw a slight change in her eyes. Excitement? He didn't think it was fear or worry. He studied them and then it struck him. Inviting.

Simon picked a spot just to the left of the man's sternum and imagined the rapidly beating heart beneath. Then, he looked at the man's face and the tiny beads of sweat that had formed on his brow and upper lip. The teamster's eyes would not settle on any single spot, and had taken on an apprehensive look.

"Are you sure?" Simon asked quietly.

A tongue's quick pass across dry lips, and a shift in the man's weight was all Simon needed to see. With his fist bunched, he rotated his shoulder, leaned into his straightening arm, and planted the blow exactly where he'd been looking only seconds before.

The man's face contorted in pain as the sound of a breaking rib snapped around the saloon. A collective grunt filled the room as every man there felt the pain. Clutching his heart, the man sank to his knees for a few seconds, then sat on his haunches and finally fell over on his back. The color drained from his face and short jerky gasps of breath came from him as his face started to turn a grayish-blue.

The saloon owner rushed around the end of the bar and knelt beside the man. He put his ear to the quivering chest. "He ain't getting no air and his heart sounds all floppy." He lifted the man into a semi-sitting position, his arms around his chest, and shook him once, then twice, and suddenly the man gasped. And gasped again, and then started to breathe rapidly. Gritted teeth and tightly closed eyes attested to the pain he felt in his chest.

"You gonna be okay?" the owner asked.

"He'll be all right," an onlooker said. "Let his freight-wagon mouth overload his buckboard ass, that's all." Several loud laughs dispelled the tension, and the noise in the saloon picked up again. Two men hoisted their fallen comrade off the floor, and sat him in a chair, his shoulders and head slumped over the tabletop.

"I don't think I've ever seen anyone that calm before, mister," Martha said.

"I don't understand it either. You ready to go somewhere?"

"If you promise not to be that quick with me." Quiver.

Simon took her arm and together they went upstairs . . . where it was quiet.

An hour later Simon lay on his back and pondered why sin had such a sweet taste. Martha was gone, and so was over half the bottle of brandy and twenty dollars. He suffered that vague feeling of disappointment he always felt after being with a woman, and he envisioned his father, serious as a snake's bite, droning on and on about what he had just done, and why he shouldn't do it. His mother had always put it in a positive light: Sarah was a good girl, and when they were together proper, she would make a good wife. The connotation of "good" and "proper" had not been lost on him then, and he thought about it now.

Martha enjoyed her job, had been light, cheerful and . . . he looked for the right word . . . diligent. Yeah, that said it, diligent. And she'd made him feel good. There, that word again, but in a different context, and his mother would no doubt point out he could not say anything about "proper."

And then there'd been the short fight. He'd always avoided confrontations, hated it when men started throwing fists, and busting up furniture. He remembered one fight at Fort Laramie where every table in the saloon had been smashed flat. This time there had been something in his head that refused to consider backing down. He'd simply picked a spot, and waited for the man to give him a reason to punch him there. Something else he could thank Reed for? It would be wonderful to be back in the valley, and enjoying the peace and solitude he'd come for. With an image of the meadow, still and calm, in his head, the soothing sound of the breeze in the twin spruce trees carried Simon off to sleep.

CHAPTER 29

He'd only been back home three days when the packer showed up. Spud, as usual, heard him coming fifteen minutes before Simon could pick any sign. A man on horseback led two mules slowly up the valley, and nearly passed by the cabin.

"Hey, we're over here!" Simon shouted from the shade of the spruce. The man's head snapped upright, spotted him, and turned toward the cabin.

It was Whiff. "Thought you'd be by the gawdamn creek." He swung out of his saddle. "Where do you want this stuff?"

"Uh . . . I . . . we can put it by the cabin. Don't you want to sit a spell first? That's a long —"

"I want to get it off and get the hell out. Gives me the jivers being back in here." He still had the lead rope in his hand, and gave it a tug as he headed for the cabin. The mules followed, their heads down in resignation.

Taken somewhat aback, Simon asked. "You're gonna stay the night, aren't ya?"

"Nope," Whiff said over his shoulder. "Sooner I'm across that river with the sun in my face the better."

Fifteen minutes later, packsaddles empty, the mules patiently stood. One shook vigorously.

"Mr. Sutton says I'm s'posed to bring back a list," Whiff said. "For next time."

"I haven't made one yet. I thought you'd camp here overnight."

Whiff puffed out his breath. "Well, I ain't." He glanced down the valley and then up at the sun. "Write it down then."

Minutes later, Simon printed the last entry on the list, folded the paper, and handed it to Whiff. The packer stuck it in his shirt pocket, and climbed into his saddle.

"When can I expect to see you again?" Simon asked.

"Olsen said five weeks." Whiff sawed on the reins and turned toward the creek. With a kick to the horse's flanks, he led the mules into the sun, and was gone without another word.

Simon shook his head. "That's got to be the most unfriendly cuss I've ever met."

August's suffocating heat drove Simon out of the cabin and into the open air to sleep. The kettle and knife still hung in the tree where he'd left them a month before. The sight of them when he'd gone for water that evening had put Red Socks on his mind. And then the Indian was there, standing just at the edge of the firelight. Simon scrambled to his feet, momentarily panicked, until he saw Spud, standing immediately behind the man.

"Damn, Red Socks, scare the hell out of me."

The man stepped into the light, a smile on his face. Peace, he signed.

"Good to see you too." Simon returned the hand signal. "Sit?" He pointed to the ground. Spud saw the finger, too, and head down, walked over and sat down submissively. "I didn't mean you, dog." He stooped to stroke the dog's head.

Red Socks walked up to the low fire. He carried the kettle, the pair of socks visible over the edge. He put the pot on the ground, took the butcher knife from inside his leather shirt, and laid it down as well. *Thank you,* he said with a sweep of his hands.

"You're welcome, friend." Simon nodded his head and pointed at the things. He pointed at the ground again. "Sit."

Red Socks sank to the ground in one graceful movement, legs folding almost mechanically.

Simon sat as well. "Coffee?" He held out his cup.

Red Socks nodded. Simon got back up, went into the cabin, and brought out another cup. He filled it from the pot by the fire, then went to the table for a piece of sugar cone. The Indian took the cup, and grinned widely as Simon offered him the sugar. Red Socks dropped the entire piece, enough for six cups of coffee, into the dark liquid, and watched it dissolve.

Simon stared, fascinated. "I guess if you don't get it often, it's a real treat when you do."

Red Socks swirled the coffee in the cup for a few seconds and then took a sip. "Hmmm. *Tsaa'n,*" he said. Satisfaction lit his round face.

"San?" Simon thought he'd heard a soft "T" sound, but wasn't sure.

"*Tsaa'n,*" Red Socks said again, and smacked his lips deliberately.

"*Tsaa'n,*" Simon repeated. "You mean it's good, don't you?"

"Mmm," Red Socks grunted and smiled broadly.

Simon and his visitor lapsed into a comfortable silence, both occasionally looking at each other and nodding. He wondered if he should offer him some food. There was so much he wanted to ask this friendly man, and tried, but two attempts led to frustration for both of them. Simon resorted to feeding Red Socks coffee and as much sugar as he wanted. The Indian seemed content to simply sit in the moonlight and watch the embers of the cooking fire slowly die.

After what must have been two hours or a little more, Red Socks stood. Simon, caught off guard, dumped half a cup of cold coffee on his foot as he followed suit. Red Socks laughed out loud. Simon had wondered if Indians did that. Red Socks reached inside his shirt and took out a leather packet. He pointed at the kettle, then presented his gift. Simon accepted a soft-tanned scabbard whose shape said it held a knife. The pale yellow of a bone handle was barely visible, set deep in the safety of the leather sleeve, and he could feel the blade.

"Thank you, Red Socks." Simon stuffed the knife into his waistband, and made the sweeping sign of appreciation with his hands.

Red Socks pointed again at the kettle and did the same. With that, he took hold of the handle, and walked toward the spruce. He paused by the tree for a moment to pick up a three-foot bow and a leather sack that contained what looked like a dozen or so arrows. Simon had not noticed them before.

"Come again. It's good to see you," Simon called at the quickly disappearing figure.

The Indian didn't pause or turn, and vanished into the dark forest.

"Well, that was interesting, wasn't it, Spud? Course, I think you and him have done that before, haven't you?" Simon sat by the fire ring and threw a few small pieces of wood on the embers. After smoking for a minute, they burst into flame, and he slowly pulled his new knife out of its scabbard. The gentle curve of the horn handle continued into the blade, a piece of intricately chipped, reddish-brown flint. The countless concave marks that covered the surface reflected the flickering light of the fire, and came alive in his hand. As he stared at it, a lump formed in his throat. He looked into the darkness. "And they call you a savage," he murmured.

The next morning Simon sat up in his bed by the tent and looked across the camp. He'd dreamt again of Buell and the many nights they'd spent sitting around a fire, silent, content with each other's company, with no need to speak. He picked up the leather scabbard that lay beside him. In daylight, the blade had lost some of its magic, but the work, the incredibly fine detail, was now even more apparent. He touched his thumb to the edge and was rewarded with a stinging nick in the skin. He licked his finger, put the blade away, and got up.

August simmered down to a slightly cooler September. He'd made three forays into the higher country just to enjoy the air, but, for the most part, the never-ending task of cutting firewood made the days pass quickly. Late one afternoon while they were at the creek, Spud let him know someone was coming. As he walked back across the meadow toward the cabin, he saw Whiff and two mules swing into view. It had to be Whiff; the short torso wobbled from side to side as he dozed in the saddle. It was a wonder he didn't fall off and break his neck. Again, Simon had to shout at him or he'd have walked all the way to the hot springs. "Hey!"

Simon knew that even with the full moon, Whiff couldn't possibly ride out immediately. He decided to make the best of a bad situation. "Hello, Whiff," he said as the rider stopped his horse between the spruces. "Nice to see you."

The packer ran a hand across the lower half of his face, then dug a knuckle in his eye. "I hate this country. Either freezing your ass off or fryin' your damn brains in the sun."

"It is hot."

"Ain't just the heat. No matter which way I'm going, the dust from these gawdamn mules is all over me." He hawked in his throat and spit a brown gob on the ground. "And the gawdamn bugs, everywhere . . . in yer mouth, ears, up yer nose. Sonsabitches have followed me for fifteen miles." He swung off his horse and swatted at the gnats that swarmed his head. "Jesus wept, drive a man crazy."

"Lead the animals into the shade," Simon said. "The bugs like it out here in the meadow grass."

With the reins in one hand and the lead rope in the other, Whiff led the mules and his horse toward the cabin. Simon hoped the animals would cooperate, because it looked like the unhappy packer was ready to explode in exasperation.

Half an hour later the packs were empty and off the mules. Staked in the meadow by the creek, the tired animals looked content. Whiff sat on the bench in front of the cabin, and sullenly watched Simon cut up a rabbit.

"How in hell do you manage to keep your head, stuck up here?" Whiff said after a while.

"It was hard at first, but now I kinda look forward to the solitude."

"That ain't what I'm talking about. The winters. And the gawdamn snow. It must get ten feet deep up here."

"Actually no. Three or maybe four, but not ten. I'll grant you the cold, though." Simon dropped the last piece of meat into the cornmeal, flipped it over a couple of times, and put it the frying pan. "It's really quite beautiful up here. The blue of the sky in dead winter will make you look twice."

"Wish I was back in Arizona," Whiff said.

And that was the end of the exchange. Simon watched the rabbit cook while Whiff smoked his pipe. He'd hoped for some conversation during supper, but Whiff silently ate more than his share of the rabbit and pan bread, then unrolled his bed by one of the spruces and lay down.

Breakfast the next morning was a repeat of the evening meal. Finished, Whiff handed him the bill, and Simon scanned the items. He dug the correct amount out of his shirt pocket, and handed it over along with a folded piece of paper. "That's what I want next time."

"Olsen wants you to pay in advance. So does the storekeeper."

"How so? Neither of them mentioned that."

"Next trip might be late, and it might be in another gawdamn snowstorm. They ain't gonna risk their asses unless they's paid for it. Neither give a farmer's fart about me, mind ya, but the mules or a bag of Arbuckles, that's different. Sonsabitches."

Simon puffed his cheeks. "Well, how much do I pay? I don't know what that's gonna cost."

"Sixty dollars for the mules and sixty-five for the supplies, same as you paid just now. Sutton said he'd get square in the spring, or if we're lucky, a trip in November. More likely the sonuvabitch is hoping ya freeze to death."

Simon shook his head. "Just a minute then. I'll get it."

"And . . . uh, they want gold."

When Simon came out of the cabin, he counted out the coins, and then offered Whiff a piece of paper. "If you don't mind, sign that, or put your mark on it. It's a receipt."

Whiff chuffed, then took the paper and

pencil, and laboriously wrote his name, holding the paper against his saddle. He handed it back to Simon, and climbed on his horse. With a rough gig to the animals' ribs, he led the mules to the center of the meadow, and trotted north. The sound of the packer's voice, cussing the swarm of gnats that followed, faded to silence as he disappeared from view.

Simon watched him out of sight, thinking. Whiff was one of those people who wasn't going to be happy anywhere. And they blamed their unhappiness on whomever or whatever happened to be at hand when the inevitable daily calamity befell them, the logic of the situation be damned.

September 2, 1874. Packer visited again. Ordered supplies. I am looking forward to winter. Experience has banished my fear.

CHAPTER 30

Simon was at a loss. Whiff had been gone a week, and for the first time since he'd been a boy, he had absolutely nothing to do. The pot of coffee was gone by midmorning, and after a trip to the bathing pool, he'd messed around camp all day. Now, in the late afternoon, he sat on his bench and basked in the golden splendor of fall. The aspens and willows were in full flair, and the grass in the meadow had taken on a subdued gray-green color. The day before he'd heard a flock of geese raucously discussing plans for winter in warmer climes.

When the sun sank below the ridge, he stood and stretched, then went inside to find his supper while he had plenty of light. He unhooked a hanging ham, and cut a slice. The aroma made his mouth water. For doing nothing, he found he was hungry and cut another one. An hour later, his belly full of corn fritters with red gravy, ham, and green beans, he leaned back and watched dusk turn into dark. The night air turned cool, and he pitched three pieces of wood on the fire. As he waited for them to catch, he went to his saddlebags and got out his journal. Opening it, the remaining piece of Sarah's letter fell into his lap and his heart sped up as he looked at the frayed thread to his past. A wave of melancholy swept over him, and he visualized her.

He held the half-sheet of paper in his hand and thought about the piece that was lost. Over the past year, he'd memorized the words of the first half, and silently recited the letter's contents from the beginning. He spoke the last sentence out loud.

"Please understand that I am happy, both with my life and with what I am doing. If you wish me happiness, wish me success here."

As always, his eyes brimmed with tears as he heard the finality of her words.

"Wish me success here."

She had no time for him. There it was again, plain as day. His heart ached for her as the peace and calm of his wonderful valley settled around him. Despite the tranquility, he felt so unhappy he wanted to cry.

It was the sixth of October, a Tuesday, and he was kind of expecting Whiff to arrive.

Both times before he'd come on a Tuesday, and he didn't want to leave camp and miss seeing the packer. Be just like the man to turn around and go back. The first snow of winter fell during the night. Just a dusting, but the warning was clear. Simon spent the day in camp, frequently looking down the valley. Wednesday came and went and Simon stewed.

Sunday morning Simon busied himself splitting stove wood into kindling. Spud lay by the fireplace and watched. "I expect they're just real busy. And that little skiff of snow ain't gonna make any difference." Taking a short grip on the ax handle, he lifted the blade and dropped it. A slim shaft of wood split off the piece of pine. "They'll be along. Besides that, if darn it comes to damn it, we can always go to town ourselves." He glanced at the dull gray sky. "If it don't snow, that is." He adjusted the chunk of wood, dropped the ax again, and another piece of kindling fell on the ground. His spine told him that he'd knelt over the splitting block long enough. He dropped the ax-bit into the top of the block and rocked back on his heels to stretch.

Just then, Spud stood up, ears erect, and sniffed the air. "What do you hear?" Simon stood and followed the dog's gaze. "That's ol' Whiff, ain't it?" He stepped into the open and stared at the gap in the trees that marked the trail half a mile away. Concentration made his eyes water, and he squinted the tears out, brushing them away with the back of his hand. They watched for fifteen minutes, the dog pacing back and forth, and saw nothing. Finally, Spud grumbled, and went back to the fireplace to lie down again. "You hear an elk or something?" Simon took a last look, and went back to the chopping block.

For the rest of the day, he cast glances down the valley and across the meadow at the trees. Instead of sleeping soundly like he usually did, that night he left the cabin every hour or so. Each time, he found Spud sitting by the spruce tree, alert. Something was out there. What, Simon could only sense, but the dog knew.

The next morning he stoked the fire for breakfast. He cussed when he went to fill his coffeepot. The disruption of his daily routine the day before had left the water bucket unfilled. With a sigh, he picked it up and opened the door. Instead of turning right toward his toilet as he usually did, he turned left toward the path to the creek. An odd, solid "thunk" sound confused him for the second it took for the dull but unmistakable report of a big rifle to reach his ears. He snapped his head around in time to see the wisp of white smoke in the trees across the meadow. His breath stuck in his throat as he turned on his heel and ducked. "Get back here, Spud," he shouted and charged back into the cabin. The dog scurried in, and turned around to bark furiously at the open door.

"Did you see him?" Simon reached out and pulled the door shut. Just as he stepped back, splinters flew from the inside and another booming report reached him. "Gawdamn, get out of the way, Spud." Simon moved to one side of the door. His breathing was quick and his heart pounded. Who could that be? And how close did he come with that first shot? Where the hell was he?

Another neat round hole appeared in the door, this one lower down, and the bullet smacked into the back wall as more fractured wood scattered on the floor. Safe enough behind the thick log walls, he thought. *Just stay away from the door . . . and the window. Oh, shit, I hope he don't hit that.* He reached down and tugged absently on Spud's ear.

Several minutes passed, maybe as many as twenty, and his nerves started to settle a little. Then another bullet flew through the door and into the stack of wood beside the stove. Four-inch wedges flew off the pile like so much tinder. His attacker was apparently shooting one of the plains hunting rifles his customers at Fort Laramie had used to kill buffalo. They had told him that it could shoot over half a mile. Simon felt trapped. For the rest of the day, randomly timed shots continued to perforate the door. He counted twenty-three holes. Just before dark, the last shot struck the outside wall. Simon spent the night sitting up, wrapped in a buffalo robe with his rifle in his lap.

The next day was a repeat of the first, and by midafternoon he realized he'd been dozing when the sound of another heavy bullet ripping through the door snapped his head upright. He stared dumbly at the riddled door for a moment, then counted the bullet holes again. His anger rose as he recognized his helplessness. His attention went to the window. At least that was intact. Stupid thought. He shuddered as he remembered sitting like this with only an oil lamp.

Then a question popped into his head and raised his eyebrows. Why hadn't this bastard shot his window out? One more slim chance that a bullet might find a soft mark inside the cabin. He looked at the pocked door again. The answer! All the holes were in the left two-thirds. He wasn't shooting the window because he couldn't see it. Simon visualized his cabin from across the meadow and immediately thought of the four-foot-high rock upstream from where he drew water. From there, the fireplace and the tent frame were out of sight, as was the window side of his house. He was shooting from the rock, and it was over four hundred yards away. That made a sure shot impossible.

Simon swallowed hard. He stood and faced the door. Next shot, he'd bust out and turn right. The shooter would never be able to reload and fire before he was in the cover of the trees. Then they'd see who hunted whom. "Sonuvabitch," he muttered, "you're in my valley."

He waited. A sweat bead formed between his shoulders, and he felt it start to crawl down his back. Sweat? It was by no means warm in the cabin. Scared then? Hell, yes. How long had it been since the last shot? Over an hour, more like two. He had to get out of there. Fatigue was starting to make him dizzy. Maybe, if he suddenly appeared, he could catch the shooter unprepared. All he needed was a couple of seconds, just two, and he'd be out of sight.

The dog. He wouldn't know what to do,

and like as not, would take off after whoever was shooting. Across that meadow, he wouldn't stand a chance. "Spud, you're going to have to stay in here awhile." He tied a piece of leather around the dog's neck and tugged hard to make sure it wouldn't slip, then tied him to the bed. Spud struggled against it. "Sit," Simon said. The dog sat and started to whine.

Simon didn't have to lift the latch; it was gone, blasted to smithereens. He took a deep breath, gripped his rifle, and pushed open the door. His left foot hit the ground as he rushed out and started to the right.

"Don't move!" Reed's voice shouted. He stood by the fireplace, the heavy gun pointed right at Simon's face. "Don't!" he screamed again.

Simon stood paralyzed. Then furious. Then dismayed.

"I knew you'd figger it out. And you've got that gawdamn dog tied up, don't ya?" Reed chuckled. "We'll do it my way this time. Drop the rifle." When Simon did so, Reed stepped away from the fireplace so he could see inside the cabin. He smiled. "Now, step over to the door and push it shut, real slow."

Simon did as he was told, and as the door swung shut, Spud started to growl. Then

Simon heard the protest strangle as the collar pulled tight. He kicked the door shut, and was relieved to hear Spud whine.

"I know you've got gold, Simon, lots of it. I just couldn't find it all last time." He stepped back toward the fireplace. As he did so, he lowered the gun from his shoulder but still held it leveled at Simon's chest.

The face that looked back at Simon made his eyes go wide. What had once been a nice-looking one, almost handsome, was now a red, angry-looking mass of scabbed flesh. His right eye drooped open, and the eyelid didn't close completely when he blinked. The overly wet socket seeped tears down his cheek. A yellow crust caked the eyelashes.

"Pretty, ain't it?" Reed said. "Hurts, too."

Simon said nothing, and watched his tormentor.

"Your dog did what he had to do. I don't hold him responsible."

Right. Now you're my friend again, thought Simon. He watched for the muzzle to drop.

"All I want is enough money to get to Denver or St. Louis and get this fixed. And you have it. If I didn't think so, you'd be dead now."

Simon said nothing, and continued to stare at the long rifle.

"I know what you're thinking," Reed continued. "You give up your cache, and I shoot you anyway. That's what's called a dilemma."

The strange calmness he'd experienced at the saloon in Challis came to him again. He felt no fear, and for a few seconds he watched Reed's chest rise and fall as he breathed. The muzzle of the rifle was huge, maybe fifty-caliber, and it didn't waver. Reed's bullets had hit the wood by the stove a dozen times, and he imagined what that heavy slug would do to his body. Death would be instant. What could be wrong with that? But what about the dog? Tied up, he didn't stand a chance.

"Are you crazy, Simon?" the voice he talked to at night asked. "You're about to die, and you're worried about a dog."

Yeah, but he's my dog. No, he's my friend, the only one I've ever been sure of.

"If you let the dog go, and I see him gone, I'll do as you say," Simon finally said.

Reed cocked his head, grimaced, and straightened it up again. It must have hurt because the tears flowed heavily. He lifted his hand and wiped his cheek, but the rifle's muzzle held rock-steady on Simon's chest. "You and that damn mutt. Didn't fool you for a minute, did I? I'd love to gut that sonuvabitch with a dull knife. But I'm a practical man and —"

Reed's left arm flew backward, and the heavy rifle fell to the ground as the sound of a gunshot smote Simon's left ear. He spun around to see Whiff lower a short carbine, and start toward him.

"Whiff." It was all he could get out.

The packer strode toward him, fumbling in his ammunition pouch, alternating glances at the open breech of his rifle and the prone figure of Justin Reed. By the time he'd reached him, Reed's legs had quit thrashing and he lay still. The Sharpe's clicked as the lever closed.

Whiff poked Reed's hip with the muzzle. "Sumbitch is dead as a horse turd," he muttered.

Simon stepped up beside him and looked at the body. The amount of blood that had spread toward the fireplace made his stomach turn. "Why are you here?"

Whiff screwed up his face. "That's kind of a dumb question, ain't it?"

"I mean, how did you know . . . how come you walked through the trees like that? Didn't just ride up like normal?"

"Oh. Yeah, I see what ya mean. I saw his horse. It's tied up nearly a mile downstream. There's enough horse shit around to know he'd been there a day or two. I figgered I'd either find you dead and him in the cabin, 'er vice-versy. Weren't gonna take no chance. There's a reward for him. And they don't care dead or otherwise."

"A reward? That means the marshal is sure he killed that prospector."

"Ain't just that. Little feller at Spring Creek, lives in that house right by the river? He found Toad's body hanged up in a brush pile. His head was near 'nuf blowed plumb off. That's when Marshal Hess posted the reward." He looked at the sky and winced. "Now, I'll go get the mules and unload." Moving as fast as his older legs would let him, he shuffled off toward the south.

Simon looked down at Reed again, and then heard a low bark. He turned and hurried into the cabin. Spud pulled at his restraint and tried to jump up.

"Sit still and I'll get you untied." Simon worked on the knot. Pulled so tight he couldn't unfasten it, he reached for his knife and cut the thong. He grabbed the dog by the scruff of his neck and stepped through the door. The growl that came from the dog when he spotted Reed gave Simon a chill. It was a vicious and serious growl. He tightened his grip.

"You leave that alone. You hear me?" He

stepped in front of the dog. "No." When he released his grip, Spud took a couple of steps to the side and sniffed the air. Then he turned to face downstream, and started to grumble.

"I know, boy. That's Whiff." Simon went back into the cabin, and came out with a piece of canvas. He threw it across Reed's body.

Fifteen minutes later, the packer led his two mules between the trees and got off his horse. "I don't think I can get out of here today." He pointed at the canvas-covered corpse. "You got a little bigger piece of that? I try to throw his ass on the mule, and all hell's gonna pay. Look at their ears. They don't even like being this close."

"I wish you wouldn't refer to him that way. Ain't Christian."

"That sonuvabitch ain't either." Whiff looked at Simon, and then at the rifle Simon had leaned against the cabin. "I see you want the rifle."

"Not really. I just moved it. You can have it."

Whiff shook his head. "Yer an odd one, I'll grant you that." He led the mules to the woodpile, and tied them up.

Whiff accepted Simon's invitation to sleep in the cabin, and after arranging his bedroll, he sat and watched Simon make supper.

Whiff struck a match, and lit his pipe. "Ya seem to have two minds, or maybe even three or four, about that yahoo laying across the woodpile."

"I suppose I see the sense in doing that, but it didn't seem right," Simon replied.

"Come mornin', that bastard's gonna be stiff as an ax handle. This way, all folded up nice, he'll hang on that packsaddle like a couple of hundred-pound sacks of feed."

"Why couldn't we just bury him, like I did that prospector?"

"Ain't the way it works. Folks is funny about their pound of flesh. Toad weren't all that friendly a feller, and he stunk like a July gut-pile, but he was considered one of the town folks. And those town folks want to see the sonuvabitch that killed him all laid out, cold, and still. 'Sides that, I've gotta go back and gather up my goods. Ain't no bother."

"Sounds like you're leaving."

"Gonna make one more trip, son. That carcass out there is my stake. I don't like this country, not even a little bit. And I don't like my boss or my job."

"Appears to me you don't like mules either."

"Yer talking about the first time we met,

right? That wasn't about the mule. He just got in the way. I'd just asked Olsen for a bit more money and he said no. You know you pay more for them mules than you do for me?"

Whiff's furrowed brow and tight lips gave Simon pause. Was this another example of being too quick to judge? How many times had he felt like hitting a horse, or booting Spud in the butt for something a human had done? "I've always tried to pay a man what he's worth."

"Well, I ain't suckin' hind tit no more. Two weeks from now, three at most, I'm gonna be in Tucson, sittin' in the sun drinkin' Mexican licker."

"Was the reward that much?"

"One thousand United States dollars, gold." Whiff enunciated every word, and then smiled for the first time since Simon had met him.

"That seems a lot."

"What folks is thinkin' is, Reed probably killed upwards to a dozen men and maybe even one woman. And the worst part is, he could cuz they trusted him. That makes him a particularly evil man to my way of thinking."

"That does shed a different light on it. Funny how a person sees a situation only as it applies to themselves."

"Don't get ya."

"Reed took advantage of me, and maybe thought about killin' me, but —"

"But you're still thinkin' that maybe he wouldn't, and that maybe he wasn't so bad after all."

"Well, kind of. I —"

"Mind you, it ain't my part no how, but I think you ought to put that out of yer head. He'd have killed you, sure as spring itches." Whiff looked at his pipe, took a pull, and fished another stick match out of his shirt pocket.

Simon turned the steaming batch of spuds over in one pan, and poked at the four plump sausages cooking in another. What he didn't want to talk to Whiff about was the fact that his own turmoil wasn't caused by Reed's death. It was about his own acceptance of the experience. It felt almost casual. There was another human being outside, bent across a woodpile for the sake of convenience, and he'd helped drape the body. What was becoming of him? There had to be some loyalty to your own kind.

"That's startin' to smell damn good," Whiff said.

"Uh . . . yeah, it'll be ready in a few minutes." Simon hastily turned the potatoes again — just in time.

Ten minutes later Simon sat and stared at his food. He tried but could not make the first bite go down. Whiff, grinning now, and relaxed, speared the two sausages on Simon's plate and relieved him of his charade.

October 14, 1874. Reed was killed as he would kill me. My thoughts are confused and unworthy of paper.

CHAPTER 31

Whiff would be in Tucson by now. Simon sat at his table looking out at the snow-covered meadow, trying to imagine a hot day. A month had passed since the incident. He thought it significant that, mentally, he referred to it as just that, the incident. Two feet of snow had fallen over the course of three days, and then the temperature had plunged. He'd made one hurried trip to the hot springs to check on the horse, and from then on he'd restricted his outside activity to trips to the creek for water, and out past the woodpile to his toilet.

The window made all the difference in the world, changing the cabin from a mind-suffocating dungeon to a rather pleasant home. Deep snow on the roof kept the heat in and buffered the sound of the wind. He recalled the last winter and how, pre-occupied with just keeping warm, he hadn't had time to think. Now he did, and what he'd thought would be a luxury turned out to be drudgery.

No man can be expected to examine his soul and not wish for a mystic eraser. Tainted by death and betrayal, Simon had journeyed to this valley seeking to restore his spirit. And what had he found, even in this beautiful place? Death and betrayal. He'd become hard, like the granite ridges above him, but without the grandness.

Since the incident, even Sarah had abandoned him. Several times, he'd sought solace in her mental image, and all he could conjure up was a vague figure walking away in the mist. He'd taken Reed for who he was because he didn't know what he was. How could he? Now he felt hardened against others, suspicious. Had he gained nothing by coming here? He looked down at Spud, sound asleep by the stove, and smiled to himself. If only that was the stuff of men. Without guile or deceit, his dog had total faith that he was the same.

October delivered to November a landscape frozen solid as a splitting wedge. And November kept it that way for December to carry into January. His fresh meat was gone, the last of a small deer boiled with some carrots and parsnips, and the cabin walls had started to lean in on him.

"Let's go find us a deer, Spud. Or even a hare. I gotta get out of here for a while." Simon shrugged into his buffalo coat, folded back the overlapping hides that blocked the draft of his bullet-riddled door, and stepped outside. His nose hairs froze with the first breath, and the skin on his face felt stiff. He pulled his rifle out of the scabbard, checked for a shell in the chamber, and strode away from the cabin.

He and the dog had trudged south, well past the frozen lake, and hadn't seen so much as a crow. It was now afternoon and they were headed back to the cabin. The frigid air sneaked past the fringe of his fur-trimmed hood and he scrunched his shoulders to close the gap. He could hear Spud behind him, snuffling in the grainy snow back some fifteen feet or so. Simon glanced back when the sound stopped to see Spud with his head buried in the snow, his tail arched over his back. Simon trudged on.

They still had well over a mile to go and he was thankful the snow wasn't so deep he had to wear snowshoes. He detested the damned things on the flat. Here, on the narrow trail, they would have been a real pain in the ass. The weight of the liver and heart in his tote sack was a comfort. It had been nearly two weeks since they'd eaten really fresh meat, and he was looking forward to it. He remembered how lucky he'd been.

When he'd about given up seeing anything, the sleek doe had simply risen from her bed in a willow grove near where he was standing, catching his breath. He put one shot right behind her ear and she'd dropped without a sound. He hated gutting the animals he killed in any event. And the twenty minutes he'd spent getting her innards out had been a trial. Blood up to his elbows, a sticky, miserable mess, he'd nearly froze his hands cleaning them in the powdery snow. He'd stashed the carcass under an outcrop and moved a couple of big rocks to partially cover her, safe enough until he came back in the morning with the horse.

Another jolt of icy air passed his bristled cheek, and chilled the sweat on his neck. He gave another shoulder hunch to cut off the flow. The temperature had dropped when the lackluster sun abandoned them, probably ten or fifteen below zero. He hurried his steps a little and wondered where the dog had gone.

As he approached the twin rocks, the streambed narrowed sharply. He couldn't see it here, but the creek's incessant babble rose through the snow. A chill crept through him, and it wasn't from the cold. This time getting wet would mean dying for sure. He picked his way along the narrow part and breathed a sigh of relief as the creek bottom opened up again, and he could see the steam from the hot springs.

He sensed, rather than heard or saw, the attacking animal. The short hairs on his neck bristled, and his sixth sense seized his groin. The beast hit him in the back with such ferocity, he was momentarily stunned. It leapt onto the meat-filled sack and held on, its hind feet digging into the backs of his legs. The snarling, coughing grunt of his attacker, and the ripping pain in his left leg, cleared his head, snapping him back to reality.

Claws, sharp as an awl, tore his wool pants as they dug in. Then, the smell hit him, and he knew he'd have to fight for his life. The wolverine! The animal had obviously sunk its teeth into the fresh meat, and the taste of blood seemed to fuel the ferocity of the attack.

Simon shook off his mittens, and tore at the rifle's shoulder strap, trying to free his Winchester and get it around to his chest. Finally, it came loose and he seized the rifle, left hand on the grip, right on the barrel. He jabbed the butt behind his left hip as hard as he could, once, twice, three times.

Each blow met solid muscle, and each blow made the wolverine grunt. The fourth strike drove the curved steel butt-plate deep, and a bone snapped. With a snarl, the wolverine let go of the pack and dropped to the ground.

Simon started to turn around. Out of the corner of his eye, he saw the flat, ugly head with the torn ear. In the time it takes to think it, the animal pressed his attack, boring in as Simon moved. In an instant, it had its yellow teeth clamped on the calf of his leg, missing the bone, but securely set in the flesh. The flash of hot pain nearly took his senses away. Up came the butt of the rifle, and as it came down, a flash of color brought Spud into the fray.

Canine teeth snapped shut on the wolverine's rear-end and testicles just as the butt of the Winchester crashed down on the beast's back. The wolverine tore its teeth loose from his leg, and seemed to turn in its skin to face the dog. Powerful jaws clamped down on Spud's paw, and with a snap of its head, the beast ripped away half of the foot. The tendons parted with a wet snapping sound. With an agonized howl, the dog let go and reared back, but not before another fierce swipe ripped into his neck. Then, both the dog and the beast sat on their haunches, rampant.

The pause in the fight lasted only a second or two, but to Simon's perception, it seemed to last forever, dreamlike. The Winchester, now a club, rose, Simon gripping the barrel with both hands. It ascended above his head as he stretched to full height and then, descended. Slowly, so slowly it came down, the steel and brass glinting in the late sun, the light scribing a deadly arc that would meet the wolverine.

The back of the steel action crashed down and the hammer spur disappeared into the top of the flat, dark triangular head. A spray of dark blood fanned out, and the sickening, yet satisfying, crunch of live bone being crushed declared the wolverine's defeat. The beast screamed defiance with one last spitting snarl of rage. The fresh blood flew all over the wounded dog, and the wolverine sagged to the ground, dead.

Simon laid his rifle in the brush and went to the dog. The glistening white of exposed bone in the dog's paw was an insult. Blood gushed from it and the wound on his neck, staining an ever-widening blotch on the torn-up trail. The dog tried to lick the wounds clean, but failed. As Simon stood looking on helplessly, the pain in his legs reminded him that he, too, was in bad shape.

His leg hurt like hell and threatened to fold when he tried to put his full weight on it. He struggled to look at his wounds around the bulk of his coat, but couldn't, and in the cold, he didn't dare take it off. He looked at Spud again. The dog licked his savaged paw furiously, all the time whining softly. A lump grew in Simon's throat. Suddenly, the dog quit and looked up at him with a stare that seemed to ask a question. Then the dog laid its head down in the snow and closed its eyes. Simon knelt beside him, and gently stroked his friend's head. Heartbroken, he didn't know what to do. Could he carry the dog a mile? A terrific stab of pain in his leg answered the question. He trembled with frustration, and his tears froze on his cheeks.

Struggling to his feet, he hobbled to his rifle, then wondered if he should use a cartridge. With the cold settling fast, what little warmth the dog had left was leaking out on the ground. Spud opened his eyes and looked up at him. Did Simon see understanding there, or was it his conscience seeking release? The dog's mouth opened a little and his tongue moved ever so slightly through his teeth. His tail twitched in one final wag, then his eyes shut again.

The ache that had been moving up in Simon's throat breached as a sodden sob, his shoulders convulsing. He knew he was letting the dog down in the most terrible way. His head dropped, his spirit failing rapidly, while the motionless dog shimmered in his tear-filled eyes. He turned in the trail, picked up one of his mittens, then searched till he found the other one. Sniffing against a streaming nose, he leaned on his rifle, and started the long journey to his cabin.

He took a shuffling step, then another . . . then stopped. The ties to his friend lying on the cold ground had drawn tight, and he could go no farther. Four steps back, and he was beside his dog again, using his rifle as a crutch to lower himself to the ground. The excruciating pain in his leg locked his jaws tight. He shifted to get as close as he could to the dog, and Spud struggled to get up. Simon gently pushed him back down.

It was only a mile. Surely, he could get them home if only he'd try. Maybe they could get to the hot springs and rest there. His dog deserved that much. He'd try. He'd rest for a little, and then he'd try. Yeah, that's what he'd do.

With unsteady hands, he draped as much of his coattails as he could across the dog. The cold rose through his buttocks, and soon the pain in his leg faded to a dull throb, then to nothing. Holding the coat snug under his neck, he leaned forward with shoulders hunched, and relaxed. Slow and ever so sure, the cold gripped more tightly. Pretty soon, he'd get up and go. Pretty soon, but not quite now, just a few more minutes . . . a few more minutes as his sight darkened and he sank closer to the edge of nothing.

Strangely warm and comfortable, he looked deep into the shimmering depths of his new realm. Pretty soon? The question floated, feather-light and drifting, at the farthest reach of his consciousness. "Noooo," someone replied, half whisper, half moan. Then, with a barely audible sigh, he put his hand on the dog's chest, and settled down to wait awhile with his friend.

CHAPTER 32

Suddenly, he was being swept aloft, lifted gently by strong hands. Relaxed and without fear, he went willingly. He knew where he was going; his ma had told him this was what happened. What do they look like, the angels? He tried to open his eyes, but they were stuck shut. He tried again. Why wouldn't they open? Was there a reason he couldn't see them? Maybe soon he would . . . or maybe not. Cold as steel, fear stabbed into him.

If not angels, what? Oh, God! He tried to fight, but his arms refused to respond. When he opened his mouth to scream, his terrified protest came out muted as the mewing of a newborn kitten. Thoughts of his dog flooded over everything, and he struggled to see him. Suddenly, in the brilliant flash that is pure truth, he knew his friend was dead.

Savaged and abandoned, Spud lay in a vast white wasteland where the only color was his prone form, splashed in brilliant red, and Simon knew he deserved what was coming. His whole being collapsed in on itself, and at last, his brain retreated into the total darkness that shields it from madness and dropped over the edge.

Slowly he drifted free of the abyss. His first conscious thought was of seeing light. It came through a small window. It looked like his window. Reed had thought him crazy when he'd spent fourteen dollars on it. But Reed didn't know what Simon knew. That aside, there it was, letting the sunlight stream in. His window? Was he home? The sudden swirl of conflict made his head ache, and he drifted back to the place where it didn't.

And back again, his mouth so dry he could barely move his tongue. He had to have some water soon. He stared at the ceiling for a few minutes, and let his eyes become accustomed to the light. Without moving his head, he looked around at what he could see of the room. The hides over the door were in place. He was in a cabin, and it was winter. There was his rifle, leaning against the table.

Slowly, he moved his head. It hurt to do so. Why? Then he saw what he was looking for, the water bucket. Had he left it full? He hoped so. What did he mean, had he left it full? Why was he lying in bed in the daylight? He flexed the muscles in his right leg, ready to throw away the heavy robe and was rewarded by a sharp pain. The attack! The wolverine had bitten him. Spud! The scene by the creek overwhelmed him, and he sank back in his bed, panting.

How did I get home? Oh, Lord, how is my leg? Motionless, he considered how he was going to get up. He did a mental and muscular search of his body, twitching his toes and flexing his ankles. They seemed to work okay. His hands worked, too, but the right one had a couple of fingers that didn't look so good, purple and swollen. Everything seemed to function all right, although he was stiff as a piece of whang-leather and sore almost everywhere. Slowly, he started to uncover, the heavy robes damp next to his body. The air in the hut was cool but not really too bad. He gritted his teeth and raised his head, grunting at the pain.

Then, clear and distinct, he heard something outside. It assaulted his fragile sense of security. Something or someone was at the door. Disappointment swept over him like a damp cloud. His head sank back onto the beaver pelt pillow. Eyes closed so tight his eyebrows met, he raged silently at the injustice. He was defenseless. Then he thought, no! He had Red Socks's knife! He was sure of it. He carried it in his pants pocket.

He fumbled under the covers, cursing the heavy robe. Finally he found it and gripped it as he waited for the door to open and the hides to be swept back. How fast could he strike? Fast enough? He sucked in a deep gulp of air — he'd stopped breathing in an attempt to be silent. Then he feigned unconsciousness. The door opened and the rustle of the stiff hides as they parted sent fear rushing through his body.

"Sadee'."

A single word, its meaning unknown, sent a thrill through him. "Red Socks?" His own voice was unrecognizable, a harsh rasp, and then something wet and warm swept across his face. He jerked his head off the pillow and there was Spud, struggling to get closer. Simon looked into the mellow brown eyes of his dog and knew there was goodness in the world.

His father's words, spoken so long ago, came rushing back. "Compared to the soul, the pain of the flesh is trivial." Not understood then, the meaning now struck him deep, hard, and true. He'd betrayed a creature that had never let him down, and now he'd been given another chance. He knew that was something not guaranteed in life. His scalp tingled with sheer pleasure as the warm smooth tongue made another swipe across his face. Spud's tail wagged furiously, his butt moving in time with it.

Suddenly the dog sat down, and Simon levered himself up on his elbow. The Indian moved quickly to his side and pushed him down on the bed, shaking his head. Simon persisted, and ignoring the pain, swung his legs from under the robes and sat up dizzily on the edge of the bed. He took the dog's head in his hands, and his tears splashed with abandon on his friend's muzzle. How had Red Socks managed to save them? Then he noticed that Spud wouldn't put his left paw down. Held aloft, it was wrapped in something.

Convulsive sobs racked Simon's body as he held his beloved dog, and he sent a prayer of thanks flying out the fourteen-dollar window. Both he and the dog were thankful for each other. For different reasons, to be sure, but sitting together again, safe and alive, the reasons didn't seem to matter much.

Red Socks stayed with Simon, and took care of both him and the dog. Spud's left front paw was a mangled, weeping mess at first, but somehow it healed with whatever the Indian put on it. The same wet mixture, — it looked exactly like fresh cow plop — went on Simon's legs. The first time Simon looked at the wounds, he despaired. Red and puffy, heat rose from the long slashes and the bluish-gray teeth marks.

Red Socks brought two deer to the cabin in one day. He cut up the liver, heart, and kidneys and heated a few pieces slightly by holding them over the fire in the stove. It was all Simon could do to keep the offering down. Red Socks insisted, signing "eat" over and over again.

After four days, Simon managed to make it to the table where Red Socks unwrapped his leg and rubbed the inflamed flesh with snow. Three days of similar treatment, and the shiny, tight appearance disappeared, and for the first time since he'd been bitten, he drained his bladder outside instead of in a pickle jar.

At the end of the tenth day, he took the bandage off, and left it off, the scabs exposed. The crusty accretions itched like a hundred mosquito bites, and with his peeling fingers, Simon scratched while Red Socks nodded his head and laughed.

Spud was not faring as well. A piece of bone stuck out where one of his toes had been. It refused to heal, and as soon as Red Socks took off the bandage, Spud was at the wound with tongue and teeth. After some discussion, the vast majority of which Simon didn't understand, Red Socks simply took off the leather wrap, and left it off. Simon could barely restrain himself as the dog whimpered and chewed at the offending spot.

Three days later, when Simon looked at the foot, he couldn't believe his eyes. The bone was gone. The wound that remained was deep, but a healthy pink. Red Socks looked too, signed "good" and said, *"Sadee'."* Simon figured it either meant "dog" or it was a name the Indian had given Spud.

Then Red Socks was gone. They had finished breakfast, and the Indian started signing and talking in his music-like language. Some of it, Simon caught. Most of it he didn't, but he knew Red Socks had to leave and would be gone until spring. The overhead sweep of his hands told Simon three moons would pass. April.

January 13, 1875. Dog and I wounded. Red Socks came and is now gone. Wolverine is dead and I am glad to be alive.

CHAPTER 33

Winter had been slow to release its hold on the valley. The extra five weeks of frozen mud, snow flurries, and cold nights brought its rewards as well. The deer remained low, and Simon had managed to kill three, one a two-hundred-pound buck. They were also spared the ravages of the flood that had nearly drowned them the year before. As it was, Simon, fed up with the cold, sat on his bench in the bright sun and dozed, once again enjoying the valley like he knew he could. Spud lay on a small scrap of canvas beside the door.

Simon's right leg still itched, and two fingers of his right hand tingled when they got cold, but physically, he'd healed. He still limped a little, but he thought that was more out of habit than anything. On the other hand, Spud refused to put his left paw on the ground except when he got up. Simon could see nothing wrong with it, but it slowed the dog considerably. He hoped that in time, he'd start to use it.

He thought he heard the dog grumble, but didn't want to open his eyes. The sun felt wonderful, and today he was actually warm all over. He shifted his back a little bit and tried to drift away again. The second time Spud left no doubt, and he opened one eye to look. Spud's head was up, muzzle pointed downstream. Simon watched him for a minute, then shut his eyes again.

Spud barked, and Simon was wide awake in a heartbeat, just in time to see the dog scramble to his feet. With his hand on the rifle barrel, Simon jumped up and followed the dog past the spruce trees to stand on the edge of the meadow. Shading his eyes with one hand, he studied the trees at the north end of the valley. Was something or someone there? The dog certainly seemed to think so, because the deep growl continued in his throat as they both stared.

Then, Simon caught a glimpse of movement well to the left of the trail. He moved back until he stood behind the spruces. "C'mere Spud." He patted his thigh. Who would be avoiding the open? Was it Red Socks? His scalp relaxed a little with the thought, and he unconsciously loosened his grip on the gun. Then a man on horseback appeared, clearly visible as he moved out of the striped shadow, and into a bright clearing . . . it wasn't Red Socks! He rode across the open, too far away to recognize, and then he was gone again, lost in the trees. Simon waited and watched. In another few minutes, the rider had to move around the rocky knob that marked the end of the meadow.

Then his elusive visitor rode into sight, only now he moved at a run, spurring his horse back into the trees. This man was deliberately staying out of sight. Simon glanced over at the cabin's chimney. Nothing showed from the morning fire, and he breathed easier. He focused on the next clearing, and was rewarded when the man moved into it and stopped.

The man wore dark clothes and a dark hat. His horse was either a black with winter-white hair or a maybe a gray; hard to tell because it stood with its rump in the hatched shadow of the leafless aspens. He seemed to be looking right at the cabin, and Simon's eyes watered as he stared back. Then the man nudged the horse in the withers and moved into the clearing.

Simon's lungs seized in mid-breath. The shadow on the horse's rump defied the sun, and remained intact as they rode out of the trees. There could be only one horse like that. Buell's Appaloosa! Could it be true? Simon stared, unable to move as the beautiful animal picked up the pace, and loped directly toward him. At two hundred yards, there was no doubt. Simon stepped into the open and yelled as loud as he could, "Buellll!" The horse surged into a full gallop, dirt flying behind; the man leaned over his neck, hat in hand. Simon reached down and caught hold of Spud's scruff.

Buell's arrival was pure Buell. Thundering down on them, the horse leaned back on all four legs in a lock-kneed slide. Buell bailed off the horse before it had stopped, to land on his feet, light as a feather.

"Found ya," the grinning man said. He reached out.

Simon took the four steps needed to cross to him and grasped the outstretched hand. He pumped it, then took hold of it with his other hand, and continued to shake. He could not take his eyes off of his friend's face. Still yanking up and down on Buell's hand, Simon realized what he was doing and let go.

Buell punched him on the shoulder, then looked down at the dog. "It seems he remembers me. Hey, Spud?" He offered his hand and Spud ignored it, sniffing his leg instead. "Checkin' on who I been with I guess." Buell looked back at Simon and smiled again. "Well hell, ya gonna say something or what?"

"I guess I'm speechless." Simon's eyes blinked rapidly as he searched for something witty to say. Nothing would come.

"Okay." Buell scratched his whiskers. "Got some coffee?"

"Yeah, sure. C'mon." Simon, relieved of the moment, turned toward the cabin. "Damn, Buell, I ain't never been so surprised."

As they walked past the spruce, Buell suddenly stopped and stared. "What'n hell happened to your door. It's all shot to shit."

"Yeah, it is. Buffalo rifle from across the meadow there. By that big rock."

"Why ya limpin'? And what happened to the dog's foot? Damn, Simon, the marshal said ya come up here for the solitude."

"Shit, I've been shot at, chewed on, hunted, and drowned . . . damn near struck by lightning . . . trapped head-down in a hole till an Indian found me. And that's just what comes to mind easy."

Buell chuckled. "I see you got yer speech back. I might add, it ain't as purty as it used to be."

"Well, you ain't either. What the hell'd ya

436

do to your head?" Simon laid his hand on Buell's shoulder and squeezed. "Sure good to see ya, Buell."

"Yeah, it is that."

"Pull your gear off that horse, and put him in with mine. Corral's just through there." Simon pointed at a path into the trees. "I'll get that coffee going." He watched as Buell started to untie his bedroll, then turned and walked toward the cabin. He didn't limp.

That evening, Simon didn't spare the wood. The fire snapped and popped as it devoured the pile of tinder he'd stacked on. He didn't want to go in, and Buell seemed to feel the same way. Besides, it wasn't all that cool anyway. Simon learned that Buell had not gone to the Black Hills. He'd started to, but had met a man coming out of there who was going to the gold fields in Idaho Territory. Buell'd simply turned around and rode with him. They wound up in the Boise Basin. Exactly what he'd done there, Simon hadn't yet learned. Buell hadn't changed much in that respect.

When asked about home, Buell admitted he hadn't kept in touch as much as he knew was decent. He'd sent three or four telegrams when the whiskey melancholy got the best of him, but never stayed around to get an answer. He'd written one long letter —

long by Buell's standards meant maybe a full page. Then he admitted that it was still in his saddlebags. Finally he said, "That's enough about me. I want to know what in hell got in yer craw to come out here and live like a damn hermit."

The question caught Simon off guard. Surely, Buell remembered the disaster in the saloon at Fort Laramie. The gruesome image of the bartender's brains, hair, and blood all over the back mirror still made him half-sick. Simon had killed him, but Buell had erased the evidence with a single shot to Twiggs's head from the fully charged .44. His own words flashed back to him, "I've become just like you." That's what he'd said and then watched as Buell simply turned around and walked out. So long ago but so fresh. "I don't like to think about that," he muttered. The air around the campfire seemed to suddenly cool.

"What?" Buell chucked a wood chip into the fire.

"Twiggs." Simon was having a hard time staying calm.

"Oh, Twiggs. Whatever happened after that? Damn, I thought you'd really stepped in the deep stuff that night. Did the army swallow it? They think I did it?"

"Yeah, they did. The provost . . . what was

438

his name? Van Eyke, Van Dyke, something like that. He concluded it was self-defense."

"Sonuvabitch. I never did like him. And it was self-defense."

"Then why did you just leave like that?"

"That or sit in an army jail for six weeks while they figger it out. No thanks. The Black Hills seemed like a good idea right then."

"But you had a talk with Tay before you left. He said you were upset."

"Well, hell, yes, I was upset. You should have seen your face. I thought you was gonna die right then and there. Wanted to stay around but . . . well, me and the army, you know."

Simon sat silent for a long time and stared at the fire.

"You're thinkin' something else, aren't ya? I've known ya all my life, Mr. Steele, and I can tell when you're stewin'. C'mon, spit it out."

"Do you remember what I said when you . . . shot him again?"

"Nope. I was lookin' to leave, hurried like."

"I . . ." Simon stopped.

"If muckin' out that particular stall is givin' ya grief, leave it alone."

"I thought I'd insulted ya," Simon blurted it out.

"You. Insult me? Not likely."

"It's been on my —"

"Then get it off yer mind. We did what we had to do, Simon. That was a rough place, and we damn near got ourselves killed two or three times. We didn't. Leave it at that." Buell's eyes bored in on his own, and his head took that peculiar cant that it did when something dawned on him. "And that's why you left? Cuz I did?" Buell started to laugh. "Ain't that a snort. I was goin' back this summer. Figgered on findin' a prosperous saloon and hotel keeper. Had a hard time believin' that marshal when he told me you were up here in one of these canyons. Coulda knocked me over with a skeeter fart."

"You'll never know how good that makes me feel, Buell. I thought I'd lost a friend."

"Humph," Buell snorted.

"Knowing that sure restores a lot of what I thought I'd lost."

"Oh, gawd, here it comes. He's gonna get all damp on me." Buell rolled his eyes.

"C'mon Buell. I ain't had nobody to talk about stuff like that since . . . well, you know, since we used to talk at Amos's place. I thought I'd made a friend when I got here.

Name was Reed and he packed in my supplies. Then the lying bastard tried to kill me. Spud knowed he was a polecat. Shoulda listened to the dog."

"He the one that shot up your place?"

"Yeah, but that was after Spud tore him up some and I'd shot his partner."

"Damn, Simon, you are a changed man. Ya shot his partner? Dead?"

"No. Took a piece out of his side is all."

"Where's the Indian come in?"

"Reed hated him. Actually, Reed hated all Indians. He almost convinced me that they are no good. But he, I call him Red Socks cuz he wears the pair I gave him, he pulled me out of . . . another story. Just say he saved me from suffocating in a hole." Simon cast a glance at the cabin. "He brought me meat when I was about to starve, saved me and Spud when we got in a fight with a wolverine and would have froze to death for sure. And Reed said the Indian was the bad one." Simon paused, stared at the fire for a few seconds, then continued. "Walks Fast was right. You know a man when he shows you his heart. I think I found what I needed up here. We should enjoy the best of what's offered and learn to live with the rest. I always wanted everything to be perfect. Well, things ain't. And that's fair, because

441

we're not either."

Buell shook his head. "What in hell would've happened if you'd actually gone lookin' for trouble?" He chuckled. "Now, tell me about gettin' stuck in a hole."

CHAPTER 34

It was late morning, and Simon sat basking in the sun. They had talked well into the night, and Buell was still in bed. *Some things don't change,* he thought. It was wonderful knowing he hadn't lost his friend. Buell hadn't been very specific about what he'd been doing personally, and that bothered him a little but . . . Simon shrugged mentally. At least he'd told a lot of stories about what he'd seen and where he'd been.

The Boise Basin sounded a lot like here, only swarming with thousands of people. Should he tell Buell about the twin rocks and the secret they held? He'd admitted that the lure of gold was what drew him to the mountains. Apparently, he'd not found much, or he wasn't talking about it. Simon gazed across the meadow and tried to imagine a tent city that stretched as far as he could see. It wasn't a pleasant image. The door opened.

"Mornin'," Buell said and hurried away.

" 'Bout time," he replied without opening his eyes.

A couple of minutes later, Buell returned and sat beside him on the bench. "I can see why you like it here. Did you make coffee yet?"

"Nope, didn't want a boot in the head. Remember that? The Texans?"

"Yup."

They sat in silence for a few minutes. "Besides that, I thought we agreed it was your job," Simon said.

Buell continued to stare at the far side of the valley for a bit, then sighed and got up. "Got anything ground?"

"Bag's on the right-hand end, top shelf. Water bucket's half full." Simon leaned back against the wall, looked up at his friend, and grinned. "Deal's a deal."

"The deal wasn't supposed to last forever," Buell muttered as he walked over to the fireplace and picked up the pot.

Simon shut his eyes and listened to Buell fuss around inside the cabin. He soon came out and set the coffeepot by the fireplace, then put the coffee bag and two cups on the table. In a couple of minutes he'd expertly coaxed the campfire back to life, and put the pot on to boil. He walked back to the bench and sat down.

"There, coffee soon enough. That does bring back memories though. Good ones."

"It does that," Simon replied. He recalled their trip across the plains from Carlisle to Fort Laramie. Simon had agreed to cook, but only after Buell had agreed to have a fire and coffee going first.

"What made you pick this spot? I saw several downstream that looked nearly as good."

"Those two trees."

Buell looked up at the towering conifers, then back at Simon. "You know what they remind me of?"

"No idea."

Buell's eyebrows went up as he cocked one leg on the bench and faced Simon. "Have you thought much about home? I mean, it's been seven years."

Simon suspected it wasn't really home he was referring to. Apparently Buell hadn't forgotten his promise not to talk about Sarah. "I got a letter from her," he said quietly. "It didn't help much."

"I'm sorry. I thought maybe . . . well, I don't know what I thought."

"She more or less told me that she'd reconciled — come to grips, with what had happened. She was teaching college. I suppose that's what she's doing now in a school back east somewhere." Simon felt somehow relieved to be talking about it. "What's home got to do with those trees?"

"They reminded me of you and her. Soon's I saw 'em, I thought that. A perfect pair, side by each."

"I always got the impression you didn't really like her much."

"I was jealous, plain and simple. I can admit it now."

"Jealous? You? Buell Mace didn't want a girlfriend. Not the Buell Mace I knew."

"There's a difference between not wanting and not needing, Simon," Buell said.

Buell's face became serious. Simon had only seen that side of his friend once or twice.

Buell went on, "That thought come to me real clear right after the first of the year. I was sittin' in a saloon, playing cards, and slowly gettin' drunk again. Fella come in, pissed as a newt, and wanted to fight me. I halfway knew this guy. He worked at the bakery."

Buell paused, and Simon could see he was recalling the incident. Buell did not talk like this. Always, he'd been reluctant to speak his thoughts. Simon nodded his head slightly.

"That happened a lot, Simon. And I was always glad to show 'em it was a bad mistake. It wasn't a matter of thinkin' about it. I'd just let fly at 'em with whatever come to hand. A bottle, beer mug, my fist, hell, I even brained a guy with a piece of foot rail once. But this time, when I stood up to get clear of my chair, something suddenly changed. And I mean sudden. Instead of seein' something I wanted to hurt, I saw something that was hurtin' already. I didn't need to do that anymore. Somehow, I knew hurting him wouldn't make me feel better, Simon. And I realized it never had." Buell swallowed hard a couple of times.

For the first time ever, Simon saw his friend's eyes glaze over. "So what happened?"

"I wrestled him to the floor and sat on 'im. I swear it would've been better if I'd just shot him. He got so mad, he couldn't holler. Just puffed air and spit. Pretty soon, three of his friends come over, so I got off and they took him outside. About a week later, I run into the marshal. He told me you was here. I kinda got the feeling that you were looking for some answers too. Right then I decided I needed to see ya again."

"And this happened when, exactly?"

"Right after the new year, maybe a week or so. And in the middle of the afternoon. That's why I remember it so clear. I thought, 'What's a working feller like him doin' blind drunk in the middle of the day?' "

A shiver sprinted up Simon's spine and his scalp contracted. "I'd say a demon climbed off your back . . . or was taken off."

"Yeah, that's something I'd expect you to say. You still like to talk in riddles and shit like that." Buell shook his head. "Anyhow, that's what happened, and here I am."

"And I'm glad you're here. You gonna stay awhile?"

"I wanna go home, Simon."

It was said, simple and clear. Simon didn't know how to respond. The same thought had slipped into his mind several times since he'd been hurt. But the thought was always transient, banished when he imagined home without Sarah.

"Why don't we go?" Buell asked.

"That's simple. Sarah. It ain't home without her."

Buell sighed. "And that letter was definite? I mean, she said she didn't . . . uh, love ya?"

"More or less. I never really read the bottom half. Couldn't get past the part where she said to leave her alone. And now that's gone."

"Gone?" Buell sat up straight.

"Yeah. When those yahoos sacked my place, they ruined the top half of her letter."

"Can you tell me what she said?"

"Exactly. I read that letter a hundred times. She said, 'Please understand that I am happy, both with my life and with what I am doing. If you wish me happiness, wish me success here.' That's plain enough."

"Not to me it ain't. She was going to school. She cared what you thought, and asked you to wish her happiness. That ain't sayin' to leave her alone. Damn, Simon." Buell frowned.

"You think?" Simon's heart sped up. "Let me get the bottom half. I'll let you read it." He stood. "And you better move that pot unless you want to boil all the water away."

Buell read the faint writing slowly. The paper looked almost soft in his hands. Simon watched him read it twice.

"Gawdamn, Simon. I ain't *never* seen you so wrong about something."

"All she talks about is stuff that's past." Simon was confused. "What could have been. Ain't that the first sentence?"

"But then she talks about your time together and how beautiful it was. She says

449

for now, you idiot, not forever." Buell looked down at the paper again. "Things can't be changed except with time. That's what she wrote. You dumb shit, she's saying she needed a little time. You both needed a little time. And why do you think she cries? She misses you and waiting for that time to pass is real hard on her. Gawd, you're stupid."

Simon took the letter from his friend and read it again slowly. The faded words distorted to indistinguishable blobs as tears formed. He got up and shuffled over to stand between the spruce trees. How had he missed it? It was so apparent once he read the bottom without the top part to upset him. He turned around.

"Let's go home, Buell."

CHAPTER 35

Carlisle now had three crossing streets, boardwalks, and a dozen two-story buildings, two of which had the name "STEELE" incorporated in the sign on the front. The town had grown up north of the railroad tracks, and the first place they stopped was the Mace Transportation and Portage business next door to the train depot. The barn was still there, but another, newer building stood alongside. Simon thought Buell's father was going to break both their necks as he hugged them collectively. It was all Simon could do to get loose. Yes, Simon's folks were fine. Yes, the town had grown. Yes, Ruth was well. And yes, Sarah was a schoolteacher and she was here.

Mace had said the school was where it always was, only bigger. A lot bigger, Simon saw, as he walked across the playground. Still the dusty place it always was, his shoes, so carefully tended and brand-new, took on a covering of the fine powder. There were several children playing on a teeter-totter and a swing, but not enough of them to indicate school was in session. Mace had said it wasn't yet.

Simon's mouth and throat were so dry, he felt hoarse. He climbed the three steps to the double doors and paused. The celluloid of his collar cut into his jaw, and a trickle of sweat left his armpit and slipped down his side. Then, he grasped the knob and pulled the door open. He'd expected to see one large room. Instead, he stood in a foyer that had desks on either side. A hall ran down the center of the building. There were four doors, two on each side. Three were shut. He headed for the open one.

The scent as he approached the door left no doubt. The lavender perfume drew him into the room, and there she was. She'd heard his footfall and stood, mouth open, staring at him. He could not take another step. Her face, now slightly narrower, and even more beautiful with maturity, was framed in the soft brown hair of memory. The sudden urge to flee surged into his legs. She said nothing. Did she recognize him?

Then she blinked. "Simon?"

He saw her eyes glaze, and his feet were free to move.

"Oh, Simon." The familiar tilt of her head, the one he'd seen a thousand times in his dreams, drew him across the floor in a rush. She opened her arms and he leaned into them as they closed around his neck. He shut his eyes and pulled her tight to his chest, hardly daring to breathe for fear he'd lose control of the moment. The sob that came from her nearly broke his heart. He held her close until he thought he could speak. Then, slowly, he relaxed his hold until he could see into her eyes.

"Oh Sarah, my Sarah," Simon murmured, fighting for control of his voice. "At last, I understand why you cried."

EPILOGUE

Simon left his rifle and cartridges at the "gift tree" and told the woman by the river that his household was free for the taking. He'd considered burning the cabin, but decided to leave it intact. The source of the gold that Simon loaded on his horse the last day was never discussed. His friends at Fort Laramie received promises of future visits, and a reply from his old partner Amos confirmed that Simon's investments had made him a prosperous man. Sarah and Simon were married in late winter at the biggest wedding in Carlisle's history. And Buell? Well . . . Buell is another story.

ABOUT THE AUTHOR

Wallace J. Swenson was born and raised in a small rural town in southeast Idaho. From the very beginning, he lived a life of hard work supported by a strong family. He was taught by example the value of honesty and loyalty, and it is about such that he wrote. His family numbered ten, and though poor in a material sense, he considered himself blessed beyond measure in the spiritual. He resided with his wife of fifty-plus years, Jacquelyn, near where both were born, and close to all their children and grandchildren. He intended to live there the rest of his life and spend that time putting down on paper the dozens of stories that whirled around inside his head. He did just that. Wallace J. Swenson died suddenly in February of 2015. He left a literary legacy of which this book is a small part.

The employees of Thorndike Press hope you have enjoyed this Large Print book. All our Thorndike, Wheeler, and Kennebec Large Print titles are designed for easy reading, and all our books are made to last. Other Thorndike Press Large Print books are available at your library, through selected bookstores, or directly from us.

For information about titles, please call:
    (800) 223-1244

or visit our Web site at:
    http://gale.cengage.com/thorndike

To share your comments, please write:
    Publisher
    Thorndike Press
    10 Water St., Suite 310
    Waterville, ME 04901